Summer of 1840
On the Shores of Singletary

Arthur L. Martin

ISBN-10: 1546698227
ISBN-13: 978-1546698227

"If there ever comes a day where we can't be together, keep me in your heart. I'll stay there forever."
Winnie the Pooh

CONTENTS

CONTENTS

DEDICATION

To the many dedicated interpreters at Living Museums
everywhere who help to keep history alive in our hearts and in
our souls, especially my friends and colleagues who work at
Old Sturbridge Village in Sturbridge, MA

PREFACE

I had the pleasure of restoring the house that Lucinda Bixby grew up in. She was six years old when it was raised in 1822.

It was a letter entitled "Happiness," written by Lucinda when she was twenty-five, tucked away at the bottom of a small leather chest, a chest handed down from owner to owner for nearly 200 years, that inspired me to write the "Summer of 1840."

When I first embarked on the project, nearly three years ago, I had no idea where it might lead me, or Lucinda for that matter.

I hope you will enjoy reading the tale as much as I enjoyed writing it.

ONE

LUCINDA... *SATURDAY, JULY 4, 1840*

The ominous screeching of coyotes interrupts the silence of darkness. I toss and turn relentlessly, hoping to steal just one more moment of sleep. In the distance, muffled sounds of gunshots quiet the howling. Silence frightens me. The scar on my inner thigh begins to burn. It does that when I am frightened. Sliding my hand gently over my warm belly, my fingers find the scar, caressing it... How will I ever be worthy of love?

The light of dawn slowly warms the darkness, bringing with it the promise of a new day and the optimism for another prosperous year for America. Fourth of July is a special day for me, a day of celebration, moreover, an indicator that my birthday is a mere nineteen days away. It is also a vivid reminder of that dreaded evening nearly ten years ago, when I was only fifteen. I awoke in a pool of blood on the floor of the Faulkners' barn, my leg torn open, a nearby pitchfork the obvious suspect, my virginity taken, having had no carnal knowledge of man. My memory of that night is vague, leaving me no recollection of the perpetrator.

Slipping out of bed, I make my way over to the mirror. It welcomes me with a warm smile. The burning is gone. I murmur to myself, "Maybe this is the summer that my fear of love will finally soften."

The curls of my brown hair fall shoulder length; red highlights shimmer in the morning sun. The freckles on my nose have become too faint to recognize, a reminder of my passing youth. The sparkle of my green eyes instills a sense of hope of better days to come. Lifting my chemise up and over my head, I expose the innocence of my tender breasts. I am compelled to touch them. I do... ever so gently. The sensation reawakens the burning of my scar. My optimism withers.

∞

My dearest mother has been working diligently with Mr. Lovell to prepare the church hall for this morning's Fourth of July gathering; I am quite sure it will be a success. Mr. Lovell oversees the event, more likely than not because he lives near the hall. He selected Mother to assist him in the preparation due to her attention to detail. My father has nothing to do with such events; crowds make him uneasy.

Carefully, I navigate the steps down the narrow staircase. I am surprised to see Mother hunched over the fire, busily preparing breakfast at such an early hour. Looking up, she smiles. "Good morning, Lucinda, I hope we did not startle you with the forty-eight rounds we fired off at 3:00 a.m. Mr. Lovell and I were quite finished with decorations of evergreen and spruce in the hall, and so we delightfully fired them to begin the day of celebration. I fear we woke the entire village."

My mother, Hannah, is a dear woman. She is short and stout. Although she would never disclose it, her hair is darker than mine, featuring highlights of gray instead of red. She is a bit old-fashioned, never allowing her hair to escape from under a proper cap. Her face appears melancholy, surely because of her rapidly aging skin. However, underneath those wrinkles lives a rather jubilant woman, always involved in the community in one way or another.

"Mother, you have worked so hard to prepare the hall; please let me join you this morning to help with the finishing touches. And let us pray that the rain diminishes, and that the day turns out to be a pleasant one."

Mother replies, "Of course my dear, let us hurry with our chores and make our way down to the village. Perhaps it is best that we take the carriage; I hear that the Whigs are going to roll the ball in a parade down by the Lower Tavern later this afternoon. It surely would be fun to watch the festivities."

∞

The rain has ceased; the sun peeks faintly through the breaking clouds. The sensation of mud between my toes is delightful. For a moment, my mind floats into a realm of ecstasy. I experience a sensation that I welcome and fear both with the same amount of passion. I quickly regain my senses, continuing my short journey to the barn. Upon my arrival, a flock of curious chickens, a cow with an overfilled udder, and my beautiful horse, Shadow, welcome me. The barn has become one of the few places in my world where I feel safe and fulfilled. It is a place without persistent conflict and confusion, a place where I feel the presence of a loving God, a God that finds me worthy of love, pure and simple.

Embracing Shadow tightly around her neck, I whisper in her ear, "Oh, my dearest Shadow, are you ready for a most adventurous day? I just know that it will bring forth a little bit of happiness for us both, well... at least we can hope that it does."

The loft is full of fresh cut hay, prompting me to treat Shadow to an extra helping, knowing that we both have a long day ahead of us. I place the milk pail properly under the cow's udder, positioning my stool just right, in anticipation of a quick and bountiful session. Gently, I begin to massage her udder to help let the milk down, and then I carefully begin to squeeze off her teats, doing my best not to cause too much discomfort. Again, sensuous thoughts begin to provoke me. I quickly turn my attention to the task at hand. I finish the milking, keeping my thoughts directly on the completion of my morning chores, and the activities planned for the day. When her udder is empty, I move the pail out of harm's way, and then proceed to collect nearly two dozen fresh eggs from all the likely locations. With everything in order, I fetch the milk and the eggs and head back to the house.

∞

Once back in the kitchen, Mother is singing loudly, as if she was already down at the hall celebrating. *"Hail! Long expected glorious day, illustrious memorable morn."*

I do not remember ever seeing her as excited as this—maybe it is the politics of the day that has everyone taking one side or another with an absurd fervor. I make my way upstairs to freshen up and finish getting dressed for the adventurous day ahead.

∞

What started out as a rather dreary day has slowly turned into a most pleasant summer morning. The road remains wet from the earlier rain. Shadow is quite content pulling the carriage through the mud. As we make our way up the hill toward the common, I feel blessed by the sight and scent of the wild flowers that line the road. My optimism is rekindled.

We pass by the open lot where the church used to stand before they moved it a ½ mile down the road, closer to the mills. There had been quite a population explosion in Burbank Village in the 20's and 30's, prompting the elders of the church to move it closer to where the population has gathered. Reminiscing, I turn to Mother and ask, "Do you remember the days when we could walk to the hall in just five minutes? I know that moving the church was surely in the best interest for the majority who work at the mills, but I sure do miss the convenience."

Mother replies, "Oh Lucinda, there have been quite a lot of changes made around here in the past few years." She pauses for a moment, continuing, "However, change can be good. For instance, I am rather happy that they cut a more direct road to the church. Do you remember when they first made the move and the journey was nearly two miles?"

The road is very steep, but Shadow continues to do a superb job navigating around the mud and the ruts.

When we finally arrive at the hall, there is a small gathering of folks outside. A sense of anticipation radiates from the crowd. The excitement is infectious. After quickly tying Shadow to the post, we make our way to the gathering of probably fifty or more. Mr. Leland shouts out to Mother, "Hannah, what was that ruckus before dawn this morning? You made enough noise to wake up the dead!"

Mother quickly responds to Mr. Leland in a triumphant shout, "Fourth of July comes only once a year, and after spending all evening decorating the hall, I just wanted to have some fun in celebration of our great nation!"

This is an election year, and so far, it has been the most controversial in history. Van Buren is spending money like a drunken sailor, while the Whigs have created an image of Harrison that suggests he will save the world sitting on the porch of his log cabin, sipping on hard cider. The Whigs have gone so far as to write nasty sayings about our president on large red, white, and blue balls, some being as tall as twelve feet, and rolling them down the streets in parades. Why, anger can fester up at any moment.

Just as Mother shouts out, the energy in the crowd begins to turn angry. Mother becomes increasingly animated. There is sinister laughter and yelling of filthy remarks about the Whigs. All of this becomes rather discomforting to me. I am surprised with Mother—she has always taught me to be humble and kind. I must try to stop this silliness. Turning to Mother with words clinging to my tongue, I recognize Reverend Holman approaching the crowd. It is as if God was suddenly manifested amongst a crowd of sinners. The silence is surreal.

My leg begins to burn; it always does when in the presence of so-called reverent men. I do not know why.

Only a few seconds pass before the mockery begins to rekindle. Reverend Holman eventually joins in, exclaiming his own views regarding the misfortune of the Whigs and a political party so marinated in evil, his eloquent words spoken in such a way as to turn the love of God into a weapon against other fellow Americans. All of this seems so senseless to me; I just want it all to stop. My leg pounding in pain, I decide to limp away toward Shadow. Her presence brings me peace; the burning of my leg begins to quiet.

Mr. Lovell calls out for the crowd to come to order, asking

everyone to gather into an organized formation so that we can begin our parade of celebration. Moving back toward the crowd, I make a promise to myself that I shall take my exit with the next outburst of jeering.

We begin to march, the crowd doing so in what appears to be a much stronger spirit of happiness and joy than I saw at the church. I am pleased to see that Mother is enjoying herself, singing songs of celebration with the others. The parade route leads us up the hill toward Ezra Lovell's place and then back again, directly across from Lovell's Hotel. It is nearly 11:00 by the time that we arrive back to the hall to continue our celebration. Upon entering, the decorations that Mr. Lovell and Mother had prepared overnight stand out distinctly as a work of art. The burning is gone.

∞

As the crowd begins to gather inside the hall, Mr. Lovell shouts out, "To all in attendance, please join us upstairs for a short oration from our guest, Mr. Benjamin Hallett."

We pass by a table lined with refreshments, making our way up the stairs, taking our assigned places in the meetinghouse. Mr. Asa Waters makes his way to the podium, and with a political fanfare, introduces our guest: "I want to welcome you all to this very special celebration of our nation's 64th year. It is with a special honor that I introduce Mr. Benjamin Hallett, who has prepared an oration promoting the cause of Democratic principles, rational liberty, and sound morality. Let us all stand and welcome him with applause."

The crowd seems overtaken by excitement. My thoughts are still with the refreshments downstairs in the hall. The politics of the day have become quite difficult for me to embrace. The controversy over what party is right and what party is wrong is causing untold friction everywhere. It is difficult for me to take sides, for my heart seeks peace, and I find no peace in the rhetoric of politics.

Mr. Hallett begins, *"Fellow Citizens: Where are we now, in the progress of that great struggle between the rights of the many and the power of the few, which to-day numbers its 64th anniversary in the march of time?"*

My thoughts begin to slip away as Mr. Hallett continues his rant. *"What a bigoted and insolent faith in humanity is that which sets up, in government, a class of men as especially designed to rule over the rest? What an insult to Deity, who created man equal and in his own image; that a few of his miserable creatures should have set themselves to work, to mar his great purpose by making inequity and injustice the only conditions on which it is pretended society and government subsist?"*

The speech continues. Mr. Hallett is turning red in the face as he continues to draw the attention of an enthralled crowd. For me, the thought of heading to Union Street in Armory Village to join the Whig celebration, with the promise of no long speeches, is becoming more and more appealing.

The oration continues, *"Shall the trash of lying newspapers suffice for a moment to convince a people that, in fact, honesty and good faith and trust-worthiness and inviolate promises are no longer to be found in 'unaccommodated man,' but must be sought for in soulless Banks and Corporations."*

The speech goes on for what feels like an eternity.

Finally, he begins his closing remarks: *"And while they lament the*

8

obstacles to human progress on the one hand, and rejoice in the sure
promise of its advancement on the other; with all the elements of
improvement so bountifully bestowed upon society in this favored land,
'The charities that soothe and heal and bless, The generous inclination, the
just rule, Kind wishes and good actions and pure thoughts,' they will find,
that it is not the necessary inequality in life, but unequal laws; not God
but man, who, in his social and political condition, has made, 'So wide a
difference betwixt man and man.' "

The crowd stands, acknowledging the passion with which Mr.
Hallett delivered his oration. Reverend Holman seems quite
delighted as Mr. Hallett makes his way from the podium. They
lead the crowd back down the stairs to the hall, where the
refreshments have been waiting with extreme patience. There
is quite a lovely spread of treats, prepared by many of the
members of the crowd. There is delicious looking ginger
bread, an election cake and caraway cakes, just to name a few.
The drinks look delightful as well; I see raspberry shrub and
ginger beer. Everyone seems overjoyed with the event, which
assuredly will please Mother.

Reverend Holman approaches. My disdain for ministers is
evident; the basis for it remains a mystery. I immediately begin
to get knots in my stomach and hot flashes that race through
my forehead, eventually consuming my entire face. The scar
on my leg begins to burn. His mannerism portrays his
uncanny ability to read one's mind, while rewinding and
replaying every thought and action from previous days, both
public and private. "Miss Lucinda, are you enjoying the day as
much as it appears? What a delight it is to see you smile. The
twinkle in your eyes portrays a happy young lady, unlike the
one I observe during most Sunday services. Let us hope that
you can contain your enthusiasm, and not let it get the best of

you."

I assure him, "Quite the contrary Reverend Holman, my enthusiasm is for the Lord, and all that He has done to bring such happiness to our great country."

As he walks away, a dreadful feeling comes over me; I pray that he really does not have the ability to read my mind. If he did, he would know that my enthusiasm is more for the excitement that lay ahead at the celebration in Armory Village.

∞

Left standing alone on the top landing of the granite steps, I turn my focus to finding Mother in time to make our journey to Armory Village before nightfall. From afar, I see my brother Sumner approaching. He is a tall man, two years my elder, married four years ago to his dear wife, Louisa. He is named after our brother Sumner, who died at the age of four, three weeks before our Sumner was born. My brother's namesake surely has much to do with his self-assurance and the honorable manner in which he conducts himself. I just love him to pieces.

He surprises me when he suggests, "Lucinda, Mother is going to get a ride home from Mr. Lovell and asked if I would accompany you to the celebration on the other side of town."

With much enthusiasm, I reply, "Yes, Sumner, that would be delightful, and now is certainly not soon enough."

We hurry to the carriage, both of us jumping up and onto the seat. Sumner gives a gentle jerk to the reigns prompting Shadow to begin the 1 ½ mile journey down to the Lower

Tavern. The weather has turned quite pleasant, the sun is playing hide and seek behind the fluff of the summer clouds, and the breeze gently makes its way under my dress, creating an exhilarating feeling of freedom. I yell out to Shadow, reminding her of my promise for an exciting day, "We are on our way!"

As we approach Armory Village, the Gowan Bridge is in sight. It provides a safe passage over the Blackstone Canal. Activity on the canal has slowed dramatically over the years, its demise bringing new hopes for a railroad that would connect Worcester and Providence. Taking a moment to dream, I imagine railroad tracks as far as the eye can see, and a glorious steam engine coupled with several coaches chugging its way toward Worcester.

Once we make our way over the bridge, it is as if we enter another world.

"Sumner, look at how beautiful Mr. Waters' home is. Have you ever wondered what it would be like to live in such a magical place?"

Sumner, being a tad more practical than I, responds, "Not at all, just more to take care of. But I have heard that the Christmas Ball is a wonderful event, and that Mr. Waters enjoys it so much that he begins preparing for it months before Christmas."

The thought of attending a Christmas Ball intrigues me. Closing my eyes for a moment, I envision myself in a beautiful dress, elegantly dancing with the man of my dreams. While I twirl in splendid delight, the scar begins to burn; I tumble to the floor, the wound is bleeding profusely, the brilliance of the ballroom transforming into the darkness of that dreaded barn.

I wake to a gentle hand holding my arm. Sumner quietly asks, "Lucinda, are you quite all right? I did not mean to disturb you with my comment about your living in a magical place."

Reaching my hand over, I lay it upon Sumner's, assuring him, "There will come a day when this curse is broken and I will feel worthy of love. I promise."

Bewildered, Sumner continues to guide Shadow toward the celebration.

∞

When we reach the stable on the corner of Main and Elm Streets, I am able to refocus my thoughts back to the excitement of the day, but not without a certain toll paid due to allowing my mind to wander. Shadow appears excited that she will be spending the afternoon with other horses. I assure her, "Shadow, you will feel safer here, and I promise we will take the long way home so that we can enjoy the beautiful evening weather together."

Sumner and I begin our walk to the celebration, sparing Shadow the noise and confusion of fireworks and a loud parade. The walk down Elm Street toward Union is less than a ½ mile. The excitement on the street accentuates the fervor for political change that seems to be inevitable. Groups of people are gathered to discuss the upcoming election, emphasizing the need for change. Passing the arcade, I am surprised with the progress that has been made on the new Methodist Church. The Village has grown quickly; there are so many new faces in town that I feel like a stranger. There is an explosion by my feet, causing me to jump nearly out of my shoes. A band of boys run behind the arcade, throwing fireworks and yelling in delight.

When we arrive on Union Street, we find that the Fourth of July celebration at this end of town is a well-organized Whig rally. Doing my best to speak over the loud voices and music, I turn to Sumner in dismay. "Brother, it is as if the devil himself is rolling that ball. They are making a mockery of our government and provoking sinfulness right here on the streets. Why the Whigs are no better than the Democrats."

Sumner smirks, "Oh Lucinda, loosen up a little, one day you will find happiness in this world, and it may very well begin with a drink of hard cider."

Sumner is right, while bothered by the craziness that I see, I am also strangely fascinated to be a part of it all.

Out of the corner of my eye, I notice a most gorgeous man walking directly toward me from across the street. There is something unique about him; his appearance simply enchants me. His stride is hypnotic. In my nearly twenty-five years on this earth, I have never experienced a gentleman so stimulating. The thought of this man's nakedness sends a tantalizing sensation throughout my entire body, settling just below my belly. His hair is dark and curly, his face slightly in need of a shave. Only a few steps away, he stares at me through his intriguing dark brown eyes. Expecting my scar to be burning in excruciating pain, I am rather surprised that instead, the tantalizing sensation below my belly just gets stronger.

I whisper to myself, "What do I say? I must say something."

I straighten my bonnet and stand as upright as I can, hoping sincerely that he will recognize me. To my dismay, he simply walks past, not stopping for even a moment.

I murmur to myself, "Why did I not say a word?" Oh, I feel so ready for love, and yet when it knocks on my door, I shudder in fear.

Turning to watch as he melts into the crowd, I feel compelled to chase him down. Sumner grabs me by the hand and jerks me toward the parade. Out of shear angst, I begin singing loudly amongst the rest of the sinners, *"Tippecanoe and Tyler too… and with him we'll beat little Van, Van Van is a used up man…"*

Just as I thought that it could not get any louder, Sumner turns to me and shouts, "Lucinda, your eyes are twinkling. You have a glow about you that is out of character."

I am embarrassed to disclose that the excitement seems to have gotten the best of me. We continue to sing in glee. The tingle in my lower belly is a constant reminder of that stunning man.

As we make our way toward the end of Union Street, we come upon the Lower Tavern, with patrons crowding the porch, sipping on mugs of ale. There is a broadside hung on one of the posts, just outside. Normally I would not have taken notice, but today, with thoughts of love fresh in my mind, it catches my attention:

DANCING SCHOOL

Commencing in the Lower Tavern Hall on Monday, July 20th.
Afternoon for ladies, and evening for gentlemen.
For instructions in the elementary principles of Country Dancing.
The first part of the lesson will be devoted to proper manners,
And the last part to the figures and proper etiquette of dancing.
No pains will be spared to make it both profitable and interesting.
For a course of 15 lessons, the terms will be $2 for
Gentlemen, and $1.50 for ladies.
Followed by a Harvest Dance to be held on Oct. 31st.
Millbury, July 3   *Obadiah Griffiths*

In a whirlwind of enthusiasm, I turn to Sumner announcing, "This surely is the summer that love will find me. I will learn to dance!"

Sumner cautiously responds, "Are you not getting a little on in age to be attending a dancing school for youth?"

Sumner is right, but I must. Moreover, I will.

∞

Keeping my promise to Shadow, we head out toward the Park Hill District by Dr. Jewett's place, taking the longer way home. While there has been a threat of rain most of the afternoon, the early evening is much less threatening with the temperature hovering around 70. I am delighted with the outcome of the day, despite a few setbacks. The happiness of it all is encouraging; thoughts of that charming man linger on. I cannot wait to tell Mother about the dance school, she will surely be as pleased with my newfound optimism as I am.

∞

The temperature has become comfortable enough to allow for a good night's sleep. It feels refreshing to slip out of my dress and petticoat. Changing into a freshly washed chemise, I lay down on my bed, thinking of that intriguing man that passed by me today. I feel safe enough to fantasize. Our conversation leads us to a quiet and secluded place. I become inebriated with a warm desire. My thoughts become blurred. As if in a trance, my fingers begin to stroke my cradle of pleasure. I try so hard to fight back, knowing where it always ends. Just at the height of it, the room begins to spin. The scar on my leg erupts into a mass of burning pain, causing me to scream out in agony, "Why must you torment me so?"

TWO

OBADIAH... *SATURDAY, JULY 4, 1840*

It is late in the afternoon by the time I arrive at the tavern in
Sudbury. The taproom is lively with music and cheer. The
ride from Providence was uneventful, except for a diversion
through Millbury to post the broadside announcing my
upcoming dance school at the Lower Tavern. There was quite
a bit of activity in the streets, including the rolling of a gigantic
ball by what appeared to be singing maniacs.

A charming but rather frail lady meets me in the foyer by the
entrance of the taproom. She is no more than five feet tall,
displaying a melancholy demeanor—a spinster no doubt. She
greets me with a forced smile: "Good day, you must be
Obadiah. My name is Jerusha Howe, Lyman's sister. We are
delighted to welcome you here to the Red Horse Tavern.
Please let me show you to your room so that you can drop
your belongings and freshen up. We will be dancing in the
upstairs hall this evening at seven-thirty. The fiddler, Elias
Howe, has not yet arrived from Framingham."

Jerusha's saddened demeanor influences my first impression of
her. Although quite reserved in appearance, I sense the soul of
a once vibrant woman, who surely must have stolen the dance
floor. "Thank you, Madam Howe. I am looking forward to a
most pleasing evening. Your kind hospitality has already
helped to make my trip a more pleasurable one."

∞

My accommodations are quite welcoming. Jerusha has

prepared a warm pitcher of wash water, placing it by a rather large washbasin, complemented by a freshly laundered washcloth. I strip myself naked, scrubbing from head to toe, finishing with a refreshing shave in front of the wall-hung mirror. My itinerary has me staying here at the tavern for four nights, and then heading off to Millbury for an extended stay there. One can only hope that the accommodations at the Lower Tavern will be nearly as superb. I fall onto the bed and sprawl out on my back, legs spread, taking in the freshness of a cool breeze gently blowing across my dampened body. With satisfaction, I mutter, "This truly is Heaven on Earth."

Closing my eyes, I slip into a dream state. Envisioning an overcrowded street with hundreds of celebrating people, the sound becomes muffled and the crowd becomes translucent; the lucid vision of a most attractive lady demands my attention. I recognize her from earlier this afternoon as I passed her on the street. She is wearing an attractive red dress and the most handsome sunbonnet; she is remarkably sweet. I stop to introduce myself.

Upon reopening my eyes, lying naked and alone, thoughts of her sustain the pleasure of love. Well-rested and unusually relaxed, I am ready for an evening of dancing and celebration.

∞

The taproom is crowded, pungent with the stench of stale tobacco. Two men stand by the cage, both contentedly sipping ale from their pewter tankards. I recognize the older fellow as the owner of the hotel, Lyman Howe. He appears a tad tipsy, wobbling back and forth, raising his tankard with every other breath, as if making a toast to every exchange. The other fellow looks to be no more than nineteen years of age, and particularly good-looking. Lyman turns, and with the raise of his tankard, hails a welcome, "Why Obadiah, I want to thank you for traveling here to Sudbury, all the way from Providence, to serve as our dance master for this evening's Fourth of July celebration dance. It is my pleasure to introduce you to my dear friend, Elias Howe. He joins us from Framingham. He is finalizing his publication of a compilation of music that he refers to as, *The Musician's Companion*, and he has generously offered to play the fiddle for our dance this evening."

I reply to Lyman, "Thank you again for inviting me. I was welcomed earlier in the day to the tavern by your lovely sister, Jerusha. The accommodations are wonderful, and I look forward to an exciting stay here in Sudbury."

With a flair of enthusiasm, I make a well-intentioned bow. "Elias, it is a pleasure to meet you, I look forward to working with you this evening. Let us find some time before the dance to go over the evening's playlist together. I am working from my Uncle John's playbook, which I am sure you will find most pleasing."

Elias replies, "It is most delightful to make your acquaintance, Mr. Griffiths. I look forward to the opportunity to work alongside you this evening. Let us fetch ourselves another pint of ale and go look at that music."

I respond with gratitude, "Excellent, and please call me Obadiah."

∞

The Willard banjo clock on the wall strikes seven, welcoming Elias and I to the hall. There are three magnificent chandeliers ablaze with what appears to be a hundred candles each. With a bid of confidence, Elias assures me that he is familiar with my uncle's work, suggesting that it will require little time at all to prepare. With that, we take a few moments to look through the playlist of music I plan to follow. Elias nods, suggesting, "A splendid selection of fine dances."

Enthralled by Elias's well-developed body and good looks, I bravely ask, "How do you keep yourself so fit as a writer and musician?"

Elias turns to me with a grin, replying, "Don't let my physique fool you. I am obsessed with having my works published, but have little money to do so. I have been most fortunate to work it out with a publisher in Boston to publish my work on credit. As a result, I am working my legs off, farming from dusk to dawn to pay them off. I must say, it does keep me fit."

I find my uncharacteristic attraction to Elias unusually arousing. I murmur to myself, "It certainly does."

Guests begin to arrive with spirits in hand, suggesting the night may well turn to day on the dance floor. Apparently, the celebration is well on its way; many dancers are already under the influence of that concoction of rum and ginger brandy that the tapster has been pouring at the bar. So much for temperance—all the talk about hard cider is having a positive effect on bar sales, while creating for me somewhat of a mob scene. I mumble under my breath, "The spirits will certainly animate the dance floor tonight."

As I prepare to form lines for our first dance, my attention turns to Jerusha as she enters the hall. Gracefully, she strolls to the front of the room, finding a seat that distances her from the others. A sweetness radiates from her face. Her eyes are translucent, providing a conduit to her soul. Her presence, shadowed by a cloud of gloom, depicts an affliction that is troubling to me. I am curious to know her better, but at the same time, reminded by a slight nudge from Elias, that the crowd is getting restless.

I begin by shouting, "Welcome to our celebration dance. Let us begin."

Elias plays a few bars of the opening dance. There appears to be six couples that are ready to indulge, and so I instruct them, "Ladies and gentlemen, let's get into position. Gents on my right and ladies facing your partner to my left." I continue with the instruction, "I like to start with a very simple dance, to help us all get acclimated. This will also assist those who are not as familiar with dance to learn the basics. It is called 'The Morning Gazette,' and we will dance it to a famous tune known by the name, 'News from Denmark.'"

The first gentleman appears to be intoxicated. I thank the Lord that his very attractive partner seems willing to provide the support he needs to get in position. Beginning the instruction, "The figures are as follows: The first couple set to the second lady, then to the second gentleman, lead down the middle—up again, and cast off. And let us not forget our manners."

Elias begins with four beats for nothing and the dance begins. I am immediately impressed with the results, giving me a good feeling about the rest of the night.

While the dance is progressing, my attention again turns toward Jerusha. I sense a unique connection between us, but remain at a loss as to the root of what seems to be an enigmatic attraction. Judging by her appearance, she has not gone to any length to impress her guests. I might go as far to say that she displays no interest in the festivities. Staring at the doorway, there is a certain sadness in her eyes, presumably waiting for someone with a waning anticipation, one that has aged over time, tarnished by years of disappointment.

The hall is alive with dancers and onlookers alike. There are ten to twelve couples dancing at a time; Elias continues to do a remarkable job with the music. The level of inebriation of the crowd, in general, seems to have settled out to a reasonable level. There appears to be only a couple of gents that look potentially disruptive.

We are well along into the dance "Young Widow," when one of the more tipsy gents trips over himself, causing a domino effect. Two ladies and four gentlemen end up lying on the floor, rather than circling six hands 'round. The ladies and three of the gentlemen reclaim their standing position, while the gent that caused the wreck remains passed out cold on the floor. The gents stop to assist the man to his feet, escorting him out of the hall.

∞

Time passes quickly; the clock is ready to strike midnight. Jerusha remains contently seated in her original place. I am bewildered that no one has approached her to dance. There is an untold story here that I am compelled to explore.

No sooner than my thoughts pass, the gentleman who was escorted from the dance floor earlier in the evening returns and heads directly toward Jerusha. He appears a bit tattered from his experience, although, most certainly, a tad more composed than before. He extends an invitation to Jerusha to dance; she quietly responds, "Zachary, you know I have no interest in dancing. But thank you for asking."

Zachary quickly snaps back, "Don't you think after fifteen years it is damn well time that you let go and enjoy an evening out? Now come dance with me." He grabs Jerusha by the arm, pulling franticly, trying to lift her from her chair.

I shout out, "That is enough!"

Immediately making my way over to where Jerusha is sitting, I remove Zachary's hand from Jerusha's arm. I begin to escort Zachary from the hall; he turns suddenly and takes a feeble swipe at me. He mumbles aloud, "She is none of your business, now let me go; find someone else to bother." I pay no attention to him, continuing to escort him out of the hall and out of harm's way.

Sitting him down forcibly, I respectfully ask that he get a hold of himself. He blurts out to me, "You have no right to interfere!" His breath stinks of rum. It is obvious that he has a strong attraction toward Jerusha.

Doing my best to remain calm, I quietly ask, "Zachary, my friend, I understand that you may have feelings for Jerusha, but is this any way to show them? Is it not obvious to you that the lady does not wish to dance?"

Zachary mumbles something and slowly takes his leave. It is difficult for me to comprehend the hurt that someone like Zachary harbors; I silently wish the best for him. With that, I must make my way back to the hall to begin winding down the celebration.

∞

When I return, Jerusha is no longer in her seat; apparently, she has had enough for the night. Twenty or so people remain in the hall; Elias is keeping the dance alive, playing "La' Belle Catherine." The dancers are flowing gracefully on the dance floor. The perfect form of the dancers reflects my love and commitment as a dance master; I am inspired to continue my roaming from town to town.

As Elias plays the final bars of "La' Belle Catherine," I begin planning for the final dance of the evening. Returning to the head of the hall, I announce, "I want to thank you all for making this a most memorable Fourth of July evening for Elias and I. It has been quite our delight to share with you my Uncle John's most popular dances. The final dance for tonight is a favorite of mine entitled 'Constancy.' It features Elias on the fiddle, playing a most pleasurable tune, entitled 'The Ton.' "

Elias plays the first few bars of the tune while the eight remaining couples line up for the finale. The dancers are quite seasoned by now, so a quick go-through of the figures should do. "Cross hands – then back again. Lead down the middle – up again and cast off one. Couples balance – turn your partner quite round and right and left at top." Elias plays a few bars as the couples make their manners for the final time tonight.

The dancers are a most wonderful sight to see while Elias, most graciously, plays the hell out of that fiddle. It is nearly one in the morning when the music finally stops. The guests that remain look worn from the evening's activities, but all are smiling nevertheless. I turn to Elias to ask what his plans for the rest of the evening are. "Will you be staying at the Inn this evening?"

He responds, "Lyman has offered me a bed for the night but he was unsure at the time where he would put me."

Lyman enters the room. "Thank you Obadiah and Elias! What a wonderful evening. The guests were all so extremely pleased, although I did hear that Zachary might have given you some trouble. He is actually a very nice man, with a bit of an infatuation for my sister that goes back more than fifteen years. It's a long story."

I respond, "Yes, the spirits did seem to get the best of that gentleman. But it is not likely he will remember much of the evening's events by morning."

Thinking of my earlier conversation with Elias, I suggest to Lyman, "Have you a room for Elias? My room is quite accommodating, and I would be happy to have him share it with me tonight. With only a sliver of the moon showing, it would be quite inconvenient for him to make the ride to Framingham."

Lyman agrees, offering, "There is a freshly stuffed tick available right down the hall from you. I would be pleased to give you a hand moving it into your room."

The silence of the tavern suggests that the celebration is over. The three of us make our way to my room. Two wall-mounted argand lamps dimly light the hallway. The light makes the moving of the mattress a more reasonable task at two in the morning. With the bed in place on the floor, we thank Lyman for his help, promising him that we will join him for breakfast in the morning.

∞

Finally, we are alone in my room, a candle providing just enough light to see. I look at Elias; the prospect of laying with him is tantalizing. Extended travel can be quite lonely at times, resulting in a gripping thirst for companionship. A wave of excitement comes over me while watching him remove his vest and slowly untie his cravat. He slips his braces from his shoulders, letting his trousers fall to the floor. His shirt hangs down just above his knees, I discreetly turn away to avoid any embarrassment. Quickly, I remove all of my attire, including my shirt. The stiffness of my member demonstrates my intentions. For the moment, I choose not to act on them.

Once comfortable in my own bed, I turn to Elias in his, thanking him for a most wonderful evening. He looks at me as if he knows my intentions. I continue the conversation: "I have made arrangements with Mr. Sibley at the Lower Tavern in Millbury to hold a dance school throughout the summer; it will end with a Harvest Dance to be held on October 31st. I have yet to find a fiddler to accompany me. Although you are twenty miles from the tavern, I thought you might be able to use some extra money for that publication of yours. I will be holding school on Mondays, in the afternoon and the evening. You would of course be invited to stay with me in my room when you are in town."

Elias enthusiastically responds, "A very generous offer; let me consider it over a good night's sleep. We shall discuss it further in the morning."

Elias stares at me with obvious anticipation; the desire to join him gnaws at me. Thinking of the ramifications of such an encounter, I force myself to roll over. Extinguishing the candle that flickers by my bedside, I lay anxiously, knowing it is best.

THREE

LUCINDA... *SUNDAY, JULY 5, 1840*

My eyes open to a glimmer of sunshine, warming the tops of my tender feet. I lay in silence, entertained by the specks of dust wafting aimlessly throughout the rays. The memory of last night's fantasy that ended in that dreadful climax has faded with the hopes of a new day. The sun is shining and the sweet fragrance of summer is calling out to me. My response is surprisingly full of happiness. I am enthralled with the idea of attending a dance school. I slide out of bed, allowing my chemise to drop to my knees. I hurry down the narrow staircase and head directly to the back door.

My morning stroll to the barn is reminiscent of a walk in paradise. A frisky little chipmunk scurries across my path, disappearing into the grass, followed closely by another who has obvious intentions. There is a curious-looking brown beetle that jumps onto my foot, nestling itself between my toes, seeking quick passage to the barn, where it jumps off at the end of the journey, burrowing itself into the hay. As I make my approach toward Shadow, a most magnificent blue butterfly lands gracefully on my hand, wiggling its way up my sleeve, ultimately nesting on my shoulder. I find it most odd that it remains affixed, gently flapping its beautiful wings, as if charmed by me. I smile. "Sorry Miss Butterfly, but I do need to get on with my chores." I lightly shake her loose, joyfully waving goodbye as she flutters away.

While tending to Shadow, I begin singing, nearly at the top of my lungs, that catchy tune about the Tippecanoe: *"Twill only*

help to speed the ball for Tippecanoe and Tyler too." Without
warning, my brother Sumner enters the barn, finding me in an
unusual state of bliss.

He looks at me in dismay, and with a smirk, suggests, "Don't
let Father hear you singing that."

I reply sharply, "There is no harm in it. After all, with the way
that things are going, we are all destined to burn in Hell."

Sumner has an apologetic look on his face. He responds, "I
didn't mean to upset you Lucinda. It is simply that I do not
see you in a state of happiness very often, and I needed to say
something." After a moment, Sumner discloses his purpose
for interrupting: "Let's walk together to church this morning; it
is a beautiful day. Maybe we can stroll down to Singletary
afterward to wade in the lake."

Looking down at my feet, I begin wondering if the offer has
anything to do with how filthy they are. Looking up at Sumner
with a grin, I respond, "A Sunday walk sounds marvelous to
me, and my feet could certainly use a thorough soaking. We'll
leave right after breakfast so that we can be sure to arrive on
time. We have a guest reverend delivering the sermon today,
so we certainly do not want to be tardy."

After our short jaunt back to the house, I return to my
bedroom to ready myself. I slip into my favorite dress; it is
plum red with a delicate pattern of white webbing flowing
through it. My sunbonnet has a wide cranberry ribbon that
complements the dress just perfectly. I think to myself just
how appropriate it is to wear a cheerful dress on such a
beautiful day. After pulling on my stockings and lacing up my
shoes, I yell down the stairs, "Sumner, are you quite ready to

get started?"

∞

As we begin our ½ mile journey to the church, there is a bounce in my step; Sumner comments again on how exceptionally happy my disposition is. Cyrus Faulkner's barn is only a few hundred feet up the road; my intent is to bounce past it, not giving it a second thought. As we make our approach, the sweet fragrance of summer turns into the musty smell of that old barn floor. My bounce is gone; my scar begins to burn. Frustrated, I am still unable to recollect the events leading up to that horrible night. I only remember the blood. Blood was everywhere.

I keep walking, picking up the pace; Sumner has come to know better than to inquire of my odd behavior in this particular place on the road. I have told no one of that horrible night, feeling ashamed and without remedy. The story is simple: I chased an old cat into the barn, tripped and fell on a pitchfork. Father sutured my wound and dressed it with ointment. End of story.

As we pass the empty lot where the church used to stand, the burning subsides slightly. The pleasure of a light summer breeze blows the fragrance of a large patch of wild roses by my nose; it is soothing. Breathing a sigh of relief, I think to myself, *Ten years of torture should surely be enough*. We turn the corner by Mrs. Hinds's house, most of the bounce returning to my step. Unfortunately, like most Sundays, the joy will remain dampened, the burning sensation a constant reminder of my unworthiness.

∞

We arrive at the church to find Reverend Holman standing at the top of the granite stairs with the visiting preacher. Reverend Holman cheerfully greets us, "Good morning Sumner and Lucinda; it is a pleasant day. I would like to introduce you to Reverend Motte. He has traveled here from Boston on his way to New York to deliver today's sermon. He is going to speak of 'The Christian Patriot.' "

Having a disdain for reverends in general, I apprehensively wish them both a good morning. Sumner, with a more cheerful disposition, does the same.

As we approach our family pew, it is strange to see that the box is vacant on such a beautiful day. Grandmother has been too weak to join us; Olive and Mary have moved to another Parish. I expect that Mother and Father will soon arrive. In the meantime, it will just be Sumner and I.

I am a bit fidgety this morning. I chew my fingers when I am fidgety. This is a bad habit of mine, but it calms my nerves until I chew through my skin. Then it hurts so badly I forget all my troubles. The remedy is simply smearing a salve containing yarrow and comfrey on the wound, followed by wrapping it tightly with a leaf of lamb's ear. The kitchen garden is thriving this year; there is plenty of relief for my silly habit.

Mother and Father finally arrive, and just in time. Reverend Holman is already at the pulpit beginning the worship: "The Grace of our Lord, Jesus Christ, the Love of God, and the Communion of the Holy Spirit be with you all."

I respond without thinking, "And also with you!"

We all stand and sing an opening hymn:

"Now may the Spirit's holy Fire,
Descending from above,
His waiting Family inspire,
With Joy and Peace and Love.

Thee we the Comforter confess;
Should Thou be absent here,
Our Songs of Praise are vain Address,
We utter heartless Prayer."

My thoughts wander, causing me to lose my place in the
hymnal. Reverend Holman stares at me, as if he is the Spirit's
holy Fire. By the time I find my place, the hymn is over. He
sees me with my head bowed, in what appears to be shame,
although my soul is at the lake, soaking my toes in the water. I
sincerely hope for a quick end to this unfortunate torture.

It seems like an eternity before Reverend Motte approaches the
pulpit. The recent political turmoil assures me that we are in
for a spirited discourse. We sing of Joy, Peace, and Love, and
in the next moment, we spit fire of hate at those we fear.

He begins, *"Happy is that people, whose God is the Lord."* And he
goes on, *"One of the most common of mistaken and false forms, into
which religion is apt to run, is an isolated piety, and abstract and
independent devotion; religion separated from the business of life, instead of
being woven up, conscientiously, with all its concerns."*

One of my fingers begins to bleed; the pain helps to subdue
the anger that is building up inside me.

Reverend Motte continues with his delivery, *"Religion and politics
are spoken of as opposite poles, the positive and negative as the*

acknowledgement of God is concerned."

His words remind me of the unrest I witnessed yesterday in the streets. I concur that politics has most certainly lost its favor with God. Murmuring to myself, "But do we need to attack so vehemently?"

The rhetoric gets stronger, "*When we speak of a man as a politician preeminently, one enthusiastically absorbed in the affairs of the nation, or more probably of a party, we do not expect to find him in church.*"

I turn to Sumner, whispering a reminder that my feet are truly in need of a good soaking, not mentioning that my scar is on fire as well. He turns his head slightly toward me, whispering back, "It is nearly over."

Reverend Motte is now speaking with the same deceit that the Whigs displayed as they rolled their ball in yesterday's parade. I am inclined to find Joy and Peace and Love in the strangest places, but it is a challenge for me to find it in this attack.

He continues, "*Our festivals, again, are either political or religious; not both together. There would seem to be something incompatible and profane, or absurd, in making them both. Such an anniversary as yesterday is not strikingly a religious day; as tomorrow's published list of its outrages and truculent mishaps in all our cities will attest. And, when the day of the month falls upon the first day of the week, its celebration is postponed till Monday; as if confessedly impossible to bring its spirit into harmony with the Christian Sabbath.*"

He goes on to point out, "*All this shows, not that politics and religion are necessarily inconsistent, but that the spirit of politics which prevails is not the right one.*"

33

The accusation that every politician is immoral inflames me. I ask myself, *How is it that a politician is any less moral than the reverend of this very church? Why is it that we are not seeking happiness, but instead spreading hate in the name of our Lord?* The cloud of darkness begins to engulf me; the air begins to smell musty, my leg burns more intensely.

I choose to retreat to a better place. I drift away, going aloft, taking with me happy thoughts of dancing with that intriguing gentleman; I think sensuous thoughts of how the pleasure of love might feel.

Just as I begin to find respite in my daydream, I am jolted by the strengthened fervor of Reverend Motte's voice, *"And, then, to make all that is given to us safe for us, and to expect a blessing continuance, we must remember God, and insist on a religious morality as the very first manifestation of a true patriotism. Ay, patriotism, that most abused word. Alas!"*

Carrying on now, as if he is the devil himself, the reverend continues with his ranting, *"Therefore, every immoral republican is a traitor and conspirator against his government, as much as if, being the subject of a king, he pointed a dagger against his life. He is spreading stratagems and snares for the feet of his sovereign; for public virtue is his sovereign. He is seeking to blind, and deafen, and lame, and cripple, and make wholly inefficient, and worse than inefficient, he is seeking to corrupt, into tyrannical wantonness and cruelty, the most beneficent monarch that ever sat upon a throne."*

I turn to Father—he appears pleased by Reverend Motte's notion that equates an emerging political party with that of immoral and fallen Christians. My mother looks to be oblivious to the words, seemingly quite satisfied with ignoring the message and resting in her own world of bliss.

My mind can hardly absorb any more of this, when finally, Reverend Motte begins to wind down his message: *"Our fathers have made one more trial, knowing that past failures were from want of Christian principle, and that they had settled these shores expressly in obedience to Christian principle, and therefore they might hope. In faith and prayer they struggled; for they felt, that with God all things are possible in the cause of righteousness, and they hoped their children would feel this too."*

Going on, he proposes, *"If a majority of the citizens were sincere followers of Jesus Christ, is it not evident, the councils of this nation would be wiser and mightier, its progress more glorious, its dominion even more potent than any other world has ever seen?"*

When I awoke this morning, I was energized by the prospect of continuing the celebration of our great nation's birthday, looking forward to seeking happiness and pleasure on a splendid summer day. I am doing my best to stop this man from spoiling it further than he already has. Finally, I block out the sound of his voice. Taking a deep breath, I am delighted to smell again the fragrance of summer. The sunshine warms me, enhancing my sudden feeling of euphoria. I whisper to Sumner, "This is going to be a most memorable summer."

Reverend Motte regains my attention by concluding his sermon in a more welcoming sprit: *"And now I see his communion table before me this day… Approach his table because you would be good citizens, among the other reasons of the act; because you love, and you serve and save, your country; because you would have it long free; because you would be truly free yourselves. Where the spirit of the Lord is, there is liberty."*

I murmur out loud, "Thank God it's finally over!"

∞

Sumner and I quickly take our leave from the church, walking directly to the lake. The water feels refreshing on my tired feet. I bend down, gently massaging them to encourage the dirt to find its way to the lake. The refreshment of the cool water is such that it attracts me deeper and deeper. With every step, I lift my dress and petticoat higher and higher to keep them dry. My scar is flooded in the coolness; at last, the fire is extinguished. The water splashes gently up and around my thighs where it eventually makes its way to my most sensitive of places; it tickles, and I am delighted.

Sumner calls to me, "Lucinda, you are a silly lady. You need to come to shore before you are completely submerged!"

I agree, and begin my slow journey back to shore, enjoying peace in every step. When back on land, I look down, and my feet are clean, my chemise is dripping wet, and I feel alive.

FOUR

OBADIAH... *SUNDAY, JULY 5, 1840*

The morning sun penetrates my eyes with waves of warmth. I am surprised to discover Elias is no longer in his bed; his absence surprises me. The fact that we did not lie together is a miracle; my unusual attraction toward him is a mystery. A life of roaming brings with it some struggles, one being loneliness. With that, loneliness has never brought me to want another man. Strange.

∞

I follow the sweet aroma of bacon and molasses that has curled its way up the stairs and into the hallway. The kitchen is adorned with wide chestnut paneling, making it quite dark, but quaint nevertheless. The larger table in the far corner is set for six; a bountiful breakfast of eggs, bacon, potatoes, and hoecakes awaits my arrival. Lyman, Elias, and Zachary are in deep conversation regarding last night's celebration; Jerusha is sitting alone, mending a dress.

I acknowledge my tardiness, "Good morning all, please accept my apologies for being late."

Looking up with an inviting smile, Lyman motions toward Zachary, responding, "Good morning Obadiah; I believe you remember Zachary from last night. He is an old friend of the family. He has graciously volunteered to help you shingle that section of the barn roof we discussed yesterday."

Zachary turns to me, struggling somewhat to deliver a smile.

His pale face and bloodshot eyes reveal how he really feels.

Doing my best to stimulate the conversation, I joke, "Zachary, what a pleasure it is to see that you have survived the night."

Waiting only a few moments, I realize that Zachary has nothing to say.

Refocusing on the delicious breakfast, I cannot help but to acknowledge that the bacon tastes as wonderful as it smells! I turn to Jerusha, who has not offered a word in the conversation. "What a delightful morning. It looks to be a great day to split some shingles and bathe in the glory of it all."

Jerusha looks up, extending me a tender smile, then quickly retreats to her work. In my mind, I mull over whether to continue the dialogue, concluding that now is not the best time.

The conversation at the table continues to recount the many events of last night, concluding with Lyman's recollection of escorting Elias and me to our room. Elias looks directly at me, appearing apprehensive and disappointed. There is a silent tension that rises between us, reaching its climax as soon as I change the subject: "Elias, will you be heading back to Framingham soon?"

With a sigh of relief, Elias replies, "Yes, I have much to do this week, including a ride out to Boston to meet with my publisher."

Tentatively, I look to Elias, continuing our conversation from last night, "Have you given any further thought to my invitation to provide the music for my summer dance school in

Millbury?"

Elias responds immediately, "Yes, I have, and I would be delighted and grateful for the opportunity. However, I must warn you that my plans could change at any time. I must get my book published."

He then asks, "When does the school start?"

Delighted with his response, I reply, "The plan is to begin classes on Monday, the 20th of July, and meet every Monday until October 26th, with a Harvest Dance to be held on the evening of Saturday, the 31st of October. The first class will be mostly on manners and the basics of dancing, but you are certainly welcome to join us."

Elias responds, "Oh, a Halloween dance, how exciting!"

While the Howes are beginning their preparation for church, I begin my preparation for a lovely Sunday doing what brings me tremendous peace and happiness, which is working with my hands in the fresh air. I find it most enlightening to experience the presence of God in my work. Excited to get started, I make my way out the front door and down the path to the horse barn that sits directly across the road.

∞

Zachary is leaning precariously against the barn, more than likely relying on it to keep him upright. My understanding is that standing helps the digestive system to work more efficiently. I cannot help but to wonder if he is going to be much help at all.

I take my seat on a bolt of pine, grabbing the froe and mallet.

ARTHUR L. MARTIN

Zachary makes his way over to the pile of bolts, rolling one over to me. I begin the back-breaking task of splitting off shingles. We will need a few hundred to finish the job. I decide that once we have about fifty, I will begin nailing while Zachary continues to split. It is probably not wise to suggest that Zachary work on the roof just yet.

Once I develop a rhythm, I turn to Zachary. "So Zachary, you had quite an interesting evening."

I sense that he would rather not discuss the events leading up to our altercation, but he does respond, "I have always admired that woman. When we were both young, we were inseparable. We grew up together, and, as it turns out, I became more of a brother to her than the lover I wanted to be."

His answer helps me to understand the deep and sincere feelings he obviously has for Jerusha. I felt it in his anger last night; I feel it in his sincerity this morning.

Feeling compelled to confide to Zachary my genuine concern for him, I offer, "I must admit that I was angry with you last night, but I definitely feel your pain. I want to wish you the best in working through it. Love is a very strong emotion, but love should not beget anger. If you love Jerusha, then you must learn to respect her and support her feelings, even if those feelings are the love for another man."

Zachary turns his head slightly toward me, with his eyes looking sheepishly down at the ground, responding quietly, "You are right, Obadiah, it has been a long and dark fifteen years for me, since Jerusha met Benjamin. It is time that I accept this reality and become the friend she wants me to be. Thank you so much for your sincere understanding; it has helped me to ascertain a more positive path forward, a path that will reveal my true desire, which is simply to bequeath comfort on a dear friend."

I continue to split shingles until we have enough to begin nailing them down. I suggest to Zachary, "Why don't you take over splitting? I will get started on the roof." I gather up a bundle of shingles in my arms and begin my way up the ladder. Halfway up, I encounter a magnificent blue butterfly that gently lands on my shoulder. Her wings flutter slowly, reminding me of the beauty bestowed upon us. Once on the roof, my little friend flies off.

No sooner than I lay the shingles down, I turn to find Zachary slumped over on the bolt of pine where he was sitting. I scurry down the ladder and rush over to him, finding him unresponsive and turning a pale blue around his lips. Lifting him by his shoulders, I drag him from the woodpile and onto a patch of grass. He remains unresponsive. With uncertainty, I run toward the tavern to summon Lyman.

"Lyman, Lyman, come quick. Zachary appears to have stopped breathing for no reason at all."

Both Lyman and Jerusha rush out. They follow me down the path to where Zachary is lying. Hoping to find him revived, I am distressed to see that the bluish tone has now spread to his cheeks and hands. Kneeling next to him, I lift his hand into mine; it is cold.

Looking up, I cannot help but to blurt out, "Why, I was just talking to him. I went up on the roof to nail some shingles and when I turned around, he was on the ground."

Stunned, Jerusha attempts an explanation, "Surely, his heart must have stopped."

Lyman, obviously distressed and not knowing what else to do, suggests, "Let me gather a plank from the barn; we will carry Zachary into the parlor and lay him there until his next of kin are notified."

∞

We lay his body on the floor in the parlor. Unsure of my next words, I offer to make a coffin for him. Lyman directs me to the carpentry shop out in the barn. Fortunately, there is plenty of pine to work with and a fine set of tools. Spending nearly three hours cutting out pieces for the coffin, I am reminded of the death of my love, Abigail. It was nearly three years ago; it too was sudden. One must always be prepared; no one knows the final hour.

∞

Returning to the tavern, I find Jerusha in the parlor with Zachary. She has already washed him, trimmed his hair, and given him a shave.

Looking up at me she asks, "I have sewed this shroud for his burial; will you help me to put it on?"

"Why of course, Jerusha."

Working together, Jerusha and I manipulate his stiff body, managing to get his arms through the sleeves and tying the back closed. There always seems to be an aura of peacefulness that surrounds a corpse; Zachary appears to be at rest.

"Jerusha, the last words Zachary spoke suggested a deep respect for you. He had gone so far as to promise his intentions to bring comfort to you as a dear friend."

Jerusha, looking up at me with tears flowing from her eyes, agrees, "He was a dear friend, I trust now that he knew that."

FIVE

LUCINDA... *MONDAY, JULY 6, 1840*

The sun is unusually bright this afternoon, complemented by a gentle breeze that flows throughout the house, carrying with it the sweet smell of summer. The weather has been nearly perfect thus far this season, as temperatures are comfortable during the day and even a bit chilly in the evening.

The finger that I chewed nearly to the bone yesterday has flared up and throbs steadily with every beat of my heart. One might think I would be through with chewing on my fingers, considering the numerous infections I have lived through. If I keep up this terribly bad habit, it most surely will end in the loss of a finger one day.

I look optimistically at the number of garments in need of mending, but the pile of mending seems to grow much faster than my hands can mend, and a throbbing finger is hardly any help. I pick up a pair of worn-out trousers, contemplating whether to throw them in the rag heap. Old rags have come into demand lately; I am confident that the tin peddler will barter fairly, a large heap of rags for a new tin lantern.

Mother has finished washing the dinner plates and kindly offers to lend a hand with the mending. "My dear Lucinda, you look to be overwhelmed with work, and that finger looks extremely angry. I am happy to sit with you for an hour or more to provide you some assistance."

Nothing is more comfortable than sitting in the parlor with Mother. Her insights are most encouraging. "Mother, I am so

44

excited about the dance school that is coming to town. I know that I am quite along in age to participate in such things, but maybe I can be of assistance in helping the instructor with the younger ladies, while also learning the steps. I have missed so many wonderful occasions to dance simply because of my unwillingness to learn. I have a good feeling about this school, and, after all, I will be turning twenty-five in just a few days; I do need to learn at some point."

Mother stops her work to look up at me, replying indifferently, "Yes dear, you do."

Mother insistently suggests, "Mr. Lyman has been adamant that I mention to you that he is familiar with a gent who is quite interested in making your acquaintance. He assures me that this particular gent is handsome, interesting, and in search of a wife."

Becoming a tad annoyed, I respond, "Mother, please tell Mr. Lyman that I am quite capable of finding my own gent." I stop mid-sentence, to be sure that my words are not offensive, and then continue, "Although I am getting on in age, I am certainly not ready to be some gent's wife, whether he is handsome or not."

Mother persists, "I do not mean to push you, my dear, but if you wish not to end up as a spinster, the summer of 1840 may be a most appropriate time for you to venture out and find a proper mate."

Following her last remark, Mother smiles warmly. I sense that she is trying to irritate me; it is working. We continue without the exchange of another word, for what seems to be forever. I break the silence, "So what do you think about my interest in dancing? Do you think it is a foolish idea?"

With a bit of a smirk, she responds, "Not at all, dancing seems a most appropriate activity for you. Maybe you can attend the Christmas Ball at Mr. Water's mansion and find a husband after all."

"Mother, please!"

The pile of garments is finally down to only one shirt that needs a button. As Mother takes her leave, I acknowledge our time together. "Thank you so much, Mother, for your help with the mending, and, of course, your energetic words encouraging me to go forth and unearth a husband. I look forward to spending Monday afternoons at dance school so as to increase my chances of an encounter through the elegance of dance, with no intent to marry."

∞

The kitchen garden is doing extremely well this year, and so are the weeds. I kneel down and begin to pull them out from between the rows of carrots. With each pull, the pain in my finger becomes more and more unbearable. I dare not look at it, in fear that I will go into shock.

I change positions so that I am sitting, hoping that it will help slow my heart rate, and subsequently the pain that comes with each beat; I take a deep breath. The roses are in full bloom; the fragrance is lovely, helping me to forget somewhat the terrible discomfort of my finger. There is a rustling coming from over by the row of peas. I look over to observe a cute little chipmunk, busily shucking pods, filling her pouch with fresh peas. I pick up a small stone, tossing it gently in her direction. She stares directly at me, silently accusing me of interrupting her feast, and then quickly scurries away.

I plan to bake a savory lamb pie for dinner tomorrow. I begin the gentle process of harvesting some parsley, rosemary, and thyme. It seems a much better option for now, considering that the pulling of weeds had become quite painful.

I finish my chores in the garden, taking twenty or more trips to the well for water. The watering can is in need of repair, as half of the water leaks out through the rusted seams before I can get the water to the carrots. I decide to bring the watering can out to the barn for Father to solder, since it seems a bit silly to continue. It is unusual for Father to be in from the fields so early in the day. I approach him with optimism. "Father, the watering can is leaking quite badly. Is there a chance you might have a moment to repair it?"

Father is a rather tall man, his cheekbones pronounced, causing his unusually dark eyes to appear sunken. The darkened skin that encircles them accentuates his hollowed look. He has a stern demeanor, offset only by my knowledge of a more gentle side, a side not readily shared with many. He is busy repairing some sort of contraption on the bench, paying little attention to me. Without losing concentration on his present activity, he responds quietly, "Just place it on the shelf with the other tinware, I will tend to it when I am through repairing this gearbox. I was planning to light the soldering furnace later today anyway."

I cheerfully respond, "Thank you, Father."

I reach over his shoulder to place the can on the shelf, passing my very swollen finger in front of him. He immediately stops what he is doing, and in an alarmed tone asks, "Lucinda, what in the heavens have you done to your finger?"

I look down at it; the wound has gotten much worse since I was in the parlor with Mother. It has swollen to double its size, and a large pocket of puss has formed around my fingernail. I try to make small of it. "Father, it is nothing; I just chewed it a little bit too much. I will put more salve on it; I am sure it will heal shortly."

Obviously frustrated with me, Father puts down his tools and instructs me to go into the house and boil some water. The thought of what surely is to come is enough to make me nauseous. Passing by the axe on my way out of the barn, I briefly have the thought of simply chopping my finger off and getting on with it.

∞

I sit in the kitchen next to the window where the late afternoon sun is most prominent. Mother adds some water to the cauldron hanging on the crane, adding a few chunks of wood to the embers. Father has followed me in, heading straight away to the chimney cupboard in the parlor to fetch the bottle of rum. This, of course, is never a good sign. I take a close look at my finger, realizing now that it has really gotten much worse than I have ever seen it. There is a red streak beginning its way across my palm toward my wrist indicating a horrible infection. For the first time, I accept how serious this might be.

Father places a full mug of rum on the table next to me, instructing me to drink. Rum is not my favorite beverage, but in looking at the pocketknife that he has prepared for surgery,

I decide it best to drink and not complain.

With a tone of concern in his voice, Father asks, "Lucinda, when will you ever learn not to chew your fingers? This infection is deep; the chances that we will successfully draw it all out are very small. Since I must make a deep incision, I advise that you drink as much of that rum as you possibly can."

Father's words are not at all comforting to my soul; the anticipation of pain has me trembling. The rum begins to affect my thinking and quietly helps to soothe my anxiety. I take another sizable drink from the mug; thankfully, I begin to lose perspective of what is about to happen. Father has layered the table with freshly boiled rags. He gently pulls my hand close to him. I involuntarily drop my head onto the table. In a daze, I allow my thoughts to wander back to Saturday's celebration. There is a tingling warmth in my belly; I concentrate my thoughts on the intriguing gentleman's warm eyes. Oddly, my scar does not interfere with my desire to touch him.

Without warning, my world explodes into a burst of light, the pain shooting through me like a bolt of lightning. The room begins to spin in slow motion. The pain becomes intolerable; the room goes dark.

When I come to, there is blood and yellow puss everywhere, including Father's vest and a dab curiously hanging from his face. The pain has subsided to a bearable level, but it still sizzles as if being held over an open fire. Albeit, I am relieved that the worse of the procedure is over.

Slowly regaining my composure, I watch Father as he reaches

for the can of turpentine, pouring a good amount into the open wound. I scream, "Enough is enough!"

I withdraw my hand and look closely at my finger, remembering little before falling unconscious a second time.

"Lucinda, I am sorry." Father quickly bends down and lends me a hand to get up from the floor. Apparently, I had toppled from the chair, landing in a pool of my own blood.

Mother has prepared a poultice of comfrey and calendula mixed in lavender oil. She gently places it on my finger. She finishes by wrapping it with a strip of hot rag to hold it in place.

She tenderly asks, "Now, how does that feel?"

The rum has taken its toll on me, making it quite difficult to focus. I reply, "Mother, it all feels much better now. I truly need to stop chewing my fingers, don't I?"

∞

Taking my leave to a softer chair in the parlor, I sit and raise my hand up over my head to help stop the bleeding; this helps to relieve the throbbing pain as well. When Mother finishes in the kitchen, she comes to the parlor to sit with me.

I start a conversation, surely influenced by the rum. "Mother, why is it that I desire to be touched, and yet, am so afraid to let a man become close to me?" I feel the tears forming in my eyes, not able to control the crazy thoughts that are currently bombarding me. My finger continues to bleed and the throbbing becomes worse.

No sooner than the words roll off my tongue, I want to retract them. I know the answer; I am the only one that knows the answer, besides him. Whoever he is. Why burden Mother with such a question? She certainly knows not the root of my problem.

Mother responds clumsily with her typical viewpoint, "You have simply not found the right gent. Give yourself time my dear."

The rum replies, "The right gent will likely come into my life at any moment, now that I am twenty-five, and soon to be without a finger, or maybe worse, my entire right arm."

The room begins to spin around most precariously, soon becoming an unbearable sensation. "Mother, I am feeling quite ill. I think it is best that I make my way up the stairs to my bed."

I perceive the worry that Mother feels for me, but I can do little to assure her of my well-being. She swiftly makes her way over to me. "Please, let me provide you some support going up the stairs."

∞

The stairway is narrow; I am quite unsteady on my feet. Mother follows me, stair by stair, her hands placed on my hips; she is doing her best to keep me steady. We arrive at the top of the stairs, making our way to the bed, which is on the other side of the room. I quickly strip down to my chemise and fall onto the bed. Mother assures me, "Tomorrow will be a much happier day for you, dear. Shout out if you need help during the night." She positions the chamber pot close to my bed, knowing that I may not make it through the night without needing it.

Doing my best to smile, "Thank you, Mother. Good night."

It is early in the evening for bed; the room remains lit by daylight. The activities of the day have certainly taken their toll on me. The spinning sensation has subsided quite considerably and it appears that my finger has finally stopped bleeding. I murmur to myself, "Things are certainly looking up."

Not knowing what else to do, I pray to the Lord that Father was able to drain all of the poison from my finger. I continue by making a pact with myself to stop the nasty habit of chewing my fingers, for the last time.

Closing my eyes, I concentrate on conjuring up pleasant thoughts. My efforts are rewarded with a lucid vision of that intriguing gentleman—the one I let get away.

SIX

OBADIAH... *MONDAY, JULY 6, 1840*

The taproom is tranquil this evening, permitting me quality time for reflection. Lyman is off caring for his ill father. He has mentioned several times during my stay that he does not expect him to live much longer. I know this is taking a toll on the Howe family, but it seems to be especially hard on Jerusha, especially now considering Zachary's sudden death.

From out of the stillness, an angelic voice fills the air, accompanied by the sweet sound of a soft but commanding performance on the pianoforte.

"Thou'll break my heart, thou warbling bird,
That wantons thro' the flowering thorn!
Thou minds me o' departed joys,

Departed never to return."

I latch onto my pint of ale and make my way slowly but deliberately to the parlor. To my pleasant surprise, I discover Jerusha sitting at the pianoforte. I stand in the doorway admiring this amazingly talented woman as she exposes her melancholy soul to the empty room. She continues to enchant me with heavenly music.

"Wi' lightsome heart I pu'd a rose,
Fu' sweet upon its thorny tree!
And may fause Luver staw my rose,
But ah! he left the thorn wi' me."

When she takes notice of me, she stops abruptly. I feel as if I have intruded into her space, but to my surprise, she turns ever so gently toward me and shares that tender smile. I am relieved.

"Obadiah, it is so good to see you. You seem like such a sweet man, a quality I have not encountered around here in nearly eighteen years. I welcome you, please have a seat."

There is a tall stack of music on the pianoforte; Jerusha carefully places "Bonnie Doon" back in its proper order. When she is through, she takes a seat next to me, subtly inviting me into conversation.

"It has been a pleasure to make your acquaintance, Obadiah. Throughout the years, many men have passed through these doors, none with much decency, all seeming to have their selfish quirks about them. Most make their way directly to the taproom upon entry, engaging my brother Lyman in a strong drink or three. Any man of decency has no respite around here once the drink begins to flow. However, times are changing; temperance is becoming more like abstinence here in Sudbury. Unfortunately, much destruction has come to my life from that accursed behavior."

Surprised by Jerusha's opening words, I am careful not to burst out in response without the proper thought behind it. I stare with warmth into her eyes, quickly finding entry into the depths of her soul. My intuition suggests that she is longing for happiness, a happiness she once knew. "I must say, Jerusha, you sing lovingly, and with such feeling, as if you possess a direct connection with the heavens, and a strong desire to be there."

She looks at me in amazement. "How astute of you to know my true feelings. My love for life in this world escaped through that door when I was twenty-five years old. That was eighteen years ago. Since then, I have been laying up my treasures in Heaven. And it is true—when I sing, I feel that my soul is elevated beyond this world, as if it mingles with the promise of happiness that only Heaven can bring."

Jerusha's sincerity goes beyond the normal course of conversation. She has invited me to share in her soulful quest to understand the feelings that she has toward this world, and the world to come. My suspicion is that to some extent she has unlocked the mystery of love, somehow managing to have a foot planted both here on Earth and also in the heavens above.

I respond, "Is it not the very purpose of life to promote and foster love in this world, so as to know it in the next?"

"Yes, Obadiah, it is, but my love in this world has vanished, and will not be found again until my death. When I die, I will be buried under a most glorious tombstone; it is there that I will await the return of my beloved Benjamin."

She pauses a moment to reminisce. "When I was young, I used to ramble in the fields and the groves, admiring the view of the thickly dotted green upon the trees. This, with the numerous plants and flowers, together with the heavenly music of the mingled notes of the feathered tribe, always made my mind so tranquil and serene. I loved to sing and dance, and when I met Benjamin, it was love at first sight."

I gaze into Jerusha's eyes, appreciating her sincerity. I remind her compassionately that she is still here in this world. "You are a most gracious woman. Knowing you for these few days will forever impact my life. I feel as if I have known you for many years, and because of that, it saddens me to see you in such a melancholic way."

She replies, "I appreciate what you say, and sometimes regret that I have squandered so much of my life away in sadness. Enough about me. Tell me a little about yourself."

"Where to begin? I will begin my twenty-seventh year in less than a month. The biggest impact on my life has been my Uncle John. Uncle John was an itinerant dance master who traveled throughout New England. He would spend hours bedazzling me with his stories. I was no older than ten when I decided that, someday, I would follow in his footsteps, reliving some of those stories for myself."

A look of surprise comes over Jerusha as she asks, "So, you make your living traveling around teaching dance?"

"Partly true, I was also gifted with the ability to work with my hands, and so I also carry with me the essential tools of a carpenter. I truly enjoy the freedom of travel and the excitement of meeting new people along the way. My uncle taught me to appreciate the mystical effect that music and dance has on the souls of youth. My work as a dance master goes much beyond the simple teaching of figures to a bunch of hooligans, but instead, transforming those hooligans into responsible young adults. I find nothing does this more fitting than dancing school and the ballroom."

Jerusha appears fascinated by my story thus far. "I also find a strong sense of peace in my being unattached to the things of this world. Things of the world are transient, here today and gone tomorrow. Be not mistaken, I love everything about this world. Every moment is better than the next. I find happiness in your smile, and in your angelic voice. These treasures bring me happiness. They are the treasures that help define me. They are my Heaven, Heaven right here on Earth."

Looking up into Jerusha's eyes, I notice a tear rolling down her cheek. "My apologies Jerusha, I did not mean to upset you."

"Oh, quite the contrary Obadiah, your demeanor is very inspiring to me. So much so, I want to share with you a little secret that I hold very dear to my heart."

With a bit of apprehension, Jerusha begins, "The evening before Benjamin left to travel back to England, we sat right here in this room, gazing into one another's eyes for the last time. Our love for each other had grown beyond this world and we had everything: intimacy, passion, and commitment. We finally kissed goodnight very late in the evening."

Jerusha's voice is trembling. "I went to my room and laid down in my bed, closing my tear-filled eyes. A few minutes passed; I sensed that someone had entered the room. Opening my eyes, I could barely make out a ghostly figure before me. As the figure slowly approached the bed, my heart began to race with an anxious fear. I closed my eyes, hoping that it was just my imagination. A warm hand gently touched my cheek. I opened my eyes; to my surprise, it was Benjamin. His presence startled me. Nevertheless, the idea that he was close warmed me. He leaned into me, touching my lips ever so gently with his. It was the first time for us both; to this day, when I lay down to bed, I close my eyes and relive the enchanting memories of that night. And so, you can see, Obadiah, I do not live in regret, but instead, I live in constant anticipation of the moment that Benjamin will again kiss my lips."

Jerusha looks warmly into my eyes, smiling tenderly. "Obadiah, if only I was fifteen years younger. We have only just met, but it is as if I have known you all of my life, and I trust you. Yes, I trust you."

Having nothing more to say, I move closer to Jerusha. Embracing her, I bid her a good night.

SEVEN

LUCINDA... *TUESDAY, JULY 7, 1840*

My eyes open to another bright and sunny day. Bathing silently in the warmth of the morning air, I feel an overwhelming sense of peace and serenity. Quickly coming to my senses, I realize that I have overslept. Thoughts of the busy day ahead clutter my mind. My sister Olive is expected, and we plan to ride into Worcester to shop for dry goods. D. S. Messinger is advertising a closeout on seasonal goods in *The Spy*. Luckily, there has been a steady flow of shoes for me to tie in the past few months, enabling me to save up quite a few dollars in wages. Many of the merchants in Worcester are beginning to demand cash payment, due to the unpredictability of the economy. Oh, the woes of life on Earth.

Turning out of bed, I roll onto my hand. Stunned by the sharp pain that shoots up my arm, I am reminded of the horrible events of yesterday. I immediately sit up on the edge of the bed peering down at the blood-soaked rag wrapped around my finger. The thought of losing my finger consumes me; I carefully untie it and begin to unwrap the rag. Unsure of what I might discover, I stop the process to give myself a few minutes to gather my thoughts. Once removed, I bring my hand close to my face to observe. To my surprise, the angriness of the wound has subsided, the swollenness about gone. It appears that Father has done a superb job of lancing the wound. The poison looks to be thoroughly bled out. Reaching over to my bedstand to prepare a fresh poultice, I carefully apply it to the wound. I gently wrap a clean strip of rag around the poultice and tie it off. Once finished, I promise myself again that I will stop this silly habit of chewing my fingers.

∞

I find Mother in the kitchen busily chopping the herbs I picked yesterday for the lamb pie. "Lucinda, how did you sleep? Was that finger of yours bothersome?"

I hold up my freshly dressed finger, joyously responding, "Good as new!"

Mother is apparently not as convinced as I am. "Well my dear, there is still quite a danger, as I am sure you know. Nevertheless, I am glad to see that you are smiling. Your sister Olive will join us for an early dinner before you venture out on your journey."

"Thank you, Mother, for allowing me to sleep later this morning, and for helping to prepare dinner. I will hurry out to the barn to begin my chores so that I am ready when Olive arrives."

∞

It is a glorious day, not a cloud in the sky. Before I am very far down the path to the barn, I stop to peer into the heavens. I think to myself how marvelous the view is and how unusually inviting the deep blue sky is this morning. Fascinated by the beauty of it all, for a brief moment, the clutter melts from my mind. Falling into a state of happiness, I lose myself to the heavens. I contemplate life without the pain of the past; I pray for a new beginning. Thoughts begin to whirl. They are happy thoughts: thoughts of summer, dancing, and again, of that intriguing gentleman.

Father yells from the shop, "Lucinda, how does your finger feel after a night's sleep?"

Startled, I jerk my head around toward him, I respond, "It seems to be much better this morning. It is far less swollen and the pulsating is gone."

He nods his head with approval.

Enthusiastically, I inquire, "Olive and I are going into Worcester today to shop for dry goods. Is there anything that you are in need of that we can pick up for you?"

Father replies, "You might stop by James Green & Company to pick me up some Dr. M. Hitchcock's Snuff. Ask Mother for a twenty-five cent piece to cover the cost. And good luck with that finger of yours."

∞

Returning to the kitchen, I find that Mother is laying the top crust onto the pie. I have collected nearly a dozen eggs this morning; I place them into a bowl in the pantry. Expecting Olive to arrive at any moment, I head up the stairs to finish getting dressed. Unlike the days when Olive, Mary, and Sumner were home, the upstairs has become my own private space. I am quite particular with the placement of my belongings; everything has a purpose, and with that, a proper place. Father recently built me a blanket chest that sits at the foot of my bed. Painted in a most marvelous Prussian blue, it displays my initials stenciled in black on the front. There is a secret compartment inside, where I keep my cherished cameo brooch. My grandmother gave it to me, and I only wear it on very special occasions. I reach into the chest to get a pair of knitted stockings, laying them on my bed.

A blue painted pearlware pitcher and washbasin sit on my bedstand. Both pieces have a band of dark blue around the top, giving them the appearance that they were made special to match my blue blanket chest. Nevertheless, I know that is not true. Beneath the bedstand, I have a redware chamber pot that I use as infrequently as possible. Although I must say, it is a blessing at times; using the pot is far better than stumbling through the dark in the middle of the night searching for the privy.

The mirror hanging on the wall next to my bedstand is much worn; I consider it a luxury. My grandmother gave it to me when I was only ten. I contemplate the reflection, remembering the many times that I have spoken with it. Closing my eyes, I ponder the little girl that once stood in front of this window of time. She was so blessed with the many hopes and dreams that come with childhood. After a few moments, tears of sadness begin to mix with the tears of joy. The little girl is growing, and the memories become a complex blend of joy and sadness. The hopes and dreams of that little girl were a blessing, until that evening when darkness filled her world.

Opening my eyes slowly, I am pleased to see the reflection of that little girl who has grown into a beautiful woman. A woman who remains fearful that she is not worthy of love. A woman who has now found hope that she may overcome that fear. Wiping the tears from my face, I take a deep breath. My soul fills with happiness; I think of the abundant possibilities that lay ahead. Silently, I thank the mirror for sharing.

With happiness in my soul, my mind drifts back to that beautiful ballroom in Mr. Waters's mansion. But this time, the brilliance does not vanish, my scar does not burn. Instead, I have a lucid vision of myself twirling gracefully in a stunning printed cotton gown. A V-neck lays low on my shoulders, the puffed sleeves are finished with cuffs at my wrists. It is a cream color with woven stripes, printed with sprigs of rosebuds in green, rose, yellow, and brown. As I twirl, a foot-wide border printed in the same color, featuring large swags and sprays, comes alive. Just as I finish my spin, I reach out gracefully to my partner. My vision is of a tall gentleman with dark curly hair; his eyes are dark and penetrating, but the rest of his face is vague. His features are translucent and undefined, but I am mysteriously attracted to him nevertheless. Just as he takes my hand, beginning to pull me toward him, my thoughts are redirected to the voice of my sister Olive. "Lucinda, look at you, twirling about as if you were at a ball!"

My stance stiffens. "Olive, you startled me. I didn't hear you coming up the stairs. I suppose I must look quite ridiculous, twirling around in a trance."

My sister Olive is wearing a pretty green dress. Her disposition is always on the happy side. "Lucinda, it is such a pleasure to see you so happy on this bright Tuesday in July. I am so looking forward to our journey into Worcester this afternoon. How is Shadow holding up in the summer heat?"

Envisioning my lovely horse, I reply, "Shadow is doing just wonderfully; the summer weather has been quite pleasant after all. And how are you doing? How is your husband?"

Olive responds, "My dear husband continues his struggle to find work. He picks up an odd job from time to time, but the steady work he had at the armory has slowed considerably. I am doing fine, doing my best to make ends meet with what we have."

Olive notices my bandaged finger and immediately redirects the conversation. "Lucinda, what have you done to your finger? Your bandage is dripping with blood!"

Looking down at it, I am stunned to see it bleeding again. "Oh, I must have opened the wound while dancing around like a fool. A result of my bad habit of chewing my fingers. Father had to lance it yesterday to drain the poison. Let me just take a moment to tend to it."

The savory smell of lamb pie finds its way up the stairs, reminding me that we must hurry with dinner so as to get on the road soon. I suggest to Olive, "You should go down to the kitchen to help Mother make final preparations for dinner. I will join you shortly."

I remove the bloody rag to find that there is very little swelling and the bleeding has already stopped. I apply a fresh poultice, wrapping it up tightly. The delicious smell of dinner is calling me. I pull on my stockings, and then slip my petticoat and dress over my chemise.

There is a peg on the wall in need of a dress to hang on it. I envision that beautiful printed cotton gown on it; it is certainly a gown proper for a Christmas Ball.

∞

The journey to Goddard's Row in Worcester is approximately six miles. We hasten to complete our meal so that we might help Mother clean up before we leave. Olive suggests, "Lucinda, maybe you can go prepare the carriage while I help Mother to put things back in order here in the kitchen."

As I am leading Shadow from the barn, she appears eager to get out into the sunshine. She makes herself very helpful by positioning herself exactly in front of the carriage. It only takes me a few moments to get her hitched. I place a bucket of freshly drawn water in front of her, encouraging her to drink. I brush her mane until Olive arrives at the carriage. I stroke the side of Shadow's face. "It is time for us to go."

Olive and I climb up onto the carriage, readying ourselves for the journey. Father peers out of the workshop, quietly reminding us to be careful. "Enjoy your afternoon ladies, and take care of yourselves. Try not to forget my snuff."

The road is quite manageable, but very dusty during the summer months. The potato crops are growing well. They surround us on both sides as we make our way down the road toward Asa Hayden's place and into Worcester. The transformation from the calm of rural life to the hustle of canals and railroads is fascinating to me. As we approach Green Street passing over the Blackstone Canal, the streets become quite congested with horses and carriages. People are everywhere, shuffling from here to there. They appear to be rapt, like a colony of ants. It is both exciting and overwhelming at the same time.

As we approach Goddard's Row, we pass by a small carriage occupied by a single gentleman. I think to myself that it can't be true. I turn to Olive, blurting out, "It's him!" I turn back just in time to see him acknowledge me with a tip of his hat, and a most tender smile. He did recognize me.

Olive turns to me in a state of confusion, replying, "Who?"

"Oh Olive, that is the gent that passed me by at the celebration last Saturday. I haven't been able to get him out of my mind."

Olive replies, "He simply passes by you, and now you are in love? Lucinda, this is very much out of character for you. Are you sure that is all he did—pass you by?"

My thoughts explode; the excitement brings on unexpected chills. The attraction I am feeling for this stranger is an absolute mystery. I murmur a few words to remind myself, "I am fearful of love."

Olive looks back over at me and shakes her head in confusion. We turn on to Goddard's Row and bring the carriage to a stop directly in front of D. S. Messinger's. We had brought along the bucket of water for Shadow, who, although seeming quite rested considering the six-mile journey, begins drinking as soon as I put the bucket down in front of her. I tie her to the hitching post and we make our way into the store.

The selection of dry goods is remarkable. There are yards and yards of summer stuffs, consisting of Neapolitan cloths, Camleteens Orleans cloth, brown linen drilling, log cabins, denims, mole-skins, &c. &c. As we make our way through the store, my attention turns to the Fresh Prints, especially to the stock of printed muslins. There is an overwhelming sense of bewilderment, when I discover a bolt of printed fabric that closely resembles the fabric of the gown that I envisioned in my fantasy this morning, while dancing in my room. The details are stunning; the border is printed exactly as I remember. Olive is close by. She looks over at me as I gaze at the fabric in astonishment. She is surely beginning to believe that I am crazed. She asks tentatively, "Are you alright?"

"I must have this fabric. It is exactly what I am looking for. It certainly will make a most marvelous gown for dancing!"

Olive replies, "Lucinda, when have you ever gone dancing? Have you lost your mind?"

I ponder what Olive is implying, but I cannot escape an inordinate clarity, suggesting that my life is about to change this summer. I am turning twenty-five in just a couple of weeks, and I am elated with how I have been feeling about life. With confidence, I turn to Olive, "This is exactly the fabric I want for my gown. I have saved since winter, and I will buy it for myself as a gift."

Olive sees the excitement on my face and simply returns a sisterly smile of approval.

Picking up the bolt, I tell Olive, "It is settled, I will buy enough fabric for a beautiful gown."

We make our way over to the accessories, where I pick up a package of brass hooks. Olive continues to shop, deciding on some fabric for a new dress. When we are finished with our selections, we make our way to the counter to finalize our purchases.

Returning to the carriage, I find that Shadow has finished the bucket of water. She is quite happy to see me. I rub her neck, offering in a quiet voice of encouragement, "Just one more quick stop to pick up Father's snuff, and then we'll be on our way home."

SUMMER OF 1840

The distance to James Green & Company is not far, taking only a few minutes. The snuff Father requested is easy to find in the store. After making the purchase, I make my way back out to the carriage where Shadow and Olive are patiently waiting. The weather has remained pleasant; the journey home is uneventful.

∞

Olive seems delighted with her purchases, while I cannot flush the vision of that elegant gown from my head. Shadow knows her way to the barn, carefully bringing the carriage to a stop directly in front of the door. Father comes around the corner of the barn and welcomes us, "Back so soon? I'll take care of putting the carriage away. Mother is waiting inside, very excited to learn what you have purchased."

I hand Father his snuff, thanking him for helping with the carriage. Olive and I make our way down the worn path to the back door. Mother is standing in the doorway with an incredible smile on her face, no doubt excited to hear all about our adventure.

I begin by assuring Mother, "The journey went extremely well. We could not have asked for weather that is more beautiful. As you would expect, Worcester is getting busier and busier. The new rail line from Norwich to Worcester has begun to run, and the Blackstone Canal appeared rather busy as well."

Olive added, "There also seemed to be more people and carriages in the streets this trip. I must also report that Lucinda was rather enthralled by a handsome gent who happened to pass by on our way up Green Street. It was as if she saw a spirit of some sort."

"Olive, hush. Mother knows of the gentleman that passed me by at the celebration, without as much as a tip of his hat."

Mother is looking oddly at us both; I do my best to explain, "We passed the gentleman I spoke of yesterday, and it turns out that he may have noticed me after all. He tipped his hat, smiling directly at me."

Olive quickly suggests, "That doesn't mean he remembered you. It just suggests that a handsome young gent happened to take notice of a beautiful young lady, and took a moment to flirt."

Mother smiles, changing the subject, "By chance, might I have the opportunity to see what you both have purchased before Olive needs to leave?"

Olive displays the checked muslin and the corded muslin that she purchased, informing Mother that she plans to sew a pretty nightcap from a pattern she found in *The Workwoman's Guide*. When Olive is finished, I hold up the printed muslin I purchased. With a burst of joyful energy, I twirl about the room, "I am going to make the most beautiful gown ever seen in the town of Millbury."

It is obvious that both Olive and Mother did not expect such an outburst. With a wide grin, Mother asks, "So when will you ever wear a gown? You never leave the house, never mind leave it with a man that you are trying to impress with your beauty."

Responding confidently, I assure her, "Mother, this is the summer of 1840; surely, you of all people will agree that it is about time I do just that."

OBADIAH...   *TUESDAY, JULY 7, 1840*

The vision of her warm smile is driving me out of my mind.
Surely, I have seen it before, but I cannot recollect where.
Turning left on to Union Street from Main, I am quite relieved
that my journey is about over for the day. My detour through
Worcester cost me at least four hours, but I would have never
encountered that captivating smile if I chose not to stop by
Benjamin Goddard's to have the axle on my carriage looked at.
On the bright side, the warm smile is still with me, and I was
able to replace that broken bolt on my carriage axle so that my
wheels don't fall off. Huzzah!

There is plenty of activity at the new Millbury Branch Rail
Road Depot. The branch off the Boston to Worcester line will
certainly help put Millbury on the map. The expansion of the
rail system has been incredible. The new line from Norwich to
Worcester is running now, and trains to and from Albany out
of Boston are a commonplace. What I believe we really need
is a rail directly from Providence to Worcester. Taking that
slow boat up the canal is of no use to me. And it is so
unpredictable.

As I cross Elm Street, making my way over the canal, I can see
the Lower Tavern in the distance. It all comes back to me! I
have seen that smile before, just a few days ago during the
celebration, while hanging broadsides announcing my school.
She was the one in that pretty red dress, wearing the sun
bonnet held on with that cute cranberry ribbon. How could I
have forgotten? What was she doing in Worcester? I murmur

to myself, "How serendipitous!"

As I approach the tavern, I recognize Jonas Sibley standing on
the porch, deep in conversation with a particularly attractive
young lady. Guiding Jasper to one of the hitching posts, I
bring the carriage to a stop. Jonas immediately recognizes who
I am and waves me enthusiastically up onto the porch. It has
been quite a long day on the road already, resulting in a thick
layer of dust on my clothes, and especially on the brim of my
hat. I remove it, gently tapping it on my knee to shake some
of it off. Jumping out of the carriage, I brush my clothes off
and head directly toward the porch.

Jonas is a tall, well-dressed gentleman; his voice is
commanding. "Obadiah, good day. It is such a pleasure to see
you again. Welcome to Millbury!"

Keeping an eye on the attractive lady, I respond, "Many thanks
Jonas, I am looking forward to a productive summer working
with the younger folks, teaching them some manners and
etiquette. And, of course, the art of dancing to some of my
Uncle John's favorite tunes."

Jonas seems a tad more favorable toward my purpose than he
did when my uncle and I first proposed the idea of a dance
school at his hotel. My uncle warned me that the Honorable
Jonas was a highly respected and prominent lawyer in the area
and may look unfavorably toward the idea of having a dance
school associated with his establishment.

Jonas turns to the young lady, rolling out his hand toward her,
"Obadiah, it is my pleasure to introduce you to Salome Fisher.
Salome and her husband Dennis live close by. They are the
innkeepers here at the hotel. While I keep a small office on the

first floor, my days are quite busy with a particularly heavy case load."

Jonas continues with his introduction, "Obadiah is the nephew of John Griffiths. I met his Uncle John a few years back at the Twelfth Night Ball in Worcester. He is known to be one of the best dance masters in New England. I have to admit, when John first wrote to me inquiring about the potential of hosting a dance school led by his nephew, I was skeptical."

Looking up at Salome, I find that she is quite intrigued, and surely entertained by the long-winded introduction. She nods in acknowledgement, adding in an assuring voice, "Well, Jonas, Obadiah appears to be quite a gentleman, and I am sure he will provide the young folks with a much-needed introduction to good manners and proper behavior."

Looking at me, she continues with sincerity, "Welcome to our town. We have nearly thirty signed up for dancing school already. There is quite a heightened excitement around town to get started." She pauses for a moment before suggesting, "Now, if you would like, I will be delighted to show you to your room. Once you have freshened up, I will give you a better look at the hotel and make an introduction to my husband, Dennis. I know that he is very excited to have you as a helping hand around here for the summer."

As we make our way up the staircase, Salome maintains her enthusiasm toward the dance school. She says, "I think it is just wonderful that the young folks will have the opportunity to attend a dance school, right here in our town. My daughter Harriet is only ten, and she too has been caught up in the excitement. While she may be a bit young to dance, she is thrilled that she may have the opportunity to observe."

I assure Salome that her daughter will be invited to partake, "Of course, your daughter is more than welcome to attend the afternoon classes for ladies. I have had youth as young as thirteen in my classes, and frankly, they do quite well."

Salome appears somewhat perplexed by my answer, suggesting, "She is only ten; maybe we should agree to limit her involvement to observation."

Not wanting to overstep my boundaries, I agree. "Why of course."

∞

My room is much smaller than the one at the Red Horse, but it appears to have all the essentials. Salome suggests that I take some time to relax, offering, "Let me go down to the kitchen and get you some water to wash with. I have some in the cauldron that is still warm from dinner. It will surely be more comfortable than washing with cold."

A warm washcloth sounds rather heavenly. "Thank you so much. I will quickly get my satchel from the carriage so that I have something fresh to change into."

The stairs by my room lead directly to the side door and out to the porch. Salome is very kind and welcoming; she is quite attractive as well, although the vision of that warm smile I encountered earlier today in Worcester is consuming me. When I reach the carriage, I am pleased to see that someone has already fetched a bucket of water for Jasper. He looks quite rested and content. I reach into the back of the carriage to find my satchel, heading quickly back to my room.

Salome has delivered on her promise; the water in the pitcher is warm to the touch. Removing my boots and socks lets the fresh air cool my tired feet; it feels delightful. Enthusiastically, I anticipate the sensation of a wet washcloth on my tired body. When I unbutton my vest, I find one button that is barely hanging on by a thread. While this is not my favorite vest, the buttons are quite unique, and surely next to impossible to match. I place the button safely on the washstand, continuing to remove my clothes. I slip the braces off my shoulders, allowing my trousers to drop to the floor, causing a cloud of dust to form by my feet. My shirt is much cleaner than the rest of my clothes and so I decide to leave it on.

As expected, the warm washcloth on my face feels extraordinarily refreshing. I wring out the cloth in the bowl, adding fresh warm water to it. Reaching under my shirt, I use the cloth to wash my upper torso and work my way down slowly, enjoying every stroke. Sitting on the edge of the bed, I am able to complete the task of washing my legs and feet.

Standing up, it feels delightful to let the cool breeze envelop my entire body. After absorbing the pleasure of the moment, I fall back on the bed, closing my eyes. I drift off; the vision of her smile becomes vivid in my mind. Falling into a deeper sleep, I am consumed by thoughts of her. I dream of a time when her gentle smile greets me every morning, and that same smile is there at the end of every day, to whisper good night. While quite contrary to my life as a roaming dance master, the promise of settling with such a beautiful lady feels quite appealing. My thoughts are captured; I am whisked away by sensual feelings that warm me. Just as I am about to embark on what promises to be a most heavenly journey, a gentle knock on the door awakens me.

I open the door to find Salome staring at me from the hallway, "Obadiah, I am so sorry, I did not mean to wake you. Is this a good time to see the rest of the hotel and to meet Dennis?"

Standing in the doorway, with only a shirt on that barely covers my knees, I sheepishly reply, "Salome, I must have dozed off for a moment. Yes, this is a perfect time. Please give me a moment to put some fresh clothes on and I will meet you downstairs."

It is obvious that Salome is enjoying the moment and not in a hurry to leave; with a smirk, she remarks, "Well, if you must."

Peering beyond me into the room, she offers, "Those trousers on the floor in a heap could certainly use a wash. Moreover, I notice a button on the washstand that appears to have come loose from your vest. My daughter Harriet will be doing a wash later this afternoon, and she would be happy to include some of your clothes if you wish. She is also quite good with a needle and thread."

I thank Salome, agreeing to gather up some things and meet her in the kitchen. There is a tremendous feeling of relief as I put on some fresh clothes; one never knows how welcome they will be when traveling from place to place.

Reflecting on the dream I was having before Salome woke me, I realize how perplexed I have become by the thought of falling in love again. The loss of my dear Abigail weighs heavily on my mind. Wandering without commitment, living my life without attachments, has been a blessing. Oddly, I sense that the summer of 1840 is going to be a summer of change.

Remembering my promise to Salome, I finish dressing and head downstairs to the kitchen with a handful of clothes, my vest, and the precious button.

∞

The kitchen smells delicious. Salome is busy at the table cutting up some gingerbread and warming water for tea. Looking up at me, she suggests with a cordial voice, "Put your clothes over there in the corner with the others. Harriet is in the parlor mending some socks. She has promised me that she will be washing shortly."

The kitchen is quite cluttered, but organized nevertheless. The fireplace has a large bake oven; the fire box just about large enough to walk into. Salome is barefoot; she steps precariously close to the hot coals on the hearth while checking the water. Her feet are coated with dirt and soot; I find a lady's bare feet to be quite enchanting. She looks to be rather comfortable in her simple cotton dress. She turns toward me, surely catching me staring at her rather intrigued. She smiles and asks, "Why don't you fetch your vest and that fancy button of yours and follow me? We'll take that tour now, finishing with some tea and gingerbread in the parlor."

I gather up my vest and follow Salome out of the kitchen and down the hall. We pass by two quaint bedrooms, stopping at the closed door on the right of the hallway. Salome knocks gently, "Jonas, might we have a moment?"

The door opens; Jonas welcomes us, "Obadiah, you look much refreshed. Welcome again to Millbury." He continues, "Salome, please make sure that Obadiah finds everything he needs and that his stay is as comfortable as possible."

Salome turns toward me with a smile, "Yes Jonas, I certainly will." She goes on, "This is where Jonas works when he is here in town and not in court resolving matters."

Moving down the hallway, we enter the parlor where we find Harriet working diligently on her mending. She stands up upon us entering the room and welcomes me. "Good day, it is a pleasure to see you again Mr. Griffiths."

I acknowledge, "Good day to you, Miss Harriet. It appears that you are quite busy with your mending."

Harriet has a welcoming temperament. She stands just over four feet tall with long, light brown hair. Her bright green eyes are inquisitive; the freckles on her nose and cheeks are adorable. She replies with the cutest of smiles, "I am, but I only have a couple more pairs to finish before I begin the washing."

Salome adds, "Harriet, Mr. Griffiths has a button that has broken away from his vest. Would you please sew it back for him? Also, there are a couple of articles of clothing in the kitchen that are his. Please add them to the wash and be sure not to mix them up with the rest."

Salome hands Harriet the vest and the button, who takes them, looking verily pleased to lend a hand. She replies, "Why, of course, Mother, it would be my pleasure."

Salome leads us out of the parlor and into the front foyer. I am compelled to say something to Salome about Harriet. "Your daughter is quite the well-mannered young lady. You should be very proud of her."

She answers enthusiastically, "I am!"

∞

The front foyer is spacious, leading out to a wrap-around porch that faces both crossroads where the hotel is situated. The entrance to the taproom is directly off the foyer to the right as you enter; the door is open. There are only a couple of patrons sitting at the corner table; they are busy in conversation. The room is painted in a verdigris green. Typical of tap rooms, the walls are soiled, and there is a stench of stale tobacco in the air. The cage is rather large, appearing to be quite well stocked. The fireplace has been fitted with a good size Tyson box stove, which surely is appreciated during the winter months. Salome suggests that the tavern is busiest during the early evening hours, having become a popular meeting spot for local men. She also adds, "We used to get a lot more travelers, but with the new railroads and the canal, we have had to turn our attention more to providing a welcoming environment for the local men."

There is a stairway that leads up to the hall from inside the tavern. Salome takes me by the hand, leading me up the stairs, explaining, "There are two staircases that lead to the hall. There is this one, connecting the tavern directly to the hall, and there is the one in the main hotel, by the parlor."

Upon entering the hall, I am delighted with the overall appearance of the room. It is wallpapered in a mustard paper featuring deep red and bright white vertical patterns. It also has what appears to be white footprints throughout. It looks to be from *Janes and Bolles*, but that is just a guess. The floors are smooth, having a worn look. Obviously, they have been danced on frequently over the years. There are two candle chandeliers hanging from the ceiling. The main bodies are turned wood, painted with a dark forest green. There are six S-shaped stems with candleholders that look like acorns. There are plenty of other candle sconces around the room, and the fireplace is large. I am quite pleased with the overall size and layout of the room. Enthusiastically, I share with Salome, "This is an excellent venue for my classes and the harvest dance I plan to hold on October 31st."

Salome is thankful that the room meets my expectations. I mention to her, "I have invited a fiddler from Framingham to play for the harvest dance. He also plans to attend many of the classes to help with the music. He will most likely be spending the night when he comes, but I have already decided that he will bunk with me. Of course, I will pay for any additional charges incurred regarding his stay."

Salome appears quite comfortable with the idea. "I am sure that Jonas will be quite accommodating to anyone integral to the success of your program. Although he may work you harder during your stay."

I smile, assuring Salome, "I enjoy working with my hands, it is quite relaxing and an excellent way to express myself through the furniture I create. I have offered Jonas my full-time effort as a carpenter and handyman to cover my board during my stay. We have already discussed several pieces he would like me to craft for the hotel."

Salome seems rather excited, responding, "I look forward to seeing your work."

There is a slight hesitation before Salome continues, "I might also add that Jonas has a young black boy living with him in

Sutton that goes by the name Little Jim. Jonas is quite proud of him, and he is quite good at working the fiddle."

After a moment's thought, I ask, "So you have heard him play? While the trip from Framingham is not intolerable, it may be helpful to have an alternate to help out when Elias cannot make the trip."

Salome confidently adds, "Little Jim can play the dickens out of that fiddle."

We leave the hall through the upstairs door and walk down the hallway past several bedrooms. The staircase is to our right, leading us back downstairs and to the door of the parlor. There is a man sitting in the room where Harriet had been mending earlier. My vest is neatly folded, lying on the table with all its buttons attached. Salome introduces me to him, "Obadiah, this is my husband Dennis."

Dennis turns toward me, "Good day, Obadiah. Welcome to our town, and to our hotel. I look forward to discussing the work you will be doing while you are here. Both Jonas and Salome have expressed interest in having you repair some things around here. I am also quite interested in hearing more about the dancing school."

Dennis appears to be in his early forties, with a rather friendly disposition. I respond to him, "Good day. It is my pleasure to meet you. I have heard many good things regarding the nip cutters that you manufacture. I look forward to seeing your operation. And yes, in conversations I have had with Jonas, he seems quite happy with the arrangements we made regarding my labor in trade for the use of the hall and my accommodations."

Salome carefully interrupts, "I will go fetch some tea and gingerbread while you men get better acquainted. I will return shortly."

Dennis inquires, "Jonas had mentioned that you were good with your hands, and in particular an accomplished carpenter."

I smile and respond, "Yes, I am comfortable working with my hands. But I am not sure how accomplished I am. I do enjoy carpentry, having made some interesting pieces in the past. I am also very handy with other artisan work. I am confident that I will be an asset to you through the months."

Dennis appears assured of my worth. "No doubt. There is no shortage of work around here. Jonas had mentioned to me that he has already discussed some pieces of furniture he would like. I have a small carpentry shop up the path by my house that I am sure you will find quite accommodating."

Dennis continues, "Also, I believe Jonas has promised a neighbor of his, who lives in Sutton, a few hands to help him raise a barn. Have you ever raised a barn?"

"I helped to raise a house for a neighbor in Providence a couple of years ago. It went quite well. I learned some of the basic techniques, while also enjoying the thrill of it all. A barn raising sounds exciting!"

Salome returns from the kitchen with a kettle of hot tea and a tray of gingerbread. She asks, "Are you gentlemen settled with your affairs? If so, I would like to join you for a tea before I begin preparing supper."

Dennis replies, "Please, sit with us. Obadiah, you don't

mind?"

My answer comes easy. "Of course not! Salome, please join us."

Before settling down, Salome pours us all some tea, asking, "Would you like a small chunk of sugar with your tea?"

I nod with acknowledgement. Salome carefully nips a piece of sugar from the loaf, dropping it gently in my tea. She then passes me a good-sized portion of gingerbread. Taking it in my hand I say, "Thank you Salome, the gingerbread smells wonderful." And then, after tasting it, I immediately pay a compliment, "Not only does it smell wonderful, but it tastes divine."

Continuing with the conversation, I ask, "So how long have you two been married?"

Salome answers, "Almost four years now."

Remembering that Harriet is ten, I wonder whether I have spoken myself into an awkward conversation. Both Dennis and Salome obviously sense my loss of words. Dennis does his best to fill in the missing pieces, "Yes, I was married eleven years to my first wife, Almira, who passed during childbirth with Charles. While it was a devastating blow to me, and the children, we have God to thank for bringing Salome into our lives shortly after. Salome is a wonderful wife, and a caring mother to my children. Harriet was nearly five when Almira passed; she missed her terribly. Salome has helped tremendously in bringing up the children, graciously earning the respect of them both."

Salome adds to the conversation, "It is a blessing to have a supportive husband with two fine children. We do look forward to having another child, and, if it is a daughter, we plan to name her Almira. I think it verily appropriate to keep her memory alive in the family."

I knew there was something very special about Salome. Her attractive features go deeper than her looks. Her heart overflows with love. Looking toward Dennis, I add, "Well, I offer you my sincere condolences, but it does sound like your life is back in order, and that there is a bright future ahead. My prayers are with you."

Salome inquisitively asks, "So, Obadiah, whatever possessed you to become a traveling dance master? Have you not found a lady to settle down with that suits your needs?"

I am a bit taken back by the boldness of her questions, but understand nevertheless. "My Uncle John was a prominent dance master forty or more years back. He traveled throughout New England teaching dance, manners, and proper etiquette to the youth of rural towns such as Millbury. While he still attends dances from time to time, he no longer holds dancing schools. When I was no older than ten, Uncle John would share story after story with me about his travels. I became intrigued with the thought of passing from town to town, bringing with me a touch of elegance and graciousness that I could share with the many youths I would meet along my way."

Dennis looks to me, and after a bit of hesitation says, "That was quite a noble goal for someone so young. When did you finally begin your travels?"

"It was three years ago when I decided that it was time to live out the dream of my childhood. I was in love with a lady from my home town of Providence. Her name was Abigail; her life ended unexpectedly in a tragic accident. Shortly following her death, I felt the calling to begin my travels. Surely, much of it had to do with never wanting to become as attached to another woman as I was to Abigail, never wanting to have my heart broken like that again. I thought back on everything that my Uncle John had told me about the mystical affect that music and dance has on the souls of youth. That, combined with the memories of the fascinating stories he shared about his travels, convinced me. My mind was made up; I packed my carpentry tools in my carriage and never looked back."

Salome appears captivated by my story, asking, "Now that you have had a chance to live out some of that dream, how long do you plan to be on the road?"

"That is a good question Salome. During the early days of my travel, my mind became rested. I began to appreciate that while life here on Earth may be finite, moments of happiness live beyond death. Memories of Abigail have become part of me; her spirit of happiness helps to animate me. It remains a constant reminder to me that happiness is every step. To answer your question, I will roam the countryside until I have a compelling reason to stop."

The look on Salome's face is one of fascination. "Well, that was quite an introduction. It is certainly a blessing to have you here. Dennis and I surely look forward to your stay. Now, it is growing late, and I do need to begin preparing supper. I trust you will join us."

NINE

LUCINDA...   *TUESDAY, JULY 14, 1840*

The prospect of finding happiness this summer excites me, and
fanatical thoughts of me dancing with that intriguing
gentleman are mostly the reason why. Most everything about
the past two weeks has been delightful. Even the sweet smell
of wild roses that fill the air. The summer breeze brings with it
an invigorating sense of anticipation, reminding me that dance
school begins in less than a week. My thoughts are filled with
joy as I slowly wander up the path to the schoolhouse. It is
always a special day when I am invited by Mr. Carter to assist
the youth in their penmanship skills.

When I arrive, Lucy Chamberlin is standing in the doorway of
the schoolhouse conversing with her sister, Susan. Lucy is my
age and has been a friend since she moved down the road a
few years ago. She is a taller lady, her body rather lanky. I love
her enthusiasm; she still skips like a little girl!

"Good day, Lucy, and to you, Susan, as well."

"Good day, Lucinda. Susan is so looking forward to refining
her penmanship with you this morning. She has brought her
writing book and she is eager to fill in some of those blank
pages."

Susan smiles, opening her book to show me her progress thus
far. I acknowledge with a tone of encouragement, "You
should be proud of your accomplishments."

Lucy peers into the schoolhouse, warning me, "It appears that
your pupils are becoming restless. Before you go, we are
having an impromptu dance gathering at our home early this

evening. My father is quite determined to teach us the art of dancing a cotillion and has invited some local folks over to participate. Jonas Sibley's boarder, Little Jim, has agreed to play the fiddle for us. We expect just enough dancers to form a set. It would be a pleasure to have you and your mother join us for the occasion."

"Sounds exciting; I would surely enjoy that. I will plan to arrive shortly after I help Mother to prepare supper. And I will be sure to ask Mother to join me as well." Knowing that I am not fond of social events, Lucy appears quite astonished with my answer.

Excited at the prospect of my attending, Lucy takes her leave. "Oh, that is wonderful. It will be such a fun evening, and so nice to have you!"

∞

The schoolhouse has more vacant seats than usual. There are only twelve students of varying ages in attendance. Since school is only in session for eight weeks during the summer, the turnout is always quite a bit lighter this time of year. I address the class. "Good morning, Mr. Carter has invited me to substitute for him this morning. He has asked me to work with you on your penmanship skills. Please open your books to your first blank page."

"Before we begin, I will remind you that penmanship is a window into your soul. The formation of each letter you scribe helps to define your character to others. Carefully formed letters transmit to the reader a high level of honesty and reliability. And so, I ask that you not rush your sentences, but instead, take the time necessary to form them into a reflection of your soul."

The students seem anxious to begin; I give them the instruction to open their inkstands. When the rustling stops, I continue, "Now, please pick up your pens and carefully fill your page with the following: *Youthful enjoyment consists more of anticipation than reality.*"

Everyone gets busy to work; I begin to roam the room to observe each student's progress. Mary Mardle appears to be struggling to form the *Y* in *Youthful.* Trying not to be too obvious, I lean close to her, whispering, "Mary, it may be helpful if you begin forming your *Y* with a slight turn outward, about half character height. Let me show you."

After demonstrating, Mary tries her hand at the sentence again. I compliment her, "Much better. Just remember, the first character of a sentence is the capital one. It is used to help define the tone of the entire sentence."

When everyone appears to have completed the task, I continue to instruct the class, "The next sentence is a favorite of mine: *Religion conduces both to our present and future happiness.*" I walk to the front of the room while reciting the sentence again. The slate board is blank; I pick up a piece of chalk and continue. "Remember, form the capital *R* in two distinct steps. Begin by forming the leg of the letter from the bottom with a slight turn, ending a little above the final height of the character. Finish by forming a second line that begins with a slight turn outward, about half character, now continue the flow gracefully to form your *R*." I demonstrate on the board a few more times and then instruct the class to begin.

Several minutes later, Sarah Peirce raises her hand. I make my way over to her desk. She looks to be struggling. "Miss Bixby, I am finding it very difficult to create a letter as lovely as yours. I have made several awkward attempts with little victory. Can you help me?"

Sarah appears to be having difficulty with controlling the pen, so I show her my technique for holding it. I carefully explain, "When forming flowing characters, it is important to allow the pen to run free, while also maintaining just the right amount of grip so as not to lose control."

Sarah takes the pen from me, trying again. I encourage her by suggesting, "You have the right idea. Perhaps you should practice a page of *R*s and then I will return to look."

The hour allocated for penmanship passes quickly. Before I know it, Mr. Carter returns, and I am strolling along toward home.

∞

Walking slowly down the hill, a dreamlike sense of peacefulness finds me. Wanting a moment to reflect, I stop to sit on a stone wall; a large cluster of roses teases my sense of smell. From this vantage point, I see the inviting front door to my home. In the same instant, I see the Faulkner Barn, that place where I was maliciously violated. Remarkably, the pain of the past is distant; my scar is not burning. My attention is focused on the future; I ponder the happiness that life will someday bring. Closing my eyes, I allow my imagination to run wild; the vision is remarkable. I am with that intriguing gentleman, and we are dancing together at the Christmas Ball. Hope and happiness bury the feelings of fear and despair. I open my eyes with a brightened smile; I head directly toward the front door with a childish skip in my stride.

∞

"Good afternoon, Mother! It is such a marvelous day; might I assist you in the kitchen?"

Snapping back with surprise, she responds, "So what happy bug has landed on your shoulder?"

"We have been invited to a dance tonight at the Chamberlain's. Would you be interested in joining me? I met Lucy at the schoolhouse before class and she invited us both to come learn a cotillion. It will be so much fun!"

With a look of bewilderment, Mother replies, "A bit out of the ordinary for you to be excited about a social event. But if you wish, I have not seen Lois in quite some time; I would enjoy spending some time with her."

"Splendid, I will help you finish preparing for dinner and then go into the parlor to work on my gown. It is going to be beautiful."

The afternoon passes quickly; I finish cutting out all five patterns. It is too late to begin the fitting so I pick them up, stacking them neatly on the table. I call out to Mother, "I am finished in here; I will be up in my room getting ready."

The windows in my room face north, causing late afternoons to be a tad cooler. Removing my cap, my hair naturally falls to my shoulders; I slip out of my dress and petticoat. Grabbing the bottom of my chemise, I lift it up over my head. Nearly naked, I twirl around, coaxing the air to bathe my body with freshness. Coming to rest, I release the chemise and let it fall where it may. I am staring directly into the mirror; I hardly recognize myself. My hair is wavy; it has a pronounced glow of red to it. My eyes are a brighter green than I remember. My smile extends almost the entire width of my face. Look at those cute dimples, and just look how my plump cheeks perfectly frame my cutely shaped nose. My muscles tighten; my upper thighs quiver. Anxiously, I remove my chemise and fall back on the bed, allowing my thoughts to go wild. The urge to touch myself becomes overwhelming.

I reach for myself and it happens. Feelings of guilt and fear
overtake me. The scent of that decayed barn floor fills my
room. My scar burns with a vengeance. Looking down, I see
the pitchfork piercing my leg. There is a man; he appears
faceless. His trousers are down around his ankles; what have I
done to invite such disgust?

The image of that horrendous night slowly dissolves; more has
been revealed in this vision than ever before. I roll out of the
bed, and the mirror is not as kind. The reflection reveals the
real Lucinda: the Lucinda that lives in fear and despair. All the
hope I had for happiness begins to vanish with the sight of me.

I think to myself, *I must fight this; I will fight this.*

∞

Mother has finished in the kitchen; she leaves supper on the
table for Father. Looking at me with concern, she inquires,
"Lucinda, where did that happy bug disappear to?"

With much effort, I muster up a smile, replying, "I am well,
just a bit tired. I laid down for a moment to rest, but fell
asleep. I have yet to reawake. Are we ready to go?"

Mother appears to accept my explanation, suggesting, "We
should bring a shawl with us for the walk home. It looks as if
it will be a clear night causing the temperature to be a tad
chilly. At least there is a full moon, so we should not need a
lantern to find our way home."

∞

The walk to the Chamberlain's house is less than a half mile.
We walk in silence past the Faulkner Barn. The thought of
telling my Mother about that awful evening has crossed my

mind so many times. I begin to murmur something, but quickly become struck with fear; I am afraid that she will become angry, possibly accusing me of enticing the attack.

Mother turns to me, "Were you going to say something my dear?"

Composing myself, I confess, "I was so excited this afternoon when Lucy invited me to the dance. But now I am rather reluctant."

With every step, the fear intensifies. I murmur to myself, "What was I thinking?"

Mother assures me, "Well, I must say, you were rather excited this afternoon. It was a side of you that I have not seen in ten years. Let us at least make an appearance; if you choose to leave early, signal me, and I will make an excuse for us both."

"Thank you, Mother."

The thought of a man touching me is frightening; my leg is burning with pain. How will dancing ever be a possibility for me? I must try.

When we arrive at the house, the front door is open, revealing more than a dozen people inside. The house was originally built as a tavern; the parlor is quite large enough to accommodate the group. Little Jim is playing the fiddle in the background, while Lucy's father and mother, Nayhum and Lois, are just inside the door welcoming everyone as they arrive. Mother speaks first, "Good evening. Lucinda and I are very grateful for the invitation. We look forward to a splendid evening."

Lois responds, "Good evening to you both. Lucy is so excited that Lucinda accepted her invitation. She thinks the world of her. She is right over there, behind Little Jim, talking with her brother Horace." Lois turns to Mother, "As for the two of us, I look forward to catching up on any gossip you might have to share."

Doing my best to hide my fear, I smile. "Good evening to you both; thank you for having us. I will make my way over to see Lucy."

Walking across the floor, I recognize the tune that Little Jim is playing. I believe it is called "Elegance and Simplicity." He plays very well. I nod politely to him, acknowledging his effort. When I reach Lucy and Horace, Horace welcomes me with a slight bow. "Good evening, Lucinda. You are looking very lovely this evening. I would be delighted if you would consider being my partner tonight."

My leg stiffens with pain; the room darkens. Fear consumes me. When I open my mouth to speak, my tongue feels tied in a knot. The best I can do is stutter a few words. "I am sorry Horace. I have promised myself to your sister tonight."

Lucy looks to me with surprise, but, knowing my disposition toward men, she acknowledges our agreement, replying, "Yes, Horace, Lucinda and I did plan to dance the first set together."

Horace is obviously upset with my answer. "That is fine, thank you for your kind consideration."

Mr. Chamberlain makes his way out to the center of the room. Little Jim acknowledges his presence and stops playing. The room becomes silent. "Welcome everyone. Thank you for coming out this evening. Mrs. Chamberlain has prepared some delicious pies and shrub that we will indulge in after getting through our dance lesson. To get started, we need four

91

couples to form a cotillion set."

I am unsure what a cotillion set is; I follow Lucy to the center of the room, taking my place to the right of her. Horace and Mary Carter take their place across from us. Lucy's brother Austin and Mary Mardle take a position to our left, while David Mardle and Adelia Waters are on our right. When we are all in position, we have formed a square, with four couples facing each other across the set. Adelia is wearing a beautiful dress, and she has her hair fixed into long flowing curls. She is certainly the prettiest lady here. I turn to her and David, acknowledge their presence with a smile and a shallow curtsey. I do the same toward Austin and Mary.

My level of anxiety has become quite unbearable; the burning of my leg is gnawing at me. What was I thinking? I am wishing the whole thing over, before we even get started. My thoughts turn to the dance school; I begin to question my decision to attend that as well. My mind is in an uproar. Just when I am ready to take my leave, a warm and tender hand slowly embraces mine. Lucy begins to gently stroke the back of my hand with her thumb. I calm down, slowly turning to her. She has a soothing look in her eyes, whispering, "Relax, it will be fun. You will see."

Mr. Chamberlain introduces the dance: "For this evening, my hopes are that you will learn the art of the cotillion. No doubt some of you may already have had an occasion to learn one, but the Chamberlain family, and I am sure others in the room, have yet to experience the joy. I have selected a tune that Little Jim is proficient with and studied the figures quite extensively. The title of the dance is 'Marlbrouk.' "

Lucy and I are selected as the head couple. Mr. Chamberlain

begins his instruction: "Cotillions are always danced in a verse and chorus format. The verses are taken from a set of ten changes, and the chorus is the distinctive figure for the dance, and is repeated after each verse."

We begin by walking through each of the ten different changes. All 'round, set to partners, women set to center, men set to center, allemande and on and on.

It has been nearly an hour, and we have yet to dance a single figure to music. Little Jim seems quite content awaiting his cue to play. My anxiety has nearly disappeared; dancing is nourishing to the soul. Lucy and I have become quite proficient so far at making it through the changes.

Mr. Chamberlain finishes his instruction on changes, further asking that we dance through them with music. He nods to Little Jim to begin; he plays four beats for nothing. Lucy and I make manners to one another, proceeding to dance through all that we have learned so far. Everyone in the set seems comfortable with our progress. With the help of Mr. Chamberlain reminding us of the figures as we go, we are able to dance through all of them with only a few blunders. We all seem to struggle most with the rigadoon step. Mr. Chamberlain stops to explain the step again. It helps some of us, but for the most part, it remains quite the awkward movement.

Without much hesitation, Mr. Chamberlain announces his intention to move on and teach the figures for the chorus. "Alright everyone, pay attention. To begin, I want the head couples to meet in the center and rigadoon. And then give both your hands to your opposite and chassé out between the side couples, rigadoon, and chassé back to the center, falling back to your places. At the same time, side couples watch the head couples, and as soon as they begin to chassé toward you, I want you to chassé apart, rigadoon, and then chassé back to your places, and finish with one more rigadoon. Now, let's try stepping through it."

Lucy and I both move forward toward the center and shuffle our feet as if we were old professionals. I then allow Horace to take my hands and we whisk out the sides, almost colliding with David and Adelia, who are slow at beginning their chassé. Horace and I laugh out loud, shuffling our feet again, and then whisk back. I feel like a young child again.

As soon as we finish the walk through, Mr. Chamberlain raises his arms and announces, "Now everyone, begin by showing your manners to your partner. Little Jim, from the top, if you please!" A quick pause and then, "All 'round!"

The music is quite hasty, allowing us very little time to think as we move through the figures. When we get to the first chorus, Lucy and I move to the center and shuffle, and Horace takes my hands. As we begin our chassés, Horace stumbles and nearly falls. I hold him tight, doing my best to help him quickly regain his balance. He acknowledges with a smile and a wink. We finish the figure, moving on to the next verse.

By the time we finish the final chorus and begin the last all 'round, we have all become quite proficient, especially with the rigadoon. When the music stops, I acknowledge Lucy and then turn to Horace. "So, we had a chance to dance together after all. Thank you."

Horace is out of breath but acknowledges, "It was my heartfelt pleasure."

I am no longer frightened; the burning of my leg is quenched. Dancing was a good idea after all.

We head to the kitchen where Mrs. Chamberlain and Mother are conversing about the abolitionist movement. Mrs. Chamberlain is explaining, "For instance, the Mohammedan religion does not allow its followers to make slaves of each other. As soon as the unbelieving slave kisses the Koran, his master is obliged to free him. But among *Americans*, if the slave embraces the religion of the country, it only enhances his value as *property*."

Mother nods, and then turns her attention to the group of us who are approaching. "Did you enjoy the dance? You all look like you could partake in some refreshments. Mrs. Chamberlain has prepared some wonderful pies!"

Adelia makes her way to my side, commenting, "Lucinda, it is wonderful to see you. I must admit, you did a marvelous job dancing this evening. Will you be attending the dance school at the Lower Tavern on Monday?"

"Why yes, I am looking forward to attending. The broadside posted at the tavern caught my attention while I was at the Fourth of July celebration. Although I will be somewhat older than most that will attend, I felt it about time that I become skillful at the art of dancing."

Others around us also acknowledged the dance school, and from what I could ascertain, everyone was planning to attend. Caught up in the excitement, I offer, "If the ladies wish, I could make the rounds in my buckboard wagon; we could all ride in together."

Lucy responds to me, "I was not going to attend because of my age, but if you are going, and if we can ride together, I think I would reconsider. Susan was intending on going, so that would be two of us."

"Grand. I will plan to pick the both of you up shortly after 1:00 on Monday, so that we are sure to arrive by 2:00." Mary Carter, Mary Mardle, and Adelia are also interested in riding with us. I conclude by saying, "Then it is settled, we will all ride together."

∞

After saying our good-byes, Mother and I begin our walk home. The moon is full, providing the light we need to make our way safely down the road. The effects that dancing had on my soul are dreamlike. The warm embrace of Lucy's hand, the enjoyment I felt engaging with Horace, together they prompt my question. "Mother, is it proper to enjoy the touch of others?"

"Lucinda, it is natural to delight in the touch of others. It makes you feel alive inside. I observed you while you were dancing. The calm that came over you when Lucy gently took your hand was blessed. And the excitement you seemed to feel when you first held Horace's hands, shuffling along the floor, was obvious. Dancing will result in a much-needed nourishment for your soul."

I ponder Mother's response, turning to her with a smile.

She continues, "Now, there is a difference between touching a dance partner, and the intimate touch of a lover. The latter, of course, is saved for your husband, in which you are becoming somewhat overdue in finding."

Mother's response brings me back to that dark night in the barn. For the first time ever, I am able to fight back my feeling of guilt. While I still have no recollection of how I got into that predicament, I am certain it was not by my invitation. I recognize now that it was not an act of intimate touch, but instead the act of an overpowering beast.

TEN

OBADIAH... *FRIDAY, JULY 17, 1840*

The breeze finds its way through the open window and across my naked body. The feeling is stimulating after struggling to sleep on an unexpectedly warm evening. Rolling out of bed, I find that the washbasin still has water in it from last night. I detect a hint of lavender scent in it; Salome is curiously attentive to my comforts. Reviving the cloth with fresh water, I bathe my entire body from my face to my toes. Falling backwards onto the bed, I spread my arms and legs wide apart; the pleasure of the cool air is heavenly.

The lids of my eyes are heavy; thoughts of the past couple of weeks swirl in my mind. The memory of that warm smile is beginning to fade, leaving me with the mission of keeping it alive. While drifting in and out of a light sleep, the breeze quietly strokes me, causing a delightful sensation that progressively gets stronger. My entire body lusts for relief. The release is intense, the sensation most heavenly, and assuredly, unexpected.

Lying quietly, enjoying the utmost relaxed state of being, the delectable smell of breakfast begins to fill the room, provoking thoughts of yet another pleasant day. It is the perfect day to work in Dennis's carpentry shop. The step-back cabinet that I am making for the kitchen is coming along well. The sun is just peeking above the tree line, suggesting it must be just after 5:30. The sun does not set until well after 8:00 this evening, leaving me a workday of nearly fifteen hours.

∞

Having washed my body, taken pleasure in some excitement, and dressing in clean clothes, I am ready for the day. Following the smell of breakfast down the stairs and toward the kitchen, I notice Harriet working diligently on something in the parlor.

"Good morning, Harriet, thank you for washing my clothes; I feel like a new man! What are you working on so intensely?"

Harriet looks up at me. With a childish grin, she responds, "Mr. Griffiths, you are welcome. You do look rather refreshed. I am practicing my needlepoint."

She stops, politely moving her hands so that I can see her work. It is quite notable. There is a decorative design in blue and brown bordering the piece. A tree of life on the top, a depiction of Gabriel on the bottom, both sewn with blue and brown thread. She has stitched out: *Tis Religion that can give sweetest pleasures while we live Tis Religion must supply solid comfort when we die.* She is nearly finished stitching her name at the bottom.

"Very impressive, Harriet. I especially like what you have written, but do remember, it is only within yourself that true religion can be found."

She tilts her head to the right, peering directly into my eyes. "Thank you." A slight pause, and then she says, "Mr. Griffiths, I am really looking forward to dance school on Monday. My mother has informed me that you have invited me to come and observe." There is another slight pause while Harriet slowly tilts her head to the left. "Is there any chance that I might join in on the dancing as well?"

Harriet's eyes are full of anticipation; I ponder her request. "Well, it is quite alright with me, but only if your mother agrees."

"Splendid. I am sure that she will, thank you Mr. Griffiths."

∞

Smiling, I take my leave from the parlor, heading directly down the hall toward the kitchen. Salome is standing in her bare feet, uncomfortably close to the hot embers on the hearth. I joke, "Be careful not to burn those delicate feet of yours."

Salome looks up at me, offering an inviting smile, "Why, good morning, Obadiah. Did you sleep well?"

Allowing her infectious smile to embrace me, I respond, "Indeed, it was a very warm evening. However, thanks to you, I was able to freshen up with a clean washcloth upon awakening. It felt so remarkable that I fell back onto the bed for a quick nap, waking up totally refreshed."

Continuing to smile, Salome looks me over, simply nodding her head in agreement.

Looking around the room, I notice that she has cleared a large area in the corner. "I see that you are preparing the kitchen for your new cupboard." Taking another moment to observe, I continue, "Dennis thought it would look nice painted in sienna. He thought that he had some pigment, and so has offered to make up some paint."

Salome, somewhat hesitant, answers, "I think I remember a tin of annatto seeds in the woodshop as well. Maybe a brighter salmon color would be more inviting here in the kitchen. I do not want to seem persnickety, but since you are going through all of the trouble to build it, you might as well be able to notice it."

Appreciating Salome's honesty, I respond, "I tend to agree, and there is nothing persnickety about you at all." I pause for a moment before continuing, "I had cut out most of the pieces for the cupboard yesterday, hoping to fit them all together today. Dennis has some very nice planes and ploughs to work with. I am going to bead some of the edges and add a crown moulding around the top."

Salome is preoccupied with roasting coffee beans. She acknowledges with a disengaged tone, "I am sure it will turn out just delightful. I am anxious to see it when it is done." She is obviously paying all of her attention now to roasting the beans, just long enough not to burn them. The fresh aroma fills the room; she eventually declares, "I believe they are done just perfectly." She pours them from the chamber into a mortar, allowing them to cool a bit before grinding them.

Salome has prepared sausage and flapjacks for breakfast this morning. I take my place at the table in anticipation of a delicious meal. Harriet joins me at the table, along with Dennis, Charles, and Jonas. In an effort to begin a conversation, I query, "Jonas, you are up early this morning. How was the ride in from Sutton?"

"Uneventful, thank you for asking. It is a pleasant morning, a bit warmer than it has been, but delightful nevertheless. I stopped by the post office on the way here to drop off some parcels. The postmaster asked if I would drop this letter off to

you."

Jonas passes the letter over to me. I reply, "Thank you, this saves me a trip to the post office, allowing me more time to work on the cupboard for the kitchen." The letter is from Elias Howe. I am eager to read it, but put it aside for later.

Salome adds, "Obadiah was explaining to me some of the details of the cupboard he is making. It sounds wonderful, and the extra storage space will be very helpful."

Turning to Charles, I welcome him to the table. "Good morning, Master Charles, I am pleased that you have been spending time with my horse, Jasper. He surely appreciates your company."

Charles offers a simple smile, nodding, "Welcome Mr. Griffiths; he is a fine horse indeed."

For a child of his age, Charles is quite the mature young man. I nod back at him in acknowledgement.

Breakfast is on the table, and Salome takes a seat with us. I open the conversation with a blessing, "Let us bow our heads and give thanks to the Lord for the food we are about to receive. And for good friends and happiness, we ask these things through Christ our Lord, Amen."

Salome is quick to add, "Amen. There is butter to spread on the flapjacks and some ground sugar and nutmeg to sprinkle on them to your liking."

Harriet finishes her first flapjack. She tentatively looks up at me, and then turns her head toward Salome.

"Mother, would it be all right if I participate in the dancing on Monday? I asked Obadiah, and he agreed, if it is all right with you."

Everyone at the table turns their eyes toward Harriet, and then toward me, and then Salome. Sounding a bit stern, she replies, "Harriet, let us discuss this in private after breakfast. We do not want to bore everyone with such conversation."

In Harriet's defense, I tentatively add, "It would be no burden to me at all; the more the merrier!"

Salome looks over at me with an even sterner face. Thank God she cannot hide the underlying grin that eventually overtakes her, "Oh, all right. But she is not dancing with any gents!"

Almost blurting out, *What fun is dancing, if she cannot dance with gents*, I bite my tongue, deciding to delight in the simple victory just won.

∞

After breakfast, I return to the parlor with the letter from Elias in hand. Harriet is back at work on her needlepoint. "Thank you Mr. Griffiths; I am sorry if I got you in trouble with mother."

"No problem at all; your mother and I will both be just fine."

Paying my attention back to the letter from Elias, I find it is short and to the point. It reads:

My Dear Obadiah,

I look forward to traveling out to Millbury on occasion to provide music for your dance school. My plan is to arrive early on Sunday evening so that we can spend some time together to discuss the playlist. You had suggested I might board in your room while visiting. Hopefully this remains acceptable. I would be leaving for home first thing on Tuesday morning, since I must go into Worcester on my way back to Framingham. Unfortunately, my services to you will be limited through the summer since I am knee-deep in publishing my book. I hope that you will be able to find an alternate in the Millbury area as well. Hoping you find joy in every blessing,

Elias Howe

There is a rush of excitement as I read the letter, anticipating that Elias will be spending two nights in my room. Harriet is now staring at me, partly curious and partly grateful for my earlier interference on her behalf. I blush, though she can have no idea what I am thinking. My thoughts, of course, are fixated on the letter. I ask myself, *What is this infatuation I have with this man? Could it be that it is safe, knowing that a permanent relationship with another man would be far too complicated?* The thought of having a sensual encounter with a warm body is inviting. I simply ache for the excitement, without the long-term attachment.

∞

My attention turns to the hallway where Jonas and Dennis are continuing with their conversation. It is about time that I begin my work in the carpenter shop. I wish Harriet a good day and take my leave.

As I approach the two, Jonas smiles and comments on my work, "Obadiah, Dennis has paid you quite a compliment on the cupboard you are making for the kitchen. He is very impressed with your work, suggesting that you are quite a magician with your hands."

"Well, thank you both for the kind words. It comes quite natural to me after all. And Dennis, it is always a pleasure to work with such fine tools as yours. I wish you both a good day."

I pass through the kitchen on my way out. Salome is as pretty as ever; I thank her for the delicious breakfast. Sheepishly, I begin to ask for her forgiveness for inserting myself between her and Harriet at breakfast. Before I have a chance to open my mouth, she hands me a fresh mug of coffee and says, "Enjoy your day, Mr. Griffiths. I look forward to watching Harriet learn the art of dance under your tutelage."

Her infectious smile thrills me; I reply, "Well thank you, Mrs. Fisher, maybe you might partake in a little dance yourself."

Placing her hand on my shoulder, she gently pushes me toward the door. "We will see."

ELEVEN

LUCINDA... *SATURDAY, JULY 18, 1840*

The first thing that enters my mind upon awakening, besides the fact that my body is moist with perspiration, is whether the sponge I prepared for bread last night has spoiled due to the heat. Preparation for bake day can be quite a challenge in the summer months. Jumping out of bed, I quickly fix my hair and tie on my cap. My chemise alone will do for now. I head straight for the stairs.

The narrow stairway leads directly into the kitchen where I find Mother has already begun the preparation. "Good morning, Mother. The weather is certainly much warmer than it has been." I notice that the sponge is on the table, presenting the frothiness of a perfect batch.

Mother is loading the oven with kindling wood to get things started. "Good morning, Lucinda; yes, it is quite warm. It appears that the yeast was quite satisfied with the temperature and the humidity overnight."

I reply to Mother, "Perfect. I must run out to the barn to tend to the animals. I will hurry back so that I can help you keep things moving along."

∞

The morning dew is quite refreshing on my feet. I have purposely veered off the path so that I can drag them through the wet vegetation, being quite careful not to rub them across any of that nasty Rhus radican along the way. When I reach the barn, Shadow is thrilled to see me. Spending much more time than I should, I brush her and pamper her. "It is going to be a wonderful day, I promise."

I tend to both of the cows and collect at least a dozen eggs from the likely places. Out of breath, I stop to sit for a moment to collect my thoughts. Taking a deep breath, I close my eyes, inhaling the lovely scent of the summer air. Exhaling, I open my eyes. The sight of my naked legs and tender muddy feet stir thoughts of that intriguing gentleman again. Lifting up my legs, I wiggle my toes, allowing my chemise to crawl up past my knees. I take another deep breath; closing my eyes, I envision myself dancing with him. Exhaling once more, I lower my legs and jump up. I raise my arms and twirl once more around; the happiness is exhilarating.

With a slight bounce in my step, I cheerfully prance down the pathway toward the house. I have a pail of fresh milk in one hand and a basket of eggs in the other. The path is shaded from the morning sun, making the short walk even that much more pleasurable.

∞

The door to the kitchen is open and I make my way directly over to the table. "Mother, it is such an exceptionally wonderful day. Do you agree?"

Mother acknowledges that I am bubbling with enthusiasm. "Lucinda, your mysterious spells of happiness are becoming much more frequent. I like that."

"Me too!"

The table is quite busy with the many ingredients required for a bountiful morning of baking. The dried apples are soaking in water, and the rhubarb is chopped and stewed with plenty of sugar. Knowing that we have a fresh supply of rose water, I ask, "Mother, can you hand me the rose water from the pantry? I would like to add some to the apples."

The pantry is just a few steps from where Mother is working. She quickly fetches the water, adding, "A very flavorful touch."

The ingredients for the molasses gingerbread are mixed. I pour them into two shallow bake pans. The sponge for bread is ready for the final ingredients; the six balls of dough are ready to be flattened into crust for the three pies. Mother begins to roll out the dough while I mix in the final ingredients to the sponge.

Father comes in from the shop where he has been repairing some tools for Mr. Faulkner. "Good day, ladies. Would it be too much trouble to ask for another mug of coffee?"

I respond, "Good morning, Father. Why of course not, we have some freshly roasted beans in the pantry. It will only take me a moment to grind some up and make a pot. Mother, would you be interested in a mug as well?"

"Yes, very much so. I will gather up some embers and begin heating a pot of water."

There has been a fire in the oven for over an hour; I check the temperature with my arm to make sure it is ready, but not too ready. It seems just about right. I begin by removing the fire, followed by loading the bread and pies. The pans of gingerbread are quite large, so they will go in as soon as the bread is finished.

∞

The remainder of the morning is quite busy for Mother and me. We finish the baking mid-morning and begin to prepare dinner straight away. The fireplace is still alive with flame, providing plenty of hot embers to cook a roast in the tin kitchen. There is still a plentiful supply of vegetables remaining in the cellar from last year. I think it best to prepare some potatoes and carrots along with some fresh parsley and thyme from the garden to complement the roast.

Mother agrees to tend the meal while I draw some fresh water from the well to replenish the cauldron that is hanging on the crane. The addition of fresh water to the cauldron cools the existing water to a perfect temperature for washing my muddy feet. I ask, "Mother, would you continue to tend the dinner while I go upstairs and freshen up? It is about time that I get dressed properly for dinner."

Mother responds, "Of course. Dinner should be ready in about an hour and a half, so take your time. I have plenty to do here in the meantime."

∞

After filling my pitcher with warm water from the cauldron, I proceed up the stairs. On my way over to the washstand, I stop in front of the mirror for a moment to ponder my reflection. The heat of the day has helped to accentuate the freckles on my face. I had never really given it much thought; they are quite becoming.

Filling the basin with water from the pitcher, I thoroughly soak the washcloth. I remove my cap and take the pins out of my bun; my hair is free to fall to my shoulders. Slipping out of my chemise, I immediately take the dripping wet cloth and drape it over my head. My head falls forward, resulting in trickles of water that tickle as they roll over my naked breasts. As the water flows past my shins, the dried dirt turns to streaks of muddy water; they form captivating patterns from my ankles to my toes. Using the cloth, I scrub my hair clean. Refreshing the washcloth in the basin, I sit on the edge of my blanket chest. I continue washing my legs, carefully erasing the patterns from my feet. By the time my feet are clean, the basin has become quite filthy. I make my way over to the window to pour it out. After refreshing the basin with clean water, I finish up by washing around my buttocks and up in between my thighs. Carefully, I wash around the scar on my leg. It has been unusually calm of late; I welcome the relief.

Placing the cloth back into the basin, I collapse onto the bed and close my eyes. Before I am able to take a couple of breaths, Mother calls up from downstairs, "Lucinda, would you be so kind as to come down to the parlor? Lucy Chamberlain has stopped by and would like to have a moment to converse with you."

My eyes open; I quickly respond, "I'll be right down." I jump up, quickly slipping into my favorite chemise, the one that has a cute little bow that lays quite inconspicuously between my bosoms. My petticoat is next, and then I slip into my pretty red dress. After pinning my hair back up into a bun, I tie on my cap. Deciding not to encumber my feet with shoes and stockings, I head directly down the stairs.

∞

Mother directs me to the parlor where I find Lucy sipping on a cup of tea, "Good day, Lucy. What brings you out on this steamy afternoon?"

"Lucinda, I have some exciting news. I just needed to come by to tell you."

I think to myself, *It must be quite important.* Smiling, I sit down, lean in close to her, and ask, "So, what is this wonderful news you have to share?"

Lucy cannot wait to begin, "My father and I had tea with Jonas Sibley yesterday afternoon at the Lower Tavern. Father had needed to discuss some legal matters with him. I went along so that I could stop at Pope and Brierly's General Store to browse through the new shipment of spices."

This is obviously not the most exciting news I have heard, and so I prompt Lucy, "And this is exciting?"

"Oh no, I am sorry. The exciting news is that I met the gentleman who is responsible for the dance school! And he is divine! His name is Obadiah, and he is staying with the Fishers for the length of the school."

Lucy seizes my interest. "So tell me more."

"He is tall and extremely well-proportioned. He has curly brown hair with dark, absorbing eyes. When I stood up to be introduced, he took my hand and raised it to his lips. My knees got weak; I thought I was going to melt into the floor."

Lucy is obviously enthralled by this gent, and so I suggest,

"Maybe this is the husband that you have been searching for? He sounds perfect!"

"Yes, well that is where things got a tad disappointing. He revealed to me that he is not one for settling down in any one place for very long. Moreover, I did not get the sense that I charmed him at all. However, that won't keep me from fantasizing."

"Well Lucy, it does seem to me that you have quite a fascination with this Obadiah fellow; maybe he will change his tune after having a chance to observe you dancing. He may even decide to settle down and take you as his wife."

With a grin, Lucy replies, "Oh Lucinda, don't try to flatter me."

Lucy and I continue to chat until dinner is ready. I ask her, "Would you like to stay for dinner? We are having roast with potatoes and carrots."

Lucy replies, "No thank you, I need to hurry home to help my mother weed the garden." Lucy pauses for a moment before she adds with a surge of enthusiasm, "I can't wait for you to meet my Prince Charming on Monday! Will you be picking me up with the buckboard?"

Offering a hint of enthusiasm, I respond, "I look forward to meeting Obadiah, and yes, you are on my list, right after I pick up Mary."

∞

The rest of my day is uneventful, except for the ghostly image of that gentleman Lucy described that keeps forming in my mind. I finish the last of my chores for the day and head for the privy before it gets too dark. I find it a much more acceptable experience to visit the privy while there is still a bit of light in the sky.

Returning to the house, I find Mother and Father in the parlor. Mother is knitting and Father is reading *The Spy*. I wish them both a good night: "I am turning in for the evening. I will be up early to prepare for breakfast so that we have ample time to walk to church in the morning. Have a good night."

The stairs going up to my room creak with every step. The room is quite dark; I light the candle that sits on my nightstand. Removing my cap and the pins from my bun, my hair falls free. Slipping out of my petticoat and dress brings with it an added sensation of freedom. I fold the petticoat and slide it into my beautiful blanket chest. Finally, I proceed to hang my dress next to the other two. The empty peg prompts me again to envision the beautiful gown that I am making for the Christmas Ball. Closing my eyes, I envision it hanging there, as if it were already completed.

My feet need washing; I ring out the washcloth in the basin and jump up onto the bed. Taking a quick swipe at my legs and feet, I am ready for bed. I blow out the candle and lay back on my pillow. Closing my eyes, a vision of Lucy's Prince Charming comes to mind. I think to myself, *There is something all too familiar about that gentleman she describes.*

TWELVE

OBADIAH... *SUNDAY, JULY 19, 1840*

The upholstered armchair in the parlor has become my favorite resting place. The space is rather tranquil when the hotel is quiet. The Fishers went out to visit after church; they are not to return until later this afternoon. The overnight guests left directly after breakfast, leaving the hotel vacant. I remove my boots and slouch down into the chair, extending my legs out as far as they will stretch. My eyes are heavy. Drifting off, I envision myself running through a lovely field of wild flowers and grass, directly toward the image of a divine lady. She is wearing a stunning gown that flows in the wind. The grass is growing taller; the closer I get to her, the taller the grass grows. Eventually, it entangles me. Too disoriented, I am not able to continue; I lay down. Mysteriously, I transcend far above the field. Looking down, I see that the lovely lady is now dancing with a handsome gentleman; it appears to be me.

"Mr. Griffiths, wake up, you must be dreaming." Jerking my head back, I am startled to find Harriet smiling down at me. Somehow, I had slid forward out of the chair and onto the parlor floor. Rather embarrassed, I pick myself up and place myself back in the chair.

Once settled, I inquire, "Good day, Harriet, how long have you been standing there?"

"I am sorry, Mr. Griffiths, but you looked quite uncomfortable on the floor. Mother and Father dropped me off here on their way up to the house. They wanted to freshen up before coming back to meet your friend Elias. They asked me to begin preparing the supper table."

Harriet appears concerned about waking me, I assure her, "Oh yes, I was most uncomfortable. Thank you for being so kind." Keeping the conversation going, I ask, "Did you enjoy church service today?"

"Yes, it was fine. I like the singing. The reverend spoke about little children and how you must be like them to go to Heaven."

Harriet paused for a moment, appearing to be confused at the notion, continuing, "I want to grow up to become an adult. Does that mean I won't go to Heaven?"

"Well Harriet, that is a good question. However, I don't think that is what the reverend quite meant. Think of it this way. A child is like an uncarved block of wood. Children are the simplest form of humanity, as an uncarved block is the simplest form of wood. Before the wood is whittled into something ornate, it is simply a block of wood. When it becomes ornate, it is often unrecognizable as a block of wood at all. In the same way, a child is simply a human, in the truest sense. You might even say that a child is the personification of simplicity and love, and that is what God admires most about us humans. However, as a child grows, and is influenced by worldly things, the simple and loving can be lost. Worldly things can whittle us into ornate beings; vanity can appear more relevant than virtue. Therefore, I think what the reverend was trying to say is that one should never lose sight of how important love and simplicity is in one's life. With that, ever since I have met you Harriet, I have only known you to be simple and loving. If you do your utmost to hold on to those virtues, you will surely go to Heaven, no matter how old you become."

Harriet turns her head oddly at me, her face filling with a sincere smile, "Mr. Griffiths, you should be a preacher."

Just at that moment, Salome enters the parlor asking, "What are you two up to?"

Harriet quickly responds, "Mr. Griffiths is teaching me about how to get to Heaven."

I look at Salome, and then at Harriet; I smile.

Salome suggests, "Well, I am sure we can all use some help with that." She then turns her attention toward Harriet, continuing, "And I could use some help preparing supper."

I am left alone, relaxed in the upholstered chair. I dare not fall asleep, in fear that I might land on the floor yet again.

After a few moments, Elias makes an unannounced entrance into the parlor. I stand to greet him, saying, "Why Elias, it is good to see you." Elias is carrying a small satchel and his fiddle.

"Good day, Obadiah. The door was open, and so I made my way in. It is good to see you as well."

Knowing the journey from Framingham is quite long, I suggest to Elias, "Please, take a seat there on the couch; rest your legs."

Salome apparently overhears our conversation and appears at the doorway. Looking at Elias, and then turning toward me, she asks, "I assume this is your friend Elias?" Turning toward Elias, Salome offers him that intriguing smile, "Welcome to the Lower Tavern. Can I get you a fresh drink?"

Elias replies, "Thank you, I sure could use a pint of ale, if you are serving."

Salome nods her head, and then looks to me, asking, "And you, Obadiah, would you like to join Elias with a pint?"

"That would be splendid!"

Elias stares at me with those captivating eyes of his, asking, "Are you enjoying your time in Millbury? It appears that you have secured yourself a fine accommodation, and a splendid lady to tend to your every need."

"The accommodations are superb, and Salome has become quite an enjoyable friend. Actually, the entire Fisher family have become dear friends of mine in just the short while I have been here."

Elias replies with a show of apology, "I am sorry Obadiah, her smile is so inviting, and her demeanor was such that I thought that you may…"

Interrupting him mid-sentence, "Not a concern Elias; Salome is happily married with two wonderful step-children. Yes, I am intrigued by her simple loveliness, but I have come to respect her as a dear friend, albeit a very attractive one."

Salome returns to the parlor with two pints, more than likely hearing the end of our conversation. "Now, you gents behave yourself. Supper will be ready shortly."

Elias and I spend nearly a half hour catching up on the past couple of weeks before I suggest, "Would you like to go up to the room and get settled? It would give you a chance to neaten up a bit before supper. I will have Charles fetch your horse a bucket of water. And maybe you would like me to get you a pitcher of wash water; Salome surely has a cauldron of warm water in the kitchen."

Elias acknowledges, "That sounds like a grand idea. Who is Charles?"

"He is Salome's step-son, a strapping young fellow for the age of five. But verily a responsible boy, he has been tending to my horse Jasper with impeccable care."

Elias picks up his satchel and fiddle, following me up the stairs. The door to the room is open; we find Harriet laying out a tick for Elias to sleep on. She looks up at us enthusiastically, explaining, "I thought it helpful if I stuffed this with fresh bedstraw for Mr. Howe. I also brought up a fresh pitcher of warm water for him."

I turn to Elias, and then to Harriet. "Thank you, Miss Fisher. I am sure that Mr. Howe is quite grateful for your help."

"No problem, Mr. Griffiths. Mother thought that Mr. Howe might like his own room, since we are not too busy, but I told her that I thought you would like the company. And I know that you do not want to be a bother to Mother."

My thoughts immediately turn to the expectations I have had for this night, politely responding, "Well, Miss Fisher, thank you for being so thoughtful."

Turning my attention to Elias I say, "You will find a fresh washcloth in the basin; take your time, I will meet you back in the parlor when you are finished."

Elias has already removed his boots, socks and vest, appearing to be quite anxious about getting started with his bath. He jokingly remarks, "Obadiah, maybe you would be kind enough to wash my backside."

Harriet finds the remark quite amusing. Chuckling, she immediately begins to leave the room. I find it quite tempting, but follow Harriet out the door, calling back to Elias, "Enjoy your bath."

∞

Elias makes his appearance in the kitchen just in time for supper. Salome has fried up some patties made from mashed up boiled potatoes. She has also prepared some peas. I introduce Dennis and Charles to Elias. Before Salome takes

118

her seat, she asks, "Would you gents like me to fetch you a few pints before we start?"

Dennis replies, "Sit my dear, let me take care of that."

After supper, Elias and I take our conversation into the parlor where we continue to indulge in a few more pints of ale. Salome stops by with a carafe of brandy on her way out. She has Charles and Harriet by her side, advising us, "We are going to leave the hotel in your capable hands for the night. Dennis has put Elias's horse in the barn alongside of Jasper. You two behave yourselves, and go easy on the spirits." She places the carafe with two brandy glasses on the table in front of us, offering us her captivating smile as she takes her leave. "I will be back to prepare breakfast just before sunrise. You both have a busy day ahead of you."

Elias is obviously intrigued with Salome's attractiveness. He responds, "Good evening, Salome, it was certainly a pleasure making your acquaintance."

I pour us each a glass of brandy, handing one over to Elias. Holding up my glass, I offer a toast, "To a most pleasurable night together, and a successful start to our school tomorrow."

Elias replies, "Huzzah!" Followed by a quick guzzling of the first glass. I follow suit and then reach to pour us another.

The conversation eventually leads to a discussion about the women in our lives. Elias seems quite curious about my decision to roam the countryside alone, asking, "I find it quite remarkable that a handsome gent such as yourself has not found a wife to settle down with. Do you spend much of your time with prostitutes?"

I am not quite sure how to respond to his question. I take a gulp of brandy, swishing it in my mouth before answering, "Well Elias, I find that prostitution is quite belittling toward women. I would rather find pleasure with myself than to subject a lady to my earthly desires."

Elias looks up at me in agreement, saying, "My position exactly; there is nothing sensual about exchanging money for sex. But don't you get lonely?"

"I most certainly do. The temptation to fall in love with the perfect lady and settle down is ever present. However, the fear of losing her again thwarts any attempt. Besides, memories of my Abigail bring me happiness enough."

Elias appears satisfied with my reply; I am not sure that I am.

"My friend Elias, there is one more thing. Look at all the intriguing people I meet in my travels. Do you remember Jerusha at the Red Horse Tavern?"

Elias replies, "I do. She was an interesting lady. She seemed to be quite gloomy, almost unapproachable."

"She was, but the last night I was in Sudbury, we met in the parlor and spent quite a bit of time sharing stories. She is quite the remarkable woman, her story engraved permanently in my soul. Those are the types of encounters that keep me roaming."

Elias is obviously moved by my honesty. Raising another glass, he salutes me: "Obadiah, you are a gentleman, and I am quite proud to have you as a friend."

"Huzzah!"

It is quite late; the combination of ale and brandy have put both of us into a fairly drunken state. All of the discussion about ladies has heightened my desire for intimacy. The time is right for us to head up to the room. Looking Elias directly in the eyes, I build up enough courage to speak; but I do not. Instead, my thoughts take an unexpected turn to that lady in the red dress. Shaking my head in an attempt to make it go away does not help. Elias is glaring at me with palpable anticipation. I struggle to say, "Elias, by happenstance, I have encountered the most intriguing of ladies recently. I met her first at the Fourth of July celebration while on my way to Sudbury, and then again on my return trip through Worcester. I cannot seem to shake the thought of her from my mind. It is so frustrating."

The randomness of my words surprises Elias; he waits in anticipation to hear more. Having nothing further to add, I suggest, "I am rather tired now, and a bit tipsy. Maybe it is a good time to retire."

We both stumble up the stairs to our room. It is a clear night; there is enough light from the moon to avoid lighting a candle. We strip ourselves down to our shirts, awkwardly anticipating what comes next. Elias sheepishly asks, "It is rather warm out, would you mind if I sleep naked tonight?"

Before giving me a chance to answer, he removes his shirt; he falls back, face up on the tick.

Following his lead, I remove mine as well. The blood rushes to my groin; the excitement is there for Elias to see. I fall back onto the bed, contemplating my next move. The room begins to spin; it is best to simply say, "Good night Elias." Elias is already snoring; my attention is back on the enchanting woman in the red dress.

THIRTEEN

LUCINDA... *MONDAY, JULY 20, 1840*

My toes are frigid; the temperature can be no more than sixty. The cold air is crawling up my legs, causing a chill to wrap itself around my body. Thank God the path to the barn is short. While yesterday was unquestionably cooler than the four days of sweltering heat we had, this morning it feels too much as though autumn has arrived. I murmur to myself, "It just can't be; it is not even my birthday yet. Assuredly, the summer is not over yet."

The inside of the barn is still quite steamy. My first order of business is to gather some hay for Shadow and to refresh her bucket of water. I run my hand along her mane, reminding her, "Shadow, today is the day we have been waiting for. Lucy informs me that the dance master is charming. I cannot wait to meet him. I am sure that he is the perfect gentleman for Lucy. She is so excited."

I rush through the rest of my chores in the barn. When finished, I move swiftly over to Shadow, giving her a big hug around the neck. "I'll be back in just a short while. We are going to take the buckboard to pick up a few of the ladies on our way to the dance school!" Shadow bows her head a couple of times with agreement, and then picks up a mouthful of hay to chew on.

∞

Arriving back at the house, Mother has just finished pressing a round of cheese. She asks me to fetch her a bucket of water from the well. Making cheese gets quite messy. The well is only a few feet from the back door. Father has just replaced the sweep and has also added a new bucket to the end of it. It has a leather flap that allows the water to fill from the bottom when the bucket is submerged. Then the flap closes when I raise the bucket, retaining the water. How ingenious. I would have never thought that water would become so easy to fetch. I fill a couple of buckets, quickly heading back to the kitchen.

"Mother, I am so excited about dance school today. What do you think I should wear?"

Mother responds enthusiastically, "Why, your red dress, of course. And your bonnet with the cranberry ribbon."

"I agree!"

The cooler temperatures are perfect for me to take on the tasks of outside work. Since Mother is absorbed in her cheese making, I suggest, "Mother, the kitchen garden is in need of some watering and weeding. I thought I might take advantage of the cool morning so as to tend to it."

"That would be helpful. Would you cut me some thyme, parsley, and rosemary while you are out?"

"Why, of course."

∞

The garden is coming to its peak quickly, especially with the recent heat. The carrots look the most over-grown with weeds; I decide to start there. The bright sun has sufficiently warmed the chilly air. In delight, I pull my chemise up just beyond my knees. Sitting cross-legged, almost on top of them,

I reach for my first handful of unwanted weeds. There is something rather peculiar about my hands. My fingernails have grown to a respectable length; they look quite becoming. The nervous habit of eating my fingers nearly to the bone has subsided since my last bout with an infection. Never mind that my moments of happiness have become much more pronounced, and more frequent.

Finished with the weeding of the carrots and parsnips, I move on to the watering. Drawing a bucket of water from the well, I fill the watering can to its brim. It is leaking quite a bit around the bottom seam again, prompting me to work fast. It is surely time to ask Father to make a few more repairs to it. Standing back, I observe my work.

The sky is a crisp blue this morning; three butterflies appear from over my left shoulder. They are performing a graceful ballet in flight. In unison, they fly in a spiral, moving higher and higher into the heavens. As they continue their flight upward, they disappear into the blue sky above. The beauty of God's majestic little creatures fascinates me. Thoughts of dancing with that intriguing gentleman fascinate me as well; oh, how I wish I had introduced myself.

∞

After completing the other tasks in the garden, I finish by picking the herbs that Mother had requested. When I return to the kitchen, Mother is just finishing up. "Mother, I will leave the herbs on the table for you. It is time that I begin to get ready for dance school. I had promised to pick up some of the ladies in the buckboard."

Mother replies, "That will be fine. Who are you picking up?"

"I must stop at the Faulkners' to pick up Mary Carter, and then go on to the Chamberlains' to pick up Susan and Lucy. I also promised Adelia Waters that I would pick her up. Father has offered to prepare the buckboard for me."

Mother shares with me an encouraging smile. "You enjoy yourself; you deserve it."

Thanking Mother, I hurry up the stairs to my room. Walking by the mirror, it draws me in. The refection of myself is glowing; I concur with Mother, *I do deserve it.*

∞

As I approach the barn, my sense of excitement for the day escalates. Father has prepared the buckboard as promised; Shadow is ready to go. I give her another hug, "Are you ready?"

Father is in the shop, and I shout out to him, "Thank you, I will be home shortly."

Father acknowledges by coming to the door. "Be careful, and enjoy your day."

The ride to the Faulkners' place is short. The sight of the barn conjures up dark memories of that night. The scar on my thigh begins to sting. Closing my eyes, I direct my thoughts toward the majestic butterflies I observed earlier today; the stinging stops.

My head turns with a jerk when Mary unexpectedly jumps up into the back of the buckboard, "Good day, Lucinda! Thank you for picking me up."

Allowing myself a moment to recover, I respond, "It is my pleasure. Are you as excited as I am?"

"I most certainly am!"

With the Chamberlains' house in sight, we see that Lucy and Susan are sitting on the stone wall waiting in anticipation of our arrival. Both Mary and I wave as soon as we are sure that they recognize we are coming. Lucy is wearing one of her prettiest dresses with an attractive white collar, surely to impress the charming dance master. Pulling up next to them, I call out enthusiastically, "Good day, ladies. Lucy, you can sit up here next to me if you would like."

Lucy smiles and hops up onto the front seat. Reaching out for her hand, I engage it affectionately. "I am so glad you decided to come."

Lucy turns her head and says, "Me too."

Shadow does a superb job of changing the direction of the buckboard. We begin our journey down to Asa Waters Mansion to pick up Adelia. It is cool, but the dust is still quite annoying. Our dresses are quickly becoming coated with it. When we arrive in front of the mansion, Adelia is running down the front path with a cheerful bounce in her step. "Good day everyone; I cannot wait!"

Adelia jumps into the back; Shadow continues the journey down Elm Street toward Union. As we turn the corner, the Lower Tavern comes into sight. The excitement amongst us explodes. It is hard to believe that the time has arrived. Guiding Shadow up to the hitching post, I pull on the reins, stopping the carriage. The ladies jump out quickly, enthusiastically ready to go. A small boy comes out from the tavern. Fetching a bucket of water from the porch, he brings it down for Shadow. "Good day, ladies. Welcome to the Lower Tavern; my name is Charles."

I think to myself that he appears so grown up for such a small boy. I make a slight curtsey, saying, "It is a pleasure to make your acquaintance. My name is Miss Bixby. And this is Miss Chamberlain, Miss Carter, and Miss Waters. We are here for the dance school."

"Mr. Griffiths and Mr. Howe are upstairs in the hall waiting for everyone. Let me show you the way."

∞

Lucy and I follow closely behind Charles; Susan and Mary follow behind. When we arrive at the doorway to the upper hall, the door is open and there are a few other ladies already present. They are seated in the chairs that line the back of the hall. I recognize Margaret Benedict, Mary Mardle, and Sarah Peirce. There are two that I do not know. There are also two gentlemen in the corner of the room with their backs toward us. Lucy squeezes my hand, saying, "That is him, Obadiah, on the right."

Four more ladies arrive while we remain standing near the doorway. It is Nancy Barton, Lydia Chase, and Louisa Harrington, along with someone else I do not recognize. I decide to do the proper thing and be sociable. "Good day, ladies, are you excited?"

Nancy answers, "We are! These are my friends, Lydia and Louisa, who I believe you are acquainted with. And Lucy

Holman, who is new to Millbury."

Cordially, I offer, "Welcome."

The eight of us begin to walk toward the chairs in the back to join the others. Lucy is still holding on to my hand when the gentlemen both turn and begin walking toward the center of the hall. Lucy squeezes again, saying, "Do you see how charming he is?"

There is a sensation that overwhelms me like nothing I have ever felt before. It is a complex jumble of emotions, both sensual and fearful at the same time. I spontaneously clench Lucy's hand, whispering to her, "Are you suggesting that the gent on the right is your Obadiah?"

"Why yes, isn't he striking?" Lucy continues, "Lucinda, you are sweating, and it feels as if you are going to crush my hand. Are you well?"

Just as I am about to answer Lucy, Obadiah looks directly into my eyes, as if he somehow knows me. He offers me a slight nod and a most inviting smile. A tingling sensation shoots throughout my body, settling in my lower stomach. I mumble my answer to Lucy, "I am well, but astonished."

Before Lucy can get another word out, Obadiah walks directly toward us. He is staring at me with those dark brown eyes. He is even more intriguing up close. I murmur to myself, "What do I do now?"

He extends his hand toward mine, removing it from Lucy's ever so kindly. Slowly, he raises it to his lips, kissing it affectionately, "Good day, my fair lady. Why, you are the mystery woman who has captivated my imagination for weeks. It is such a pleasure to make your acquaintance."

I am short of breath and of words. "Why, it's you." Relaxing enough to muster a slight smile, I attempt a feeble curtsey. Regaining some of my composure, I acknowledge, "The pleasure is all mine."

Obadiah releases my hand slowly but his eyes remain affixed on mine. With what appears to be an extremely satisfied grin, he turns and makes his way to the center of the hall. Lucy and I take a seat with the rest of the ladies. I am astonished. Lucy smiles, whispering to me, "Well, there go my chances for a husband."

"Oh, don't be silly."

The room is echoing quite loudly with conversation from an excited group of young ladies. Obadiah is standing rather patiently in the center of the room. He is with another very attractive gentleman. Taking Lucy's hand again, I give it a squeeze, suggesting, "Obadiah's partner is quite striking as well. Maybe there is a husband in this for you after all!"

It appears that Obadiah is rapidly becoming agitated, when he finally makes a motion for silence, "Ah hum... might we have your attention up here, please?"

The room becomes silent. "Welcome, everyone. My name is Mr. Griffiths, and this is our fiddler for the day, Mr. Howe. Mr. Howe has graciously come from Framingham to play for us." Obadiah continues by turning his hand out toward a younger lady sitting by herself. "And this is my dear friend Harriet Fisher, who will be joining the class as my guest. As a courtesy, please stand, one by one, starting over there by Harriet, stating your name and your age."

Sitting in the last seat of the row, I have plenty of time to prepare for my introduction. Although all I need to do is stand and repeat my name and age, the anxiety builds with every lady that stands before me. When it is my turn, I get up onto my wobbly legs. "My name is Lucinda Bixby, and I will be twenty-five on Thursday. My friend Lucy and I thought that we were young enough in spirit to join the class."

Obadiah surely perceives my insecurities. He looks directly into my eyes, responding, "You are certainly not the oldest lady to attend a dance school. I anticipate it will be a pleasure to have you."

Obadiah redirects his attention toward the class, saying, "Let me begin by suggesting that there is nothing more fitting than good manners and dancing to teach the virtues of becoming a responsible adult. With this, we will spend much of our time discussing instances of ill manners that should be carefully avoided by youth of both sexes."

Obadiah is obviously passionate about his teaching. Again, he takes aim on my eyes. "This would apply to our more elderly pupils as well."

He continues, "The first instance is one that can easily be overlooked. That is, omitting to pay proper respect to company on entering or leaving a room, or paying it only to one person when more are present."

I think to myself that Obadiah had seemed to pay all of his attention to me just moments ago, and look to him with a frown. He obviously realizes his contradiction, smiles at me, and continues, "The next instance to avoid is entering a room with the hat on, and leaving it in the same manner."

Obadiah reveals a few more instances of ill manners before asking us all to stand and select a partner. Harriet is alone, and so I ask Lucy if she would mind if I ask Harriet to be my partner. She responds, "Why of course not; it is quite thoughtful of you."

Harriet seems rather surprised as I make my approach. I offer a shallow curtsey, whispering, "Would you like to be my partner?"

Harriet's face lights up with a glow. She enthusiastically responds, "Why, yes, Miss Bixby, I would like that."

Obadiah begins by explaining the meaning of a longways set, helping each couple to understand their position in what he describes as a minor set. He then goes on to emphasize the importance of listening to the music, eye contact, and the taking of hands. He goes on by explaining, "There remains nothing more important than honoring your partner, before and after the dance, with a well-executed curtsey."

Harriet and I have been asked to take what Obadiah describes as the top of the set. We practice our curtsey together, lifting our dresses just enough to reveal the position of our feet. Obadiah is walking up through the center of the set toward us. I close my eyes, envisioning myself dressed in my beautiful new gown, taking the most gracious curtsey as possible. I cannot help to smile as I do. When I open my eyes, Obadiah is standing directly in front of me. Quietly, he says, "Well, that is a very impressive curtsey, indeed." He turns to the other ladies in the set, speaking out, "Lucinda is quite accomplished at making a curtsey." He then looks at me, asking, "Would you be so kind as to demonstrate, so that all of the ladies can see?"

I close my eyes, doing all I can to muster up another vision, with no luck. As I become increasingly anxious, I open my eyes to see Obadiah staring at me with an inviting smile of encouragement. A relaxed feeling comes over me. Looking directly into his eyes, I execute a curtsey even more gracious than the first. Obadiah acknowledges with a bow, whispering quietly, "Magnificent."

Obadiah takes a position at the top of the set with Elias. Little Jim is sitting by himself on one of the chairs. He has his fiddle in hand. I quietly get Obadiah's attention, making a motion toward Little Jim. When he sees that Obadiah recognizes him, he makes his way over with his fiddle.

"Mr. Sibley suggested that I come by to meet you. My name is Little Jim, and I live with Mr. Sibley in Sutton. Would you mind if I play along?"

Obadiah smiles, turning to Elias, "Elias, I would like to introduce you to Little Jim. Would you mind if he plays along with you?" I barely hear Elias's response, but it is obviously positive since Little Jim perks up with a big smile and plays a few bars in response.

Obadiah introduces the first dance of the afternoon. "The 'Morning Gazette' is my uncle's favorite dance for learning how a longways set progresses. It is short, easy to remember, and teaches a few basic figures." I look across the set at Harriet, fascinated by her maturity and magnetic smile. She notices me gazing at her, and her smile becomes even more engaging. Obadiah goes on, "The figures for this dance are as follows, remembering to always begin and end by honoring your partner. The first Couple set to the second Lady, then to the second Gentleman, lead down the Middle, up again, and cast off."

I am suspicious to why Obadiah placed Harriet and me in the top position. When he looks at me and then at Harriet, the reason becomes obvious. He asks Harriet, "Would you mind if I demonstrate with your partner?" Harriet smiles, quickly stepping away. We begin with another heartfelt bow and curtsey. And then, Obadiah extends his right hand out to me with a most delicate flow, ending with his palm up, just perfectly positioned, nearly shoulder high. I place my left palm down in his, and he grasps it with just enough force to assure me of his presence. We turn to Lucy, who is in the second Ladies position, and set to her. His moves are gentle and bold at the same time. We continue to work through all of the figures, making our way down to the bottom of the set. We end our demonstration with a bow and curtsey. Obadiah quietly shares with me, "Quite graceful!"

I take my position at the top of the set again with Harriet as my partner. Elias and Little Jim seem eager to make music. Obadiah gives the instruction to begin, setting off an almost flawless execution of the first dance. The music stimulates me to move with the exuberance of a butterfly, fluttering happily into the heavens. The figures become a natural response to the music, permitting me to drift for a moment while still dancing. The remarkable events that have unfolded in the past hour enchant me.

The lesson continues for another hour. Obadiah describes more instances of ill manners and continues his discussion on proper posture. When it is time to leave, I gather up Lucy, Mary, Susan, and Adelia, and we begin to make our way toward the door. Obadiah is on one side of the doorway, with Elias and Little Jim on the other. I am conscious that my hair has come free from the bun it was in, and has fallen out of my cap and onto my shoulders. Obadiah has locked his eyes on me; I decide not to fumble with it. When I get closer, I stare deeply into his heavenly eyes. They are a window into his gentle soul. I smile and curtsey.

He returns the smile, bowing ever so slightly, saying, "Ms. Lucinda, you are a most gracious dancer, and your curls are most becoming. Enjoy your twenty-fifth birthday."

FOURTEEN

OBADIAH... *MONDAY, JULY 20, 1840*

The parlor is dark, lit only by two candles flickering on the wall; Elias and I find respite after a long day. The first session of dance went quite well with the gentlemen. There were twelve in attendance, all very well-behaved, except for the minor bout that festered up between David Mardle and Leonard Chase. That's to be expected.

My intrigue for Lucinda is obvious. Appearing to be the perfect lady, it is impossible for me to stop thinking of her. Surely, Elias will inquire before the evening is over.

Elias appears quite fascinated by Little Jim's performance. Shaking his head in amazement, he shares, "Little Jim can certainly wail on that fiddle." He further confides, "I was especially impressed with how natural it was for him to start fiddling, looking over at the music only but once to get started. I am much relieved that you have found someone like Little Jim to fiddle when I am out of touch."

Agreeing with Elias, I reply, "I must thank Mr. Sibley for making the introduction to Little Jim; it surely will make things a tad more manageable those weeks that you are not available. And speaking of absence, what are your thoughts on that? Will you be joining us next week?"

Sheepishly, Elias turns his head towards me. "My book publisher in Boston has promised me that they will finish the plates and print first copies of *The Musician's Companion* by year's end. I have promised them that I would pay for the copies as soon as they are printed, forcing me to focus entirely on farming over the summer and into the fall. I would most assuredly be available to play at the Harvest Dance in October, and maybe a couple of other sessions throughout the summer."

Perceiving Elias's sincerity, I assure him, "Elias, do not be concerned. You are right about Little Jim—he is a local boy and certainly plays a mean fiddle. By no means do I want this to be burdensome for you. Let us plan to stay in touch through the mail, and please know that you are welcome to attend at any time."

Elias appears to be much more relaxed after my relieving him of his commitment. He suggests, "Maybe a splash of rum would be helpful about now. I really would like to hear more about that lovely mystery lady in the red dress. It most certainly appears that those brief encounters you had with her were more than just happenstance."

I reply quite simply, "Let me go pour us some rum, and I promise, this afternoon was the first time I have exchanged in conversation with that lady. Although, she has certainly occupied a considerable amount of my imagination over the past few weeks."

Returning to the parlor, I find that Elias has taken the liberty to relieve himself of his boots and socks. He has also loosened much of his attire. He appears to be far more relaxed than he was before our conversation. I pour each of us a glass of rum from the carafe. I raise my glass. "May the spirits bring us together when apart, and may our friendship always remain strong."

Elias lifts his glass. "Huzzah!"

Elias and I are the only two remaining at the hotel for the night. Since we are alone, I too make myself a little more comfortable before sitting back down. Taking a rather large swallow of rum, I look to Elias, asking, "Now, where was I in my disclosure regarding that lovely lady in the red dress?"

There is a slight pause before Elias replies, "Obadiah, it appears that love has redirected your intentions somewhat in another direction. Your face has not stopped glowing since you embarrassed her with that most unusual greeting. If you ask me, you will soon cease from roaming and settle as close as you can to Lucinda."

"Let us not be hasty. Although I must admit that, for the moment, my heart is on fire. My thoughts have been fully occupied the past few weeks with vague visions of what I thought to be a most intriguing lady. But I must say now, the visions did not do her the justice she deserves; she is absolutely the most overall striking lady I have ever encountered."

Elias seems somewhat fascinated with my deep regard for Lucinda, especially since we have had only a few happenstance encounters. "For someone who has dedicated his life to roaming, this is certainly a bizarre way to show it. Is this your first fascination with a lady?"

Elias seems relentless in his goal to sort out the secret of my apparent falling into love. I assure him, "No, this is not the first lady that I have fancied. I was quite attracted to a lady in Providence, whom I thought might soon become my wife. When she died suddenly, nearly three years ago, shortly after being struck by a carriage in the street, I was devastated. Her sudden death triggered a spiritual search for purpose, followed by the eventual surrender of my life's possessions in exchange for a life of meaning. The experience had left me living for every moment, with the innate knowledge that life on this earth can be very short. Furthermore, it resulted in my determination to share whatever gifts I have with those that I encounter along the way. For reasons unknown, the attraction to Lucinda is like a force driven by the heavens above. I must, and will, follow my heart."

My rant has Elias spellbound. He looks inquisitively into my eyes, surely lost for words. He shares, "Obadiah, you fascinate me."

There is quite a long pause, which we both occupy with another swallow of rum, before I ask, "So, now that you know my deepest secrets, how about you?"

"Haven't much time for ladies; I am one of twelve children, always staying quite busy on top of the plough horse. When not farming, I am playing the fiddle, or writing down dance tunes. Romance will surely find its place in my life. I do fancy looking at the ladies, but for now, a lady would most certainly get in the way of progress."

I can see that Elias is quite perplexed over his answer, and so I tease him a little by saying, "Well, Lucinda's friend Lucy couldn't take her eyes off of you. It is a pity that you are so subjugated by the publishing of that book. We could have some good times together." It is obvious that Elias is quite serious about his publication, having no interest in romance at this time. "But, I understand you will surely become the savior of contra dance, and after all, that would be good for my business as well."

We empty the carafe of rum just about the same time that the candles have come to the end of their useful life. Extinguishing the candles leaves us in total darkness. Carefully, I grope around for the chair to give my eyes time to adjust. Elias appears rather despondent, most likely caused by the combination of our discussion around romance and the large quantity of rum we have consumed. The moon casts just enough light for us to make our way up the stairs and to our room, but not without a few obstacles along the way.

∞

The light in the room is much improved over that of the parlor and hallway. The moon casts its light directly into our window; there are thousands of brightly lit stars surrounding it. I stop for a moment to gaze, reflecting on the events of the day. The air is much cooler this evening; Elias falls to his tick without removing his shirt. I decide to do the same, removing my vest and trousers, and then falling back on the bed. Elias begins to hum a tune; I recognize it as *The Star*. *"Twinkle, twinkle, little star, How I wonder where you are!"*

He seems to be about finished. "Good night Elias, sleep well,"

He stirs, and continues, *"Then the traveler in the dark Thanks you for your tiny sparks; He could not see which way to go, If you did not Twinkle so..."* A few minutes of silence and then he offers a slight murmur, "Good night, Obadiah."

FIFTEEN

LUCINDA... *TUESDAY, JULY 21, 1840*

The temperature remains quite comfortable for this time of year. We finished dinner early, due to Father having to take the buckboard down to Burbankville to pick up a plough he was commissioned to repair. It is the perfect afternoon to continue the work on my gown. Mother has been cutting and stitching shoes at home as a source of income for the past twenty years. She just received a new order of shoes to sew; this will afford me some much-needed conversation time with her. I have not yet had a chance to describe to her my first day of dance, although she has been probing me all morning. I am so excited to tell her about Obadiah; I cannot get him out of my mind. The parlor is comfortable; a gentle breeze is blowing directly at me. The room receives the morning sun, but by afternoon it has made its way to the other side of the house, making it quite cozy.

The front and back pieces of my gown have all been cut and are lying neatly out on the floor. The fabric is much prettier than I had remembered. I am excited to begin sewing, but I want Mother to help me make sure that the fit is just perfect before pinning. While waiting, I turn in my chair to look out of the front window. The view is stunning. The wild carrots are in full bloom, filling the field leading to the pond with a bouquet of Queen Anne's Lace. Spontaneously, I remove my shoes and stockings, allowing the breeze to cool my feet and legs. Wiggling my toes helps to bring life back to my feet. My eyes close; I envision myself twirling in my beautiful gown, in a lovely field of wild flowers and grass. As the vision becomes more lucid, a soft voice awakens me, "Lucinda, wake up."

Mother is staring down at me with a look of bewilderment. "Dreaming? In the middle of the day?" Followed by a soft smile. "Has all of that dancing worn you out for the week?"

"Oh Mother, I simply closed my eyes for a moment to collect my thoughts. And now that I have, would you help me to pin my dress?"

I have already sewn the two back pieces together; Mother helps me to adjust the front piece so it fits my shoulders perfectly. When the task is complete, Mother helps me to remove the pieces, asking inquisitively, "So, tell me about your first day at dance. Did you meet the gent that Lucy was panting over?"

Thoughts of Obadiah begin to inundate my mind. Taking a seat again by the front window, I enthusiastically answer, "Mother, Obadiah is no other than that intriguing gentleman that I have been talking about, the one that I have encountered, quite by happenstance, twice in the past few weeks." Beginning to feel somewhat lightheaded, I continue, "He recognized me as soon as our eyes met. And then, with hardly any delay, he walked directly up to me, greeting me with a warm kiss on my hand!" Trying to contain my apparent desire for him, I continue, "He left me quite speechless; all I was able to mutter was that the pleasure was all mine."

Mother, who has hopes of me finding a suitable husband soon, wants to know more, "Is he the perfect gentleman that you imagined? Do you think, maybe…?"

I rudely interrupt her mid-sentence, "Mother, he is a roaming dance master, more than likely just a slick gent with ill intentions. I will not get my hopes up for such a man!"

Unsure as to why I answered so defensively, Mother tilts her head slightly, rebutting, "Well, it seems quite obvious to me that you are sufficiently attracted to this gent. Perhaps the most prudent thing to do is to simply allow things to take their course, before making him out as some sort of rake."

Mother is correct. Obadiah has given me no reason to suspect that he is anything but a perfect gentleman. Feeling somewhat frustrated, I say, "This is all new to me; I have never fallen for a gent quite like this. What if he is not particularly interested in me? Oh, I am so muddled."

"My dearest daughter, you will come to learn that there is nothing more distracting in one's life than falling in love. And the pity of it all is that you will have little control over your feelings. My advice: take things one day at a time, and try not to overthink those things."

I finish stitching the shoulders and stand. "Thank you, Mother. I will wait tolerantly until next Monday to see how things progress. Might you help me again in fitting my gown?"

The gown fits perfectly on my shoulders. Mother helps to adjust the fit just right around my torso and reassures that the gown lays properly on my petticoat. I clumsily slip out of the gown, and start to stitch together the front and back pieces.

Quite unexpected, my brother Sumner appears at the front door. He reaches his head around the corner, inviting himself in and saying, "Good day, ladies, I was passing by and thought it proper to stop in to say hello."

Startled, but always pleased to see him, I offer, "Come in! Mother is working on a new order of shoes and I am working diligently on my new gown. What brings you out to see us?"

"I was just down at Ithamer Stowe's farm helping him to mend some fences. He seems quite overwhelmed with taking on the care of 120 acres, but very pleased nevertheless."

Mother adds, "It was certainly nice of Captain Wood to sell the farm to Ithamer at such a reasonable price. I am sure he will adapt quickly to the tasks at hand."

Sumner looks over at me with a sinister look. "Ithamer tells me that the new dance master down at the Lower Tavern is quite a handsome-looking gent."

Sumner receives my undivided attention. Obviously, he has more to say. Sumner continues, "He also tells me that he had overheard he has a fancy for you."

I am immediately embarrassed and stunned by the rumor, although quite excited by it as well. "Now how can that be true? I have only met the gent but once." Trying hard to stay composed, I ask, "Where did your friend Ithamer hear such a thing anyway?"

"Well, I cannot speak for him, but I believe that Andreas Peirce was helping Ithamer to mend fences before I arrived. It was Andreas, who had attended the dance school last evening, who suggested it. I understand that his sister Sarah, who was at the afternoon session with you, was quite astonished at the greeting you received. But again, maybe it is all just hearsay."

I do my best not to display the excitement that has captured

143

me, replying, "Oh, it was nothing; he was just showing his respect for me, since I was so much older than the other students."

Sumner smirks, "And Lucy?"

Mother comes to my defense, "Sumner, maybe it best that we do not make accusations based on hearsay. It seems Lucinda was a subject of circumstance. She is surely more interested in learning to dance than seeking out a husband."

Sumner takes his leave, saying, "I understand; I meant no harm by it. I must be off—Louisa is expecting me home shortly. Enjoy the rest of your afternoon."

"No harm done. Good day."

Thoughts of Obadiah consume me; I feel his warm lips on my hand. The tingling sensation that I felt when we first made eye contact recurs; it settles again in my lower belly. Mother is staring at me as if I am possessed. She acknowledges my muddled state with a warm smile, suggesting, "Lucinda, you must trust that everything will turn out just as it should."

My life has changed so much since seeing Obadiah for the first time. My scar has ceased from burning; my heart is full of happiness. Lifting my head, I stare deeply into Mother's eyes, "I believe you are right."

SIXTEEN

OBADIAH... *TUESDAY, JULY 21, 1840*

Rays of warm sunshine consume the woodshop; the crisp air rushes through the open window, making it the perfect afternoon for finishing Salome's cupboard. The paint that Dennis mixed is a lovely salmon; Salome will love it.

The lyrics Elias mumbled just before falling to sleep last night are playing repeatedly in my head. *Then the traveler in the dark thanks you for your tiny sparks; He could not see which way to go, If you did not Twinkle so....* My infatuation with Elias has mysteriously vanished as swiftly as it came, replaced by a growing intrigue for Lucinda. She has become the star that twinkles, helping this traveler to find his way.

Warm thoughts of Lucinda provide me solace while reorganizing the woodshop, preparing for the next project. Salome had suggested a new seat board for the privy, complaining the present one is about to fall through.

Harriet's sweet voice accentuates the serenity of the day, announcing, "Mr. Griffiths, Mother is preparing some supper and has asked that you please join us in a half-hour."

Harriet is an angel of love; her simple ways are inspiring. "Thank you Harriet, I am about done out here. How would you like to go to the parlor and talk some more about life?"

"That would be wonderful, and what would you like to talk about?"

Hoping that Harriet had a subject in mind, I suggest, "It is a beautiful day for a walk; I am sure we will think of something along the way."

Daydreaming as I walk the path, I think of how I want to get closer to Lucinda. I murmur to myself, "What if I just surprise her with a visit?"

Harriet turns quickly, asking, "What did you say, Mr. Griffiths? Have you discovered a topic to discuss?"

"I am sorry; I was just murmuring to myself." Harriet seems anxious to talk, and I am daydreaming about a lady who probably thinks I am nothing more than an ill-mannered rake. I fear now that I should not have been so exuberant with my greeting.

We reach the parlor; I take a seat in my favorite upholstered chair, asking, "Harriet, do you mind if I remove my boots and socks so as to be a tad more relaxed?"

"Of course not, Mr. Griffiths. Mother tells me that you are the hardest working gent she has met in a long time. You deserve some time to relax." Harriet pauses for a moment, and with a look of concern, continues, "Am I of trouble to you Mr. Griffiths? I do not want to be of any trouble."

"Why of course not. You are a pleasure to have around, and even more a pleasure to talk with."

"Mr. Griffiths, I do have a few things that are bothering me." She is struggling for words, eventually blurting out, "Do you have any idea on how to store up treasures in Heaven? Do you even know where Heaven is? And what kind of treasures should I store there?"

The questions that she poses are quite complex; I ponder on how I might best answer them, "Oh Harriet, this may not be a topic that we can properly cover in the short time we have before supper. Let us see what we can do."

Beginning slowly, I suggest, "Maybe we can use an analogy. Harriet, do you know what an analogy is?"

She looks at me with a cute frown, shaking her head back and forth, "I am sorry, Mr. Griffiths, I do not."

"Well, let us just say it is a comparison of ideas. A comparison between an idea that readily makes sense to you, and one that is more difficult for you to comprehend. In this case, we want to find an analogy that may help clarify what it means to store treasures in Heaven."

Harriet continues shaking her head, muttering inquisitively, "Interesting."

"Tell me, how do you feel right now?"

In her own unique way, Harriet tilts her head. Looking directly at me, she responds, "I feel happy."

"And why is that?"

"Well, for one thing, Mr. Griffiths, you are very easy to talk to. You help to explain things that are hard for me to understand. And, you are so friendly to everyone; it makes me want to grow up to be just like you."

I did not expect that as an answer, but I will accept it. "Anything else that makes you feel happy right now?"

"It is a beautiful summer day and the wildflowers across the way are just delightful. And, I can't wait to dance again!"

It is obvious that Harriet is anxiously awaiting how I am going to respond. I suggest, "These are all certainly good things to be happy about. However, have you ever thought that all of those things are not permanent and that they will eventually pass?"

Harriet is looking a tad more perplexed, responding, "I do, from time to time, but the memory of many of those happy times tends to stay with me. And that makes me a happier person."

The grin on her face ripens into a brilliant smile; she continues, "So even though you will eventually move on from here, after the wildflowers wilt and the summer turns to fall, the happy times we shared together will live on in my heart. For as long as I cherish them."

"Why yes, Harriet, it seems that you have captured the essence of it." Her smile is contagious, and her expression morphs into one of jubilee. She exclaims, "The happiness that we receive, and the happiness that we share, are the treasures. Our times together, the wildflowers, summer weather, and dance, are the passing things that make us happy in the present. However, those moments of happiness that we welcome into our heart are the real treasures. Those are the treasures that are safe; the treasures that will live on forever in Heaven."

"Oh, Mr. Griffiths, thank you so much! I knew you could help; it is so much clearer now."

Salome enters the room, and with a noticeable smirk, continues, "And what is clear to me is that supper is ready and your presence is requested at the table."

Harriet looks over at Salome, and then back at me, "I suppose it is time for supper."

∞

The setting sun floods the parlor with light. It has been a busy day; I am quite happy to have finished the cupboard for the kitchen. The time is right to pour myself a much-deserved glass of rum. My head is swimming in thoughts about Lucinda.

Harriet pokes her head into the parlor. Her cheerful countenance is uplifting. "Good night, Mr. Griffiths, enjoy your evening."

I reply, "Thank you, Harriet, a good evening to you as well."

Harriet has become a very dear friend. Her innate wisdom of love and simplicity is profound; her childhood innocence is a virtue to behold.

The sun has settled below the horizon; the subdued light in the parlor brings a welcomed end of another day. Rum is the perfect remedy to help unwind. I take another sip; it is smooth. There is a rustling behind me; Salome appears, taking a seat on the upholstered sofa. She appears perplexed, asking, "Obadiah, excuse me for inquiring, but I have noticed that you have not been quite yourself today. Would you care to share with me?"

Having had a delightful conversation with Harriet earlier and a relaxing glass of rum, I decide to invite Salome to probe. "To be honest Salome, I am fearful that I may be falling in love. I cannot extinguish the thoughts of Lucinda from my mind; it is relentless."

"You must be speaking of Lucinda Bixby, the mysterious young lady in the red dress you spoke of earlier."

I am surprised that Salome remembered my mentioning the lady in the red dress. I cannot recollect the moment when I did.

"Why yes, I am captivated by her and do not know why. Have you any suggestions?"

Salome seems somewhat surprised with my question, responding prudently, "It certainly does not seem constructive to run from her, so my suggestion might be to run to her. At least to explore further the obvious fascination you are feeling." After pondering for a moment, Salome tilts her head; her eyes flutter, "I have an idea. Lucinda lives only two miles from here in a small farmhouse with her parents, Hannah and Simon. They are very welcoming folks, and I am certain that they would enjoy meeting the new dance master in town."

"Are you suggesting that I make a surprise visit?" Thoughts of seeing Lucinda again overwhelm me with happiness. I ask inquisitively, "Do you think she would see me without a proper invitation?"

Salome grins, "Well, it is 1840, and she is of proper age. I am sure she would be delighted. Of course, only if she has an interest in you. And what single lady in her right mind wouldn't have interest in a roaming dance master?"

I contemplate the idea of a visit, rationalizing it to Salome. "It is Lucinda's twenty-fifth birthday on Thursday. Maybe I could stop by for just a moment to wish her a good day."

Salome is quick to answer, "Why that sounds like a grand idea!"

SEVENTEEN

LUCINDA... *THURSDAY, JULY 23, 1840*

The morning sun is brilliant, the air unusually chilly for this time of year. Nevertheless, the perfect day to turn twenty-five. I pull the quilt tightly around my neck, allowing my feet to slip out from beneath it, exposing my toes to the nippy air. Turning on my side, I pull up my knees, retracting my bare feet from the cold. A sense of excitement comes over me, ushering in hope that I might soon know the happiness of love. I anticipate the next dance lesson with great desire, yearning for the opportunity to be close to Obadiah. Is it at all possible that I have finally met a man who might love me, unconditionally?

Remaining in a curled-up position, I wrap my arms tightly around my knees. I draw them ever closer to my chest. I experience a heartfelt sensation of security; it is difficult to let go. My eyes close again, just for a moment. I am unable to quench Obadiah from my thoughts; I am hypnotized both by his appearance and his demeanor. I murmur to myself, "What is it about that man?"

With much reservation, I unfold myself, poking my toes out from beneath the blanket to test the temperature. It is still chilly, but my chores will certainly not be accomplished while rolled up under my quilt like an infant. Turning around in the bed while still under my quilt, I reach into my blanket chest to retrieve a pair of clean stockings. I slip them on and hop out of bed, allowing my chemise to fall to my knees. I turn, detecting that the reflection in the mirror is being extremely kind to me again this morning. Grinning, I whisper softly, "A delightful way to start the day."

∞

The sky is a deep blue; the air is refreshing. Feelings for
Obadiah prompt me to momentarily consider making a visit to
the Lower Tavern today. After all, it is my special day, and it
would be a treat to see him. By the time I reach the barn, I
abandon the fantasy. How silly of me.

The chilly morning helps to make my chores in the barn most
pleasant. It appears that the animals are also quite satisfied
with the cooler air. The chickens have remained quite active,
providing me another dozen eggs.

∞

Returning to the house, I find that Mother has prepared a full
breakfast, consisting of delicious bacon, fried eggs, and fried
potato cakes. She certainly deserves my compliments.
"Mother, the breakfast you have prepared smells delicious!"

It turns out that the potato cakes were made extra tasty this
morning. They were most assuredly fried in lard, which always
makes them quite pleasing. When breakfast is finished, I help
Mother to organize before making my way out to the garden.
From the looks of it, the sun has begun to warm the chilly air,
prompting me to slip off my shoes and stockings before
venturing out.

The dew-covered grass is a mite biting on my toes, but
refreshing nevertheless. The garden is bursting with fresh
vegetables this time of year, providing us with an ample supply
of delicious options for meals. I fill my basket with a

hodgepodge of vegetables, quickly returning to the kitchen to find that Mother has begun preparing dinner.

Mother is heating a large cauldron of water, already having peeled some potatoes and onions. She has also prepared a large portion of salted beef that was cured in January. Placing my basket of vegetables on the table, I offer, "We have some delicious looking turnips with their greens, cucumbers, a summer squash, thyme, and parsley. I will cut up the squash, onions, and herbs, and add some butter for frying."

Mother seems quite pleased with my selection. "That would be lovely; I will wash off the turnips and cucumbers and slice them for boiling." Mother turns toward me, looking sincerely into my eyes. "Lucinda, you are such a pleasure to have as a daughter!"

Unsure of what may have prompted the compliment, I acknowledge her with a nod and a smile, continuing preparation for dinner. Most likely it was in response to it being my twenty-fifth birthday today. I am the youngest of four children, and, I am presuming, ageing faster than Mother wishes. With the table sufficiently populated with prepared foodstuff, I ask Mother, "Would you mind terribly if I go up to my room now to freshen up a bit?"

Mother responds, "Of course not, everything looks delicious here. Let us plan dinner for around noon. Father will surely be famished by then."

∞

I am not expecting visitors today, and so I decide to wear my most tattered dress. It has been mended at least twenty times;

the bottom edge is ragged from dragging on the ground for so
many years. There is water left in the pitcher, and so I decide
to fill the basin and wash quickly only the areas of my body
that most need it. I slip my petticoat on over my chemise and
then slide my dress on over my head. Looking into the mirror,
I decide to leave my hair untied for the afternoon. I add a little
grease to tame it a bit. There is mending that needs tending to
after dinner; I look forward to a restful afternoon in the parlor.

Dinner is especially delectable today, most likely due to Mother
and Father being peculiarly warm toward me. Mother refused
my help in the kitchen, nearly pushing me into the parlor.
"Lucinda, the wind is picking up, surely causing a most
comfortable cross breeze in your favorite chair. I will finish up
in here, you go and enjoy the afternoon."

There never seems to be a moment of peace; I decide to take
advantage of Mother's offer; I venture into the parlor. The
pile of clothing in need of mending has grown some, but not
close to the level it was three weeks ago. To be honest, I find a
bit of mending to be quite therapeutic.

The view out of the front window is delightful. My mind
begins to wander somewhat, provoking me to close my eyes,
just for a moment. Thoughts of Obadiah begin to take shape,
but not with the elation of the past. Doubts turn to fear,
creating a sense of darkness that draws me helplessly to that
place; that place where happiness is void. Reluctantly, my
attention is swept into a whirlwind of darkness. I murmur to
myself, quietly, "He surely has no interest in me. His
ostentatious greeting was just his way of mocking me."

Mother enters the room, asking inquisitively, "Lucinda, who
are you mumbling to?"

I look up to see Mother staring at me with a somewhat startled look on her face, almost as if she has seen a ghost, "Oh, it is nothing; just daydreaming, I guess."

Mother informs me, "There is a gentleman at the door calling on you. He addresses himself as no other than, Mr. Obadiah Griffiths. Were you expecting him?"

"Why no! Just look at me; I am certainly not fit to be seen by Obadiah."

Just then, Obadiah reaches his head in and around the corner addressing me in an apologetic voice, "I am terribly sorry if this is not a good time. I am at a loss to what I was thinking. I should have never presumed you would see me without a proper invitation. Oh, I am so terribly sorry. I will take my leave immediately!"

"Wait, Obadiah, I am sorry. I was just a bit startled is all. Please come in." I cannot help but to feel grossly unfit to be in his presence, but my attraction to him is truly magnetic. "Please, accept my apologies for my appearance."

Obadiah steps into the foyer, removes his top hat, and bows slightly, saying, "Lucinda, you are quite stunning, no matter what your appearance."

Mother is looking somewhat confused by the exchange, interrupting, "Well, you must be Obadiah, the gentleman teaching dance at the Lower Tavern. Lucinda has spoken quite favorable toward you. Welcome to our home."

Obadiah bows to Mother. "It is sincerely my pleasure, Mrs. Bixby. My apologies again for the surprise visit. But your daughter has captured my attention, and knowing it is her twenty-fifth birthday, I wanted to make a quick visit to extend her my best wishes."

Mother appears rather pleased, responding, "Well, that is quite thoughtful. It is my pleasure to make your acquaintance." She looks over to me with a grin of approval and begins to make her way out of the room, assuring me, "I have plenty to keep me busy in the kitchen."

Turning my full attention to Obadiah, I say, "Please, take a seat. You won't mind if I go upstairs for just a moment to put my hair up into a cap? Maybe we can take a short walk outside. The weather seems quite pleasant."

I don't think that Obadiah has taken his eyes off me for a moment since he entered, except for the quick introduction that he shared with Mother. He speaks in a quiet voice, "Lucinda, you look quite pleasing to my eyes, just the way you are. So please, do not concern yourself much on my account."

I smile at him, quickly taking my leave out of the parlor, through the foyer, and into the kitchen. Passing Mother, on my way toward the stairs, I get another grin and a nod of approval, "Oh Mother, stop it!"

Standing in front of the mirror, I cannot help to think out loud, "Lucinda, you are such a ridiculous lady; of course he likes you." I am so excited I can hardly catch my breath. I quickly pin my hair up into a bun, tie on my cap, and take my bonnet from the top of the dresser. On my way out, I cannot help to notice that my reflection in the mirror again reveals a confident exuberance toward love.

When I return to the parlor, I find that Father has taken a seat next to Obadiah. They are engaged in conversation, as if they were old friends. Father looks up at me. "Lucinda, I was just having a political conversation with Obadiah. His views are rather interesting." Father stands up. "But enough for now. Obadiah, it was a pleasure to meet you; I trust you will take proper care of my daughter?"

Obadiah immediately stands to acknowledge my father's departure, "Why of course, Mr. Bixby. I hold nothing but the best intentions." Father leaves the room while Obadiah exhales a sigh of relief. "Your father is quite set in his political ways. I trust I did not offend him terribly with my indifferent stance."

I can tell that Obadiah is feeling a tad uncomfortable. "Father will be fine. Would you like to join me in a walk up and around the common?"

Obadiah regains his composure almost immediately, responding quickly, "That sounds like a splendid idea."

∞

Obadiah's horse is tied to the hitch by the road. "Your horse is beautiful. What is his name?" I stroke his mane and snuggle up close to the side of his face.

"His name is Jasper; I have owned him for three years. You might say we have become extremely close over that time."

I stroke Jasper's mane a couple of more times, whispering in his ear, "We will be back in a short while."

While it is a pleasant summer day, the wind is surely enough to blow my bonnet off my head. I decide it best to remove it for now, to eliminate the annoyance. The silence between us soon becomes rather awkward, neither of us knowing quite what to say. We have walked nearly a quarter mile without the exchange of a single word. Darker thoughts begin to gnaw at me as we pass by the Faulkner barn. Knowing quite well that I must not allow myself to slip into that abyss, I muster up some words, asking inquisitively, "It was rather a surprise to see you this afternoon. Whatever prompted your visit?"

Obadiah seems quite surprised at the candor of my question. I am equally surprised for asking. There is a nervous shuffle in his stride as we approach the grassy common. As soon as my feet sense the softness of the grass, he stops and turns toward me. His dark brown eyes appear to be on fire; any thoughts of an abyss vanish. He reaches out with both hands. I instinctively drop my bonnet and accept his hands into mine. Desire fills my heart, desire such as I have never felt. He slowly closes the lids of his eyes. He whispers, "Lucinda, your presence is surely a gift from Heaven. The happiness that I feel when near you is like nothing I have ever experienced. You have turned my world upside down, and I am truly at a loss for an explanation."

My heart is unquestionably set to explode; I am lost for words. His eyes open slowly, revealing a sincerity that surely has not been contrived. My vulnerability is unbridled. Acknowledging his sincerity, I grasp his hands tighter. "Obadiah, I am overwhelmed by the feelings I have for you at this moment. You are the culmination of all of my hopes, all of my dreams, and all of my fears, all at the same time." I stop for a moment to regather my thoughts, "And I want so much to be close to you."

The desire to embrace becomes nearly unbearable. He begins to pull me closer, when out of the corner of my eye I see that Lucy is approaching. I push away and drop his hands.

"Lucy, what brings you out today?"

I can readily detect the disappointment Obadiah is feeling, as am I. He quickly composes himself and welcomes her by saying, "Lucy, why it is a pleasure to see you again."

Lucy is obviously surprised to find Obadiah and I holding hands on the common in the middle of the day. She acknowledges, "A pleasure to see you both. I was just on my way over to visit Mary Carter. She has been working on a needlepoint, and she wanted to show me the progress that she has made." Lucy appears to be quite content with not prying. "I look forward to seeing you both on Monday. Lucinda, should we plan to have you pick us up at the same time?"

"Why of course Lucy; enjoy the rest of your day."

Lucy skips off toward the Faulkners, leaving Obadiah and I awkwardly anticipating our next moves. Obadiah bends down and picks up my bonnet. He takes my hand in his, suggesting, "Why don't we continue our walk?"

An enchanting energy lifts my spirit toward the heavens. We continue to walk in silence, but the silence is no longer awkward; it is peaceful. We begin our descent down the road from the common, toward my house. The field of Queen Ann's Lace is swaying back and forth with the wind. Obadiah stops, pointing out a threesome of Eastern Tailed Blue butterflies, fluttering in the sky. He appears stirred by their appearance. "Butterflies are the most peaceful of God's creation. They dance in the sky, to music of their own making. Graceful and innocent, they invite us to soar with them, into the heavens where love is abounding."

Obadiah tightens his grasp on my hand, as if he intends never to let go. No words can adequately describe the happiness that I feel at this moment.

EIGHTEEN

OBADIAH... *SATURDAY, JULY 25, 1840*

The evening is quite pleasant; the breeze finds its way through
the cracked-open windows, reaching every corner of the
taproom. As the summer days begin to wane, dusk is upon us
a mite earlier each night. Warm thoughts of Lucinda occupy
my mind; my desire to taste the sweetness of her lips heightens
with every encounter. Monday seems a lifetime away.

The tavern is abnormally busy; Jonas Sibley and his friend
Stephen Hutchinson are expected shortly to share in an ale and
discuss plans for a barn raising. Dennis has been working
energetically behind the cage since I sat down nearly an hour
ago. Despite it, he has done a remarkable job of keeping my
mug at capacity. Jonas has spoken quite highly of Stephen,
although he informs me that they do not share much in the
way of political views. My view is no view; the election has
turned into a meaningless shouting match between the
candidates. Whatever good can come from that?

Jonas arrives, making his way immediately to the bar. He looks
over at me shouting, "Good evening, Obadiah, are you in need
of a refill?"

"Thank you, Jonas; I am at capacity for now."

The stench of stale tobacco saturates the air as patrons become
sloppier with their aim, missing the spittoons more often than
not. There is a fellow two tables over that spits out a wad that
misses the spittoon entirely, plastering the wall directly behind
it. I want to say something, but decide not to cause a
commotion. I think about my sweet Harriet. She is the one
having to scrub down the place in the morning; it just doesn't
seem right.

Jonas sits down with his ale and commences with conversation, "So Obadiah, Little Jim tells me your first day of dance school was quite the success. He also mentioned that your fiddler friend from Framingham may not be able to participate regularly."

"That is correct; Elias is working to publish a music book in Boston and finds himself quite busy preparing to purchase and sell the first production run."

Jonas appears genuinely concerned, responding, "Well, I believe that Little Jim would be a brilliant replacement. He would be ecstatic to be a part of it, and would surely do it for no charge. Although, it would be gracious of you if he could receive a minimal compensation; maybe twenty-five cents per week?"

It takes little time for me to consider the offer, responding, "Why that would be a great help, Jonas. And the twenty-five cents per week seems like a fair price to pay for such a talented musician. Please let him know that he has a job."

About a half hour goes by before a tall, well-dressed gentleman enters the tavern and approaches our table. Jonas stands up. "Stephen, it is a pleasure to see you. Please, let me introduce you to Mr. Obadiah Griffiths. Obadiah is conducting a dance school for youth, right here at the hotel."

I stand to acknowledge Stephen, "It is a pleasure to make your acquaintance. Jonas speaks very highly of you."

Stephen responds, "A pleasure it is. Thank you for joining us this evening. Let me fetch a mug of ale; might I offer to replenish either of yours?"

I hand Stephen my mug, acknowledging, "Why thank you; please have Dennis top it off for me."

Stephen returns in just a few moments with two full mugs of ale and places them on the table. He grabs a chair from the table next to ours and takes a seat. He raises his mug, offering, "To new and old friendships alike."

Spontaneously, Jonas and I raise our mugs. "Huzzah."

Jonas begins the conversation with a sarcastic quip: "Stephen, I am surprised that you are not partaking in a mug of hard cider in place of that ale."

Stephen frowns, "And you, a flute of champagne."

I choose not to take sides with either of them regarding their subtle political dual, but instead inquire, "Stephen, Jonas informs me that you are planning a barn raising in West Sutton on August thirteenth, and that you may be looking to recruit some help."

Jonas smiles, "So... not interested in hearing our political rant? How dreadful."

Stephen perks up, replying, "Why yes, Obadiah, my wife Evelyn and I live about seven miles southwest of here, directly on the intersection of Millbury Road and Main Street." He stops and points toward the parlor, indicating the direction. "It is to be a rather small barn, twenty feet square, with room enough for some pigs beneath it. On the ground level, maybe a small shop, cover for a carriage, and a stall for our horse. We have the cellar dug, stones in place, and just a couple of more beams to mortise."

Jonas is quick to add, "There will be plenty of rum, and Evelyn will surely bake some of her delicious pies."

Stephen works to enhance the occasion even further, offering, "You are welcome to invite an acquaintance as well, the *Almanac* has the Sturgeon Moon in the sky that evening, making it ideal for an evening of dancing, following the raising.

Little Jim will be helping us out and has promised to fiddle for us until our legs get wobbly!"

I reply, "It certainly does sound like an exciting time, although I am unsure of who to bring, since I have only been in town for a week. But you can definitely plan on me being in attendance."

Stephen seems quite excited to recruit another set of able hands. "Well, that settles it; we will see you on the morning of the thirteenth. And be sure to keep a keen lookout for that special lady; you have nearly three weeks." Stephen is being quite persistent that I entice a lady to join me.

My thoughts are obviously with Lucinda, but would she go?

Jonas politely reminds Stephen of the time, "The sun has set and we are only three days from the new moon. It may be prudent for us to be getting on our way."

Stephen acknowledges, "Yes, our business is done here. Obadiah, thank you again for your kind offer to help."

Stephen turns to Jonas, agreeing, "It does appear to be getting rather dark. I have my carriage this evening and candles for the lamps; you are welcome to ride with me and have your horse follow along."

Jonas replies, "A grand idea!"

The roads from Millbury to Sutton are very passable in the summer, with little or no obstructions to be concerned with. But it is always a comfort to light the way with some lamps. Jonas and Stephen stand and bid me their goodbyes. My journey is a bit simpler. To the bar for a glass of rum, to the parlor to enjoy it, and then to my room to sleep.

∞

The taproom has cleared out and Dennis is working to clean up the bar. As I approach him, he is already pouring me a glass of rum. He appears tired, but joyful nevertheless. "Obadiah, I thought you might like this." He hands me the rum, asking inquisitively, "Did Jonas and Stephen convince you to join in on the barn raising?"

Enthusiastically, I respond, "It didn't take much convincing; it should be quite the frolic!"

Dennis continues with his cleaning. "I must tell you, Salome surely appreciates the work you did on that cupboard. It will provide her some much needed storage space." He stops for a moment and leans over the bar toward me, quietly asking, "Are you planning on asking Lucinda to the barn raising? Salome tells me you have quite a fancy for her."

The question makes me a tad defensive, I respond, "Well, I hardly know the lady." Thinking quietly to myself, I murmur under my breath, "But I certainly plan to get to know her better!" Adjusting my voice back to a level where Dennis can hear me clearly, I continue, "We will see how things progress over the next couple of weeks." Lifting my glass, I salute, "Thank you for the rum; I will be in the parlor for a while before turning in."

∞

The parlor is dark; I choose not to light a candle. There is an oil lamp providing a distant light from the top of the stairs. Salome has become quite perceptive of my repetition, knowing I always take a moment in the evening to relax in the upholstered chair to ponder the day's happenings. She accommodates my habit by lighting the lamp before she leaves for home, allowing me safe passage to my room.

The rum goes down exceptionally smooth this evening, resulting in a state of relaxation beyond the norm for me. The lids of my eyes are heavy, provoking me to drift in and out of consciousness. There is a faint voice in the distance, "Good night Obadiah, sleep well."

I recognize the voice as Dennis's, and do my best to mutter, "A good night to you as well."

I return to dreamland, reliving that moment when Lucinda revealed her desire to be close to me. I envision her lovely eyes staring into mine, I pull her closer, I taste the sweetness of her lips.

A coyote screeches, startling me back to consciousness, the vision vanishes. I am left with an aching desire to be close to her. My thoughts have never been so occupied as they have been with Lucinda over the past week. I make a pact with myself; I will fulfill Lucinda's wish to be close to me, now and forever more.

NINETEEN

LUCINDA... *MONDAY, JULY 27, 1840*

The day is cloudy; there is a distinct feeling of rain in the air. As the buckboard crests the hill onto the common, Mary, Lucy, and Susan are all gathered, waiting for my arrival. They are standing in the same spot that Obadiah and I were when we exchanged those evocative words with one another, just the other day. Gently pulling on the reigns, I whisper, "Whoa Shadow."

The ladies skip jubilantly over to the buckboard, waving to me as they approach. Susan and Mary jump into the back while Lucy hops up onto the bench next to me. She reaches over, taking my hand in hers, saying, "Good day, Lucinda, it is such a happy day."

Holding the reigns in my left hand, I give them a slight shake; Shadow moves along. "Good day to you, Miss Lucy. And what brings such happiness to the three of you?"

"We were just sharing how excited we are for the upcoming dance to be held two Fridays from now. Our first chance to dance with the gents while we strut our accomplishments."

Lucy grips my hand a tad tighter. Bending over toward my ear, she whispers, "Why, I thought Obadiah was going to kiss you in broad daylight, right in front of me."

I turn to Lucy, softly responding, "He would have, if you didn't come along." I grip Lucy's hand gently in return.

When we arrive at Adelia's, she is waiting on the side of the street. Her dress is gorgeous and her hair is fixed into long curls, held together beautifully with plenty of bear's grease and tiny bows of ribbon. Lucy calls out to her, "Good day, Adelia. You look adorable today."

Adelia hops up into the back of the buckboard. In a sweet voice, she acknowledges, "Thank you Lucy; good day, ladies."

As we approach the tavern, I recognize that Charles is sitting on the stairs of the porch anticipating our arrival. He jumps up and runs toward us, shouting, "Welcome ladies, I have been waiting for you." He guides Shadow to the hitching post, promising, "I will fetch a bucket of water for your horse."

I shout out at Charles, "Her name is Shadow, and thank you kindly for watching out for her."

The four of us enter the tavern where we are greeted by Mrs. Fisher. "Welcome, ladies. Mr. Griffiths is up in the hall awaiting your arrival. There are already five others in attendance." She recognizes me, and goes on, "Why, Lucinda, it is a pleasure to see you again. Mr. Griffiths informs me that you are doing quite well with your dancing." She smiles, undoubtedly knowing more than she is revealing.

"Why thank you, Mrs. Fisher. Mr. Griffiths is certainly a fine teacher."

Harriet runs out from the parlor and takes hold of my hand, enthusiastically saying, "Good day, Miss Bixby! Let's hurry upstairs. Mr. Griffiths is patiently waiting for you!" I begin to get the sense that our secret admiration for one another is not so secret. The thought of Obadiah warms me; the thought of love makes me shudder.

Lucy, Susan, Adelia, and Mary begin their way up the stairs. Salome suggests to Harriet, "Go along with the ladies. I want to speak with Miss Bixby for a moment. You can assure Mr. Griffiths that she will be up shortly."

When the ladies are out of sight, Salome turns to me, sharing, "Lucinda, my apologies. It was I who prompted Obadiah to pay you a surprise visit on Thursday. He had been fluttering around here like a lost butterfly. I trust that the visit went well?"

Quite surprised, and pleased with Salome's intervention, I say, "No apology necessary. We had a splendid visit. He is a very intriguing gentleman."

Salome obviously agrees with my assessment, replying, "Well yes, he is, and I am pleased that the two of you are getting along so splendidly."

The anticipation of seeing Obadiah has me quite fidgety. "I must not keep the class waiting. Would you like to join us upstairs?"

Salome senses my urgency, prompting me to go along: "Thank you, but I have much to do in the kitchen. You be on your way, and do enjoy the afternoon."

"Thank you, Salome; enjoy your day!"

∞

When I enter the hall, I find that Obadiah has already begun the class. The ladies are sitting in chairs placed along the wall, while Little Jim is standing next to the window, staring out as if in a trance. Obadiah's back is toward me. Quietly, I make my way around him and into a chair. I am quite careful not to make a sound. Just as I think my effort is successful, Obadiah stops what he is saying, turning his attention to me, "Good afternoon Lucinda. It is better that you are a tad late, than not showing at all."

Obadiah's greeting seems somewhat harsh to me; I take my seat without a response. With a look of concern, he comes over and takes my hand, bending over and whispering quietly in my ear, "What I meant to say is that I am so relieved to see you, Lucinda. I have not stopped thinking of you since our last meeting." He releases my hand, stands, and smiles. My heart is on fire; I try my best not to turn a scarlet red.

Obadiah returns to the center of the hall, where he continues with his instruction. "Now, another example of an ill manner would be to interrupt someone who is anyway engaged." He looks directly at me with a smirk. "And another: ridicule of every kind, vice or folly." Now he is just displaying his wit. I reply with my own wit by crossing my arms and sitting back sloppily in my chair, staring at him with an expression of contempt.

He appears to take enjoyment from it, continuing, "And let us not forget the ill manner of lolling in a chair when speaking or being spoken to, and looking someone earnestly in the face without any apparent cause."

He smiles at me, and then calls out to Little Jim, "Are you ready to make some music?" Little Jim nods, walking out to the center of the hall. Obadiah continues, "Ladies, each of you take a partner and form a set, same as last week."

Little Jim and Obadiah move down toward the front of the room, making space for the formation of a longways set. The ladies quickly choose a partner and form two lines. Harriet and I take our positions at the top of the set. I am delighted over Harriet's apparent infatuation, enjoying the attention this special little girl affords me.

Obadiah has not stopped grinning since his tirade regarding manners. His attention turns toward me; I respond with a scowling look. He smiles; I cannot help but to return the smile. He begins, "We will open by dancing 'The Morning Gazette,' the figures are as follows: The first Couple set to the second Lady, then to the Lady in the second Gentlemen's spot, lead down the Middle—up again, and cast off." Obadiah takes a breath, continuing, "And remember, I want to see those gracious curtsies at the start, as well as when you are finished." Obadiah nods to Little Jim to begin; the ladies perform the dance flawlessly.

The next dance that we learn is quite elegant; the name of it is "Constancy." Obadiah reminds the class to listen attentively to the music. "Each figure starts and ends perfectly on each phrase." Continuing, he explains, "The steps fall on the beat and all the dancers in a set must move together so that all the figures occur at the same time."

The music is lovely and the ladies do a wonderful job with the figures. After going through the dance at least a dozen times, Obadiah stops the music, all of us remembering to acknowledge our partners with a curtsy at the end.

"Ladies, your dancing is coming along splendidly. I would like now to introduce you to a more elegant traveling step known as a Pas de Bourrée." Obadiah explains the step while demonstrating, "From the plié on left foot, rise, and on beat one, step forward on ball of right foot, then left, then right, lower heel to floor and plié on right foot, bringing left heel to right, left foot off the floor."

Little Jim begins to play, and Obadiah moves elegantly, dancing around the floor, flowing effortlessly. I close my eyes, imagining myself dancing along, twirling gracefully into his hands. When the music stops, I open my eyes and am quite surprised to find that Obadiah has ended his graceful dancing, standing directly in front of me. With his dark eyes penetrating mine, he bows, and I acknowledge with a curtsy. Surely, the other ladies have become quite suspicious of this obvious flirting.

When the class ends, the ladies begin to take their leave. Lucy, Susan, Adelia, and Mary gather together and approach me. We begin to walk out of the hall together. Obadiah is standing at the door, conversing with the ladies as they leave. When our group reaches him, he expresses his thoughts regarding our progress: "Ladies, you are performing the figures with precision and grace. I must say, I am quite proud of you all." Harriet joins us, and Obadiah acknowledges her: "And Harriet, you amaze me with your grace as well."

As I make my way through the doorway, Obadiah reaches out for my hand, "Lucinda, might I have a quick word with you? I promise it will only take a moment."

The ladies snicker; Lucy addresses Obadiah's question before I have a chance to: "Of course you can. Lucinda, we will wait for you downstairs on the porch."

Obadiah appears to be a tad jittery as he walks over to where the chairs are lined up. "Please take a seat." He continues, "I am aware that the ladies depend on you for their transportation, and so I will only take a minute of your time."

I have never experienced him quite this serious; I become rather concerned that I may have done something to upset him. I think to myself, *But what?*

We sit; he reaches out and gently takes my hand into his. The warmth of his touch is unlike anything I have ever felt before. He stares into my eyes with a tentative look, as if he is carrying the weight of the world on his shoulders. The anticipation has me searching for a clue as to what he has on his mind. I cannot wait any longer. "Obadiah, do you have something to say to me?"

He grips my hand a bit tighter and begins to mutter some words that are hardly distinguishable: "Lucinda, I was invited to participate in a barn raising on Thursday, August thirteenth, in West Sutton."

He pauses; I think to myself, *Well, he certainly does not have to ask my permission.*

172

Suddenly, he asks, "Would you consider accompanying me to the raising? There is promise of a good time and dancing into the evening."

It takes me a good while to comprehend his words, having never received an invitation such as this. I grip his hand ever more tightly, responding warmly, "Of course; it would be my pleasure to accompany you to the raising."

There is a look of relief on his face, as if the world just granted him the wish of his lifetime. He responds with excitement, "Thank God!"

TWENTY

OBADIAH... *MONDAY, AUGUST 3, 1840*

It has been a long week since last seeing Lucinda, that encounter being a memorable one, her acceptance of my invitation to the barn raising, simply delightful. This, the third week of dance classes could not come soon enough; my longing for Lucinda grows stronger every day.

I am utterly impressed with how the ladies have progressed in all aspects of the art of dancing. "Constancy," my uncle's favorite dance, has come alive; the music is energetic, and the ladies are in perfect sync with it. Now, I can only hope that the gents are granted a miracle of some sort this evening, so that our first dance on Friday does not become a ladies-only event.

Signaling Little Jim to play one more time through, I walk slowly toward the head of the set. Lucinda seems to be lost in a world of enchantment, performing her Pas de Bourrées with the grace of a princess. Dancing seems quite the natural for her. I mumble quietly to myself, "I should invite her to learn a minuet with me. We could dance the opening set together on Friday."

The music ends; the ladies make their final curtsies to one another. I speak out with enthusiasm, "I truly believe that this was the grandest performance ever achieved with only three sessions of instruction. You should all be quite proud of your achievements." I pause to allow the words spoken to settle for a moment. "Your first dance, together with the gents, is to be held this Friday at seven in the evening. Your parents are invited to attend and observe, or participate if they wish."

Taking my place by the door, I extend my farewells to the ladies as they file out. Lucy and Lucinda are holding hands as they approach me. My thoughts are tangled; I find myself in a bit of a turmoil. Lucinda looks to be perplexed by my apparently disordered state. "Why, Obadiah, you appear to be dazed. Is there something bothersome to you?"

"Why, no." Working hard to collect my thoughts, I continue, "I am mindful that you graciously provide transportation to four of your friends, to and from class." Lucinda is now staring at me rather inquisitively. I go on to suggest, "I thought that if Lucy would agree to chaperone the ladies home, it would be my pleasure to offer you a lesson in dancing a minuet."

Lucinda's eyes pop open; her expression of confusion concerns me. Have I overstepped my bounds with her? She looks at Lucy, "Would you be so kind as to accompany the ladies home and then deliver Shadow and the buckboard to my house?"

I breathe a sigh of relief.

Lucy responds, "My pleasure. I will inform your parents that you will be arriving a mite later in the capable hands of Obadiah Griffiths." Lucy looks up at me, adding, "I assume that you will be delivering Lucinda to her home safely, returning to the tavern in time to teach the gents?"

"Why, of course; I owe you a debt of gratitude."

Lucy smirks at me, "You certainly do!"

Little Jim is the only one remaining; he is sitting on one of the chairs along the wall. He looks up at me, asking, "Obadiah, would you like me to stay and play some more music?"

I respond, "Are you familiar with 'King George the 3rd's Minuet'?"

"Why, yes sir, I am."

Knowing it will take some time to introduce the steps of a minuet to Lucinda, I suggest, "Please give us an hour on the clock to practice some steps, and then return, and we will be prepared to dance to music."

I am quite cognizant that learning a minuet in an hour is foolishness, but my aspirations are exceptionally high. Little Jim responds, "I will take my leave and return in an hour."

Taking Lucinda by the hand, I move us to the center of the hall. Her expression of confusion has passed, but it appears that she remains tentative regarding my intentions. I start my instruction by saying, "Let us begin by discussing a bit about minuet deportment." Lucinda's eyes focus on mine, prompting me to forget where I left off. "The manner in which a minuet is performed is that of graciousness. We dance lightly and always with a straight posture. Our hand and arm movements always done without pretension."

Lucinda is intent on listening. Turning toward me, she affectionately takes my other hand in hers, prompting me, "Go on."

Our eyes are locked in a trance; I do my utmost to continue, "Eye contact is to be maintained with your partner, with the exception of a brief acknowledgment to the audience during opening honors, and only very tersely during points of crossing." Our eyes remain locked, suggesting that eye contact between Lucinda and I will not be troubling.

Lucinda's concentration begins to wane; an endearing grin begins to take shape. It is as if she is somehow cognizant of my next instruction. "One must always maintain a pleasant expression on one's face, neither too serious, nor too frivolous."

Her grin becomes a smile. Then, unexpectedly, she lets go of my right hand. She lifts my left, twirls under the arch of our arms, and ends with a gracious curtsy. When finished, she looks up, declaring, "Delightful!"

Quite surprised, but entertained nevertheless, I smile and respond with a bow.

Lucinda has become quite accomplished with her footwork, her presence is enchanting, and her timing impeccable. With only half an hour left before Little Jim returns, we begin to practice our minuet step. I explain, "Begin by standing in your first position, with weight on your left foot." Lucinda and I both assume the position. "Now, sink onto your left foot by bending both legs at the knee, making sure your right leg does not bear any weight." We continue through the entire step.

When finished with the instruction, we practice the step, over and over. "Rise, hold, sink; rise step, step; sink." Lucinda absorbs the steps most readily; she is already performing them with a degree of elegance. I encourage her to continue the steps while I stand back to observe. I think to myself, "This foolishness may become a reality. If she embraces the figures as quickly as she has the steps, we may open the dance together this Friday with a minuet after all."

Lucinda appears to be absorbed in the moment; she moves through the steps as if animated by the Holy Spirit above. So as not to overwhelm her, I suggest tenderly, "You have certainly mastered the steps well enough to assimilate them into a sequence of figures."

She opens her eyes, offering me an affectionate smile and a nod of agreement.

We begin by walking through the figures. We start with honors and then with our lead in, followed by a Z pattern and then a right hand turn. We come back by a left hand turn and perform a final Z pattern. We finish with our closing steps and a closing honor. After walking the figures a dozen or more times, Little Jim appears at the door. He apologizes by saying, "I am sorry to be a tad late sir, and my excuse is not worthy to be shared."

Knowing we needed the extra time to prepare, I respond, "You have arrived at the perfect moment; we are ready to put it all to music." Little Jim picks up his fiddle from the chair placing it under his chin; the bow is extended and he is poised to begin.

We take our positions facing out toward the empty chairs, our necks turned toward one another to permit eye contact. Lucinda's eyes sparkle; she presents herself with such elegance and simplicity. Little Jim begins to play. Lucinda's arms are perfectly extended to her sides in a gentle curve. She holds her dress between her thumb and the four fingers of her right hand. She turns her left hand so that her palm faces forward. I offer her my right, prompting us to turn our heads forward. We begin.

Lucinda executes the figures with grace, performing with great ease and propriety. Little Jim offers us a heartfelt rendition of "King George the 3rd's Minuet", permitting both Lucinda and I to dance in delight. Each time we perform the dance, our poise becomes further polished. By the fifth time through, I am thoroughly convinced that our performance on Friday evening will be stunning. I turn to Lucinda; the expression on her face is one of extreme happiness. She moves toward me, taking my hands, and kisses me gently on the cheek, "Obadiah, you are a blessing to me."

Salome has been observing us from the doorway. She enthusiastically comments, "You two are perfect together; you dance as if your souls are one." She approaches us both, inquiring, "Lucinda, where did you learn to dance so gracefully?"

Lucinda is perceptibly astonished by her accomplishment. She reveals, "There is nothing in my past that affords me such pleasure as dancing. Surely, dancing with such an intriguing gentleman provides some advantage. But I feel that it mostly comes to me naturally."

I interject, "It is settled. We will open the dance on Friday by performing a minuet together."

Lucinda and Salome both appear to agree. Little Jim shares his opinion as well: "It will be an exquisite beginning to a perfect night."

∞

The afternoon has slipped away; it is time that I hitch Jasper to the carriage so as to get Lucinda home in time for me to return to teach the gents. I thank Little Jim for the music, bidding him farewell until later in the evening. Turning to Salome, I say, "Thank you for your encouragement, and I must say, Harriet has become quite accomplished in dance herself. You must certainly plan to join us on Friday evening."

Salome returns a smile, responding, "Should I plan on a selection of pies and cakes?"

"That is a superb thought; we'll discuss it further upon my return."

I turn to Lucinda, saying, "We must be on our way."

When we get to the barn, Jasper is already hitched to the carriage. Dennis is in the shop working on something. When he hears us approaching, he looks up, saying, "Good day, folks. Salome had suggested you would be requiring the carriage this afternoon and so I took the liberty to prepare it for you."

"Many thanks to you, Dennis; this saves me some much-needed time, for I must be back within two hours."

Dennis responds, "If you would rather that I escort Lucinda home, it would be my pleasure."

Every moment that I have with Lucinda is a blessing to me; my response to Dennis is polite: "Lucinda and I have several topics to discuss regarding the art of dancing a minuet. But I certainly appreciate your kind offer."

Dennis does not appear terribly convinced of my reasoning, but agrees nevertheless by acknowledging, "Understandable, enjoy your ride; it appears that the rain showers have finally passed."

I assist Lucinda up and onto the seat, quickly moving around the carriage, taking my place next to her. I shout out to Dennis, "Thanks for your help; I shall return shortly."

∞

The road to Lucinda's is well-traveled; it should take us half an hour at most. As we turn the corner on to Elm Street, Lucinda slides herself close to me, her left leg stopping up against my right. She warmly places her hand atop of mine, quietly saying, "Obadiah, it was such a pleasure to dance with you this afternoon. You have brought untold happiness into my life."

I look into her eyes, discovering that they have swelled with tears. "Lucinda, why do you weep?"

"I assure you, Obadiah, I weep with overwhelming joy." She tightens her grip on my hand, showing an affection for me that excites me beyond imagination. I want to stop and embrace her with all of my heart. But the road is much too active to provide the necessary privacy.

We pass by the beautiful mansion where Adelia lives and over Gowan's bridge heading toward Burbankville. We take the road that leads up to the common where Lucinda's house is. The road becomes quite desolate; my thoughts become driven by the excitement I am feeling for Lucinda. Her warm hand continues to stroke the top of mine; my desire to embrace is immeasurable.

Just as I am about to pull the reigns, I collect myself, rethinking my actions. It is still daylight, and the thought of a neighbor happening upon us helps to corral my desire. I turn to Lucinda, saying, "My dear lady, you cannot imagine how much I want to stop right here, in broad daylight, and embrace you. But it is not the responsible thing to do. And you are much too precious to me to jeopardize your good name."

She leans toward me, placing a warm kiss on my cheek. "You are the perfect gentleman."

We pull up to the front of Lucinda's house; I tie Jasper to the hitch. I help Lucinda from the carriage and walk her to the front door. Lucinda's mother comes to the foyer, welcoming us. "It is such a pleasure to see you again, Obadiah. Lucy informed me that you extended your class to teach Lucinda the art of dancing a minuet."

"Why, yes, Mrs. Bixby, I did. Lucinda has learned it well enough to accompany me in the opening minuet on Friday night. Will we have the pleasure of seeing you and Mr. Bixby at the dance? I believe you will be quite proud of Lucinda's accomplishments."

Mrs. Bixby appears delighted with the news. "I am not sure about Mr. Bixby, but Mrs. Chamberlain and I have discussed the event and we are both planning to attend." Appearing aware of my need to return to the tavern, she bids me farewell. "Now, I should allow you to make your proper good-byes. I truly look forward to seeing you again on Friday evening."

Lucinda seems delighted by her mother's announcement. She takes my hands, drawing me in closely, kissing me warmly on the lips for the first time, "Obadiah, thank you for everything. Friday evening cannot arrive fast enough."

TWENTY-ONE

OBADIAH... *FRIDAY, AUGUST 7, 1840*

The taste of our first kiss lingers on my lips, the pleasure of it triumphing over all my thoughts. The days since I last saw Lucinda have been long, the nights even longer. My time in the upholstered chair is mainly spent reliving the happiness of my newfound love. The opening minuet is only hours away; the thought of staring into those warm and welcoming eyes enchants me.

Salome and Harriet have spent much of the day in the kitchen preparing baked goods for this evening's dance. The guest list has grown to include many of the parents. We are only three weeks into the program. I anticipate the need of drawing the elders in, after the youth demonstrate only two or three dances. Surely, it will be a pleasurable evening for all.

Harriet peeks her head into the parlor, asking, "Mr. Griffiths, are you ready for the dance?" She appears rather animated as she makes her way into the room. Before I have a chance to reply, she continues, "I am!"

Taking a seat next to me, she continues with the questioning, "Are you nervous?" Again, she answers her own question, "I am!"

I am not sure if she is waiting for an answer from me, or if these are just nervous questions that she needs to answer for herself.

Eventually, she tilts her head and looks inquisitively at me, which always means something is bewildering her. Her sweetness is endearing. "Mr. Griffiths, may I bother you with a question?"

"Of course, no bother at all."

"It has to do with my dancing; I am trying so hard, but I find it to be so difficult." Her head tilts the other way, her eyes blinking during the transition, "I cannot try any harder." She pauses, finishing her thoughts with, "You are an excellent teacher; what might I do differently?"

Never expecting this as a question, I ponder it before speaking my first words, "In my estimation, you are doing extremely well for a young lady of your age." She perks up a tad, but appears to be anticipating more of an answer than that. A few awkward moments pass as I toil to formulate a more helpful answer, suggesting, "Maybe you are trying too hard."

Harriet jolts her head back, inquiring, "How does one try too hard?"

She is perceptibly bothered by my question, and so I ask, "During our class together, you have been dancing with Miss Bixby, correct?"

She interrupts, "Yes, and she dances superbly."

I go on, "Have you ever taken the opportunity to observe her as she dances?"

"Not really, since I have been expending all of my effort on learning the steps as you teach them."

Hoping to relax Harriet somewhat, I tone my voice down, softly suggesting, "I have had the opportunity to watch Miss Bixby quite closely. She has learned the fine art of dancing more swiftly than any other student that I have ever had the pleasure to teach." Harriet's attention is immediately captured. I propose, "And I think I know why."

Harriet's inquisitive nature returns, resulting in the telltale tilt of her head. "Why?"

"A couple of years ago, while traveling from Providence to Northampton, I met an interesting Oriental gentleman at a tavern in Sturbridge. I was tired and lonely; the traveling had become quite an effort for me. While I had recently decided to make my living by traveling the countryside and teaching good manners and dance to youth, the effort to do so at that time seemed insurmountable."

I have not yet lost Harriet's attention, and so I continue, "The demeanor of this gentleman could be summed up in just one word: quiet. I went on to explain my dilemma to the gentleman, in particular, the effort that was required of me to pursue my goal."

Harriet's inquisitiveness takes over. She asks, "And so what does this have to do with my learning to dance?"

I smile and respond, "You will see."

She nods, encouraging me to continue the story, "The gentleman went on to teach me about a concept he referred to as *Wu Wei*. He explained that *Wu Wei* is the cultivation of a mental state in which our actions are quite effortlessly in alignment with the flow of life."

I go on to explain, "After my encounter with that kind gentleman, my life changed. Rather than always struggling to over-achieve, I learned to appreciate the moment. I began to embrace the simplicity of things, allowing myself to relax and to excel naturally."

"Mr. Griffiths, I do not mean to be impolite, but what does any of this have to do with my learning to dance?"

"Harriet, when Miss Bixby dances, she dances as if she is being moved by the Holy Spirit. Her eyes are in a trance, her posture is elegant; she moves upon the dance floor as if doing so without any effort at all." I have Harriet's attention again. "Miss Bixby appears to invite her natural instincts to move her, rather than extending all of her effort on controlling her moves."

Harriet's sudden expression of understanding is a relief to me. She replies, "Maybe I am trying too hard."

I respond immediately, "Exactly!"

There is a moment of silence between us. I continue, "Miss Bixby and I will be performing an opening minuet this evening. I want you to watch her intently. Watch how she is taken up by the moment; how confident she is in her moves." I go on, "And then, when it is your time to dance, do so without so much effort. Relax, and invite the music to move you."

"Thank you, Mr. Griffiths, I will try hard not to try so hard." She smiles, realizing her contradiction. "I am truly excited to watch you and Miss Bixby dance together."

As we finish our conversation, Elias walks into the parlor with fiddle in hand, saying, "Good day, Obadiah. I should have informed you by mail of my intent to come tonight, but it was only at the last moment that my time became free."

I am rather surprised to see Elias, but pleased nevertheless. He turns to Harriet, "Good day to you as well, Miss Fisher. Will you be dancing with us this evening?"

"Yes, Mr. Howe, Mr. Griffiths was just giving me advice on how to improve my technique. It is a pleasure to see you." Harriet looks toward me, then back at Elias, and goes on, "Mr. Griffiths is going to dance a minuet with Miss Bixby; I am very excited to watch."

Elias looks at me with a measure of disbelief. "It appears as if your relationship with Miss Bixby has matured somewhat. Is she quite prepared to dance a minuet?"

"Miss Bixby has been an astute learner, assimilating into the art of dancing quite rapidly. Actually, I find it quite remarkable that she learned the art of dancing a minuet in one afternoon. We will be dancing 'King George the 3rd's Minuet' at the opening of the dance. The addition of your fiddle will make the performance that much more brilliant."

Elias replies, "I am truly awestruck. The entire evening will assuredly be grand!"

We all nod in agreement, taking our leave to go ready ourselves for the dance.

∞

As the guests begin to arrive, Salome is present in the front foyer to greet them. Elias and I are upstairs, waiting at the entrance of the hall. Jonas Sibley is the first to arrive, along with Little Jim and his fiddle. "Good evening, Jonas, it is a pleasure to see you. Do you remember Elias?"

Jonas appears excited, responding, "Good evening, Obadiah. Why, yes, of course, good evening, Elias."

Little Jim appears quiet. I reassure him, "Good evening Little Jim, and thank you for coming. It will be wonderful to have two fiddlers playing this evening; the music is always so much richer with multiple musicians."

"Why thank you, sir, it is always my pleasure." Little Jim turns to Elias, saying, "Welcome back to Millbury, Mr. Howe. It is a pleasure to see you again."

Guests continue to arrive, many of the youth with their parents. Adelia Waters approaches us, adorable as always. "Good evening, Mr. Griffiths. I want to introduce you to my father Asa, and my mother Susan." Adelia appears overjoyed, asking, "Has Lucinda arrived?"

ARTHUR L. MARTIN

I reply to Adelia, "Not as of yet, but I anticipate her arrival momentarily." I proceed to welcome her parents, "Good evening; it is a pleasure to make your acquaintance. Adelia is doing quite well with her dancing. She has obviously been acquainted with the art for quite some time."

Susan is quite becoming for a woman of her age. She smiles, adding, "Adelia speaks rather highly of you, Mr. Griffiths. It is a pleasure to finally meet you."

It is getting close to the hour and there is no Lucinda as of yet. She is always on time, and so my anxiety begins to heighten. Elias, anticipating my concern, works to soothe me. "You appear anxious; Lucinda will most assuredly arrive in time for the opening."

Just as I am about to respond to Elias, Lucy appears from around the corner. My heart begins to race in anticipation of seeing Lucinda following directly behind her. Instead, behind Lucy is a lady that I have never met, most likely her mother. Lucy approaches, displaying an enthusiastic smile. "Good evening, Elias; it is a pleasure seeing you again." It is obvious that Lucy is taken back by the sight of Elias, her attraction to him becoming ever more obvious. She then turns to me, "Good evening, Mr. Griffiths. Let me introduce you to my mother Lois."

Turning my attention to Lucy's mother, I reply, "Good evening, Lois. It is a pleasure to make your acquaintance. Thank you for attending this evening."

Lois replies, "It is entirely my pleasure to be here. Lucinda and her mother are directly behind us; they became engaged in conversation with Salome on their way in."

A sense of relief warms my soul. "Wonderful, we shall need to get started soon. I believe all of the guests have arrived."

Lucy assuredly perceives my concern. She comforts me by saying, "Let me run downstairs and hurry Lucinda along. It does appear that everyone is ready to begin."

Lucy turns to leave; Lucinda and her mother appear from around the corner. Lucinda is wearing the red dress she wore the first time that I saw her; her beautiful hair fashioned with long curls. She has a bun low on the back of her head, tied with a narrow, cranberry-colored ribbon. The sight of her makes my knees go weak. As she approaches, the smile on her face becomes radiant. I reach for her hand. Slowly, I bring it to my lips; the world spins.

Looking directly into Lucinda's eyes, I welcome her. "Good evening, my dear, you look magnificent." I turn to Hannah and reach for her hand. I extend her a warm welcome, although admittedly, without the world spinning. "Good evening, Hannah, it is a pleasure to see you."

Hannah is warm toward me; her smile is inviting. "The pleasure is all mine. Lucinda is a changed lady since her introduction to dance; she is quite excited to be performing a minuet with you."

Looking into the hall, I detect that the guests have settled. I reassure Hannah, "Yes, your daughter is a most splendid dancer, and it appears that you will observe that for yourself, momentarily."

∞

There are nearly fifty people in the hall including students and parents. I take my place at the center of the room; the guests immediately become silent. I begin, "It appears that my lessons on manners have paid off; thank you all for your prompt attention."

With the dead silence comes a wave of anxiousness. I become concerned; is Lucinda ready for this? Fear becomes apparent with the sweating of my brow.

I continue, "Many thanks to our musicians for this evening, Mr. Elias Howe from Framingham and Master Little Jim from Sutton." Lucinda is standing next to Elias and Little Jim. She appears relaxed and prepared. "To open, I have asked Miss Lucinda Bixby to accompany me in demonstrating the art of dancing a minuet, to be followed by a dance demonstration performed by the ladies and gents who have spent their valuable time studying the art of dancing over the past three weeks."

Lucinda approaches, wearing a most confident and inviting smile. Her curls are bouncing in concert with her elegant steps; my heart fills with joy. She takes her position facing the audience, and with grace, moves her arms fluidly into position. The music begins; I remove my hat and lower it to my side. I turn to look at Lucinda. Her eyes are delicious. I extend my right hand to her; she delicately places her left hand in mine. The dance begins. Lucinda's movements are heavenly. Throughout the performance, Lucinda's expression remains inviting. Her eyes are fixated on mine, her body flowing with the music as if one with it. When the music ends, Lucinda tastefully removes her hand from mine, both of us turning in unison to face the audience.

There is a look of awe shared by everyone. In particular, Harriet is staring with a look of astonishment. It appears that she has affirmed the topic of our earlier conversation, and when she recognizes me gazing at her, she smiles and nods her head.

Lucinda turns to me, and with the look of an angel, reveals her thoughts: "Obadiah, that was the greatest happiness that I have ever experienced; it will forever be a treasure that I cherish!"

I am speechless; I spontaneously reach for her hand, and, again, raise it to my lips. The taste of her skin is delectable. Everyone in the hall expresses their approbation by standing and clapping their hands. We extend our manners to the audience one more time, and Lucinda makes her way over to Harriet. The performance was utterly remarkable.

∞

The evening was a complete success. The students performed three dances, flawlessly, and then the parents joined in, keeping the floor active until nearly midnight. The baked goods provided by Salome were delicious. And I had a chance to kick up my heels a bit.

As guests begin to leave, I take my place at the doorway. Lucinda joins me in wishing everyone a good night. Adelia approaches, announcing that she has exciting news. Before she is able to divulge anything further, her mother Susan offers, "Obadiah and Lucinda, you danced the minuet together superbly. You might know that Asa and I put on a Christmas Ball every year. It is held on Christmas Eve at our home. We would like to extend a personal invitation to the both of you to join us."

Lucinda immediately turns to me; the look on her face is precious, her eyes are twinkling with anticipation. I smile, extending my invitation to her: "Would you be so kind as to join me on Christmas Eve for a Christmas Ball?"

I am not quite finished with my invitation, when Lucinda answers, "I would be most pleased to do so!"

Turning back to Asa and Susan, I confirm our mutual interest. "Thank you for the invitation, Lucinda and I would be most delighted to attend."

TWENTY-TWO

LUCINDA... *THURSDAY, AUGUST 13, 1840*

The morning is crisp and clear. The sun peeks through the window, bringing the promise of a most splendid day. I have little time to complete my chores; Obadiah is expected to arrive by seven. The journey to West Sutton will take over an hour; Obadiah wants to be there to help raise the first wall.

The smell of bacon fills the air, signifying that Mother is busily preparing breakfast. I slip out from beneath my quilt, finding my way over to the window. The fields are green; the sky is a bright blue. A few plumy clouds hang like puppets from the heavens. If the sky remains clear, the Sturgeon Moon will assuredly brighten the evening, almost as if it were day.

∞

I hurry through my morning chores, taking only a moment to visit with Shadow before returning to the house. The hair of her mane is long and silky; my brush slips through with little resistance. I am anxious to share my feelings of delight with her, "My dear Shadow, you have always been here for me, especially when the darkness was most dreadful." I kiss her on the side of her face, and then take a step back to ask, "Is it not time for the darkness to be lifted?" Shadow nods her head with affirmation. I continue, "This summer has already brought me untold happiness, but I sense today may prove to be the happiest day of my life." I give Shadow a warm embrace around her neck. "Wish me the best."

∞

I hurry down the path toward the house. I fear that Obadiah will soon arrive and I am not yet properly dressed. Mother has prepared a slab of bacon, some fried eggs, and fresh biscuits for breakfast. There is little time for me to stop and enjoy, but I do manage to slice off a good-sized piece of bacon and butter myself a biscuit. Mother quite understands. "I certainly appreciate just how excited you are, but you should take a few minutes to enjoy your breakfast. Obadiah is a gentleman, and surely will not mind waiting on you for a moment or two."

Accepting that Mother is correct, I take time to sit and enjoy my meal. Just as I chew the last bit of bacon, there is a light knock on the front door. Turning to Mother in a bit of a panic, I ask, "Is it possible that Obadiah has arrived early?" I quietly motion to Mother, prompting her to inquire if it is Obadiah at the door. I have yet to put on any more than my chemise; I quickly run up the stairs to my room.

Mother calls to me from the foot of the stairs, "Obadiah is here, and he apologizes for arriving early. I will pour him a mug of coffee."

My spirits are high, resulting in a prompt reply. "Tell him I will hurry; offer him a biscuit!"

∞

The wash water is quite chilly, but there is certainly not enough time for me to fetch warm water from the cauldron downstairs. Nevertheless, I must wash myself. I tolerate the cold water, anticipating that I may have moments today where I find myself quite close to Obadiah. I choose to clean my teeth as well. Mother has loaned me a handsome paisley dress for today; I plan to complement it by wearing my straw bonnet with the cranberry ribbon. Passing the mirror, I stop to observe my reflection; I murmur to myself, "'Tis a beautiful day for an outing."

When I enter the kitchen, I find Obadiah and Mother deep in conversation over a mug of coffee. Obadiah stands to greet me. "Good morning Lucinda; you look marvelous today, as always."

Obadiah looks quite becoming in his work clothes. In an approving voice, I return the greeting. "Good morning Obadiah, it appears that you are well-prepared for a long day of hard work."

Mother interrupts, "It is getting late; you must be on your way."

∞

The carriage ride to West Sutton is a mite more than six miles. The padded seat in Obadiah's carriage is quite comfortable; sitting close to him is most delightful. It has been just over eighteen years since my last and only experience of a raising of any kind. I was only six when we raised our home in February of 1822. I do remember it quite clearly, six or seven men working together, everyone drinking plenty of rum.

As we make our way down the hill toward the church, Obadiah breaks the silence by saying, "Lucinda, it is an absolute delight that you have agreed to accompany me today."

I place my hand on his, assuring him, "Why, it is my pleasure; there is nothing I could imagine that would be more pleasing."

Our journey brings us past the grove at Singletary Lake. I point it out to Obadiah. "There were nearly twelve hundred pupils gathered on the grove for a Sabbath school celebration on July first. I did not attend, but friends have reported it was a beautiful event where hymns were composed and sung by all of those who gathered."

We continue to follow the road that winds around the lake. We pass the Millbury-Sutton line on our way toward our destination. The weather is beautiful; the air is crisp and the sky is clear. Millbury Road is a long stretch with little population. We pass the schoolhouse where I have taught penmanship on a few occasions. Although it is quite a distance from home, I thoroughly enjoy working with pupils on their writing skills, making the journey on a pleasant day most worth it.

We come to the end of Millbury Road and take an immediate left onto Main Street. There are already several men working on the barn. The Hutchinsons' home is directly on the right; they are raising the barn just to the east of it. Obadiah brings the carriage to a stop and hitches Jasper to a post. He immediately comes to the side of the carriage, offering me his hand for assistance.

The house and barn are both quite close to the road. Obadiah wishes me a good morning and makes his way to the area where the men are working on the barn. Eveline Hutchinson approaches. She greets me by saying, "Good day, might you be Lucinda Bixby? My husband Stephen and I are delighted that you were able to join us."

Eveline is a welcoming lady; I respond, "Good day; it is an absolute pleasure to be here, and to make your acquaintance."

Eveline motions me to follow. "This way. The other ladies are in the house, socializing and preparing a wholesome dinner for the gentlemen."

∞

The house is crowded; I immediately recognize Salome. "Good day, Salome; I was not aware that you would be attending today."

She replies, "Oh yes, Stephen is a good friend of Jonas's and Jonas had requested Dennis's help. It is marvelous that Obadiah has volunteered as well. It will be a fun day."

Eveline takes me by the hand, guiding me into the parlor. "Ladies, this is Lucinda Bixby, from Millbury. She is here with Obadiah Griffiths, the gentleman who is conducting the dance school at the Lower Tavern."

I smile, pleased to see there are many women who are in attendance, as well as an infant. "Good day; it is a pleasure to make everyone's acquaintance."

Eveline looks around the room and begins to make proper introductions to all. "This is Mindwell Phelps and her brand new baby daughter who was born the latter part of June. Her name is Mindwell Amelia." Eveline reaches for the baby's hand, giving it a gentle squeeze. "Sitting over there is Margaret Sibley, who is Jonas's wife. Next to her is Martha and Peregrine, both sisters of Amos Waters. Amos's grandfather Judah is the brother of Mr. Amos Waters, who was responsible for building the house we are in."

Margaret appears inquisitive. She asks, "Jonas reports that you and Obadiah danced the minuet quite elegantly at the dance that was held the Friday evening before last. It would be splendid to see a repeat performance, if time permits, later this evening. Our Little Jim is here and is prepared to fiddle for us."

I blush with embarrassment. "Why, of course, let us hope that Obadiah is willing after the day's activities." I look out of the window and count nine gentlemen helping to hoist up the first wall.

∞

By early afternoon, the gentlemen have raised all four walls. It appears that they are passing a jug of rum in celebration, surely toasting to their accomplishments before coming in to share in the dinner that the ladies have prepared.

The gentlemen begin to file in from the outside, moving directly into the keeping room where there is a bountiful spread of delicious meats, vegetables, and baked goods. The ladies move into the keeping room to assist with the serving of food. By the amount of food being piled onto plates, the gentlemen are all obviously quite famished.

I recognize Dennis, Jonas, and Little Jim. Obadiah takes me by the hand and introduces me to Stephen and his son, Stephen; Jonas's son, John; James Phelps, who is a neighbor; and Amos Waters, brother of Martha and Peregrine, who I had met earlier. I ask Obadiah, "How is everything fitting together? It looks as if you are doing quite well."

Obadiah is chewing on a piece of pork. When finished, he replies, "The preparation has been done with much precision. Once we raise the ridge timber, the rafters should go quickly." The ladies have made their way back into the parlor. He looks into the parlor at the ladies, and then back at me, asking, "Have you had a good day thus far?"

I reply, "It has been wonderful. The ladies are all pleasant, and the conversation has been very diverse." I look into his eyes with desire and continue, "But I am craving your presence." His smile is delectable. I inform him, "Jonas's wife, Margaret, has asked if we would perform the minuet this evening."

His response is immediate: "There is nothing that would please me more!"

∞

The remainder of the afternoon is spent cleaning and conversing with the ladies, mostly on the subject of abolition. The movement is gaining momentum; the subject is being discussed openly amongst ladies throughout the area.

As the afternoon wanes, the sun moves to the western sky, causing the house to cast a shadow that nearly extends to the barn. The men are again passing the jug around, taking shelter from the sun for a moment in the shade. The ridge timber is in place and nearly all of the rafters assembled. Obadiah notices me peering out of the window; he tips his hat toward me. I discreetly raise my hand waist high and wiggle my fingers, responding to his kind gesture.

∞

When the sun sets, the full moon is already beginning to brighten the sky. Eveline enters the parlor with news that the gentlemen have completed their work for the day. "Stephen has informed me that the barn work is complete. It is time that we move out to the barn floor; it will be a spectacular place to assemble for some dancing." The ladies all agree, quickly filing out of the house.

Stephen and his son have set up a dozen lanterns around the perimeter of the barn. They have also temporarily hung a pierced tin chandelier holding eight candles from one of the beams. It is an extremely still evening; the candle flames in the chandelier hardly flicker. The Sturgeon Moon, accompanied by twenty candles, provides us an abundance of light for dancing. The jug of rum is still being passed, and there is plenty of raspberry shrub for the rest.

Little Jim has already begun fiddling while everyone else gathers in the center of the floor. Eveline raises her hand, saying, "May I have everyone's attention?" She pauses until the music stops; the gathering becomes mute. "Obadiah and Lucinda have agreed to open our dancing with a repeat performance of the minuet they danced last week at the Lower Tavern."

The gathering disperses, everyone taking a place around the perimeter of the floor. Obadiah and I are left precariously alone in the center. I turn to him; his smile of confidence raises my spirits. I think to myself, *Happiness abounds in the love that I feel for this intriguing gentleman I am about to dance with.*

I immediately take my position alongside Obadiah, moving my arms as gracefully as I can to their proper positions. Little Jim begins the music; the rest is enchanting. When not staring directly into his eyes, my thoughts are consumed by the recurring vision of me twirling in my lovely gown. When I refocus my eyes on Obadiah, we are already dancing our final honors; where did the time go?

Everyone appears to be quite moved by our performance. Obadiah warmly takes my hand into his, he bows, and I follow with a curtsy. My entire world is whirling in a funnel of happiness. He turns and stares into my eyes, drawing me ever closer to his soul.

Eveline makes her way out to the center of the floor, exclaiming, "Such elegance and simplicity, something for us all to strive for." Casting a strong smile, she invites everyone to join in. "Ladies, take a partner, and form a large circle for our first dance."

Obadiah and I dance together throughout the night, with the exception of only two dances. By request, Obadiah teaches two of his uncle's favorites, "Constancy" and "Pleasure of Love." I dance "Constancy" with Salome and sit out the other. Just before midnight, Obadiah suggests we begin our journey back to Millbury. I smile in agreement; we extend our best wishes to everyone as we take our leave.

∞

The road home is lit by the light of the full moon. The temperature is rather crisp; I snuggle up close to Obadiah. Looking up at the sky, I am fascinated by the twinkle of a thousand stars. As we come up alongside the secluded shores of Singletary Lake, Obadiah pulls slightly on the reigns, "Whoa, Jasper."

He reaches behind himself, returning with a blanket. He covers our legs with it, while commenting, "It is a mite chilly out here; this will help." He stares at me, his warm and inviting eyes drawing me closer. He extends his arms around my waist, holding me tightly, as if he will never let me go. We kiss; his lips are delicious.

Our embrace becomes heated; his hands are busily at work, making their way through my clothing and to my flesh. He gently fondles my breasts, running his strong fingers gracefully across my nipples. He draws me even closer; he again brings his warm lips to mine. They are so sweet to the taste. I adjust myself in the seat by turning myself toward him. My hand wittingly falls onto his leg. My only thoughts are to somehow return the pleasure that he is providing me.

Unsure of myself, I slowly move my hand closer to the inside of his thighs and begin to slowly massage him. Having never experienced this level of desire before, I instinctively move my hand to the buttons on his trousers. Deliberately, I fumble to release a few, sliding my hand slowly through the opening. It is larger and firmer than I ever would have imagined. He immediately responds, becoming even more intimate with his touch. I begin to stroke him gently; his groans of pleasure assure me of his satisfaction. His breathing becomes more like panting. I grip him tighter, increasing the intensity of my strokes.

I am quite startled when his hand finds its way to my knee; he anxiously begins to massage my inner thighs. The scar is warmed by his touch; it has never felt so good. My desire has grown beyond my wildest dreams; I am drifting in and out of ecstasy. Just as I am about to explode, he slides his warm fingers into me, and I tremble with intense pleasure. He knows exactly how to touch me. I am suddenly overwhelmed by a warm release that takes over my entire world. Almost simultaneously, his body stiffens, and he lets out a loud and passionate sigh of release.

We embrace, as if our souls have united into one. The sensation of warmth remains with me; our lips meet again.

∞

The remainder of the journey home is peaceful and without much dialogue. When we come to a stop in front of my house, Obadiah removes the blanket and jumps from the carriage. I slide over toward him; he extends his hand to assist me in getting down. I adjust my chemise and dress. Unsure as to whether I am properly fastened, I ask Obadiah to be sure all the hooks along my back are clasped. He smiles, and pulls me toward him, "My dear Lucinda, this has been a truly blessed day." He kisses me on the cheek.

My eyes immediately become tearful; wetness begins to run down my cheeks. It is difficult for me to trust the emotions I am feeling. Obadiah continues to hold my hands, looking at me with great apprehension. The words simply slip out of my mouth, "Is this truly how it feels to be in love?"

TWENTY-THREE

LUCINDA... *FRIDAY, AUGUST 14, 1840*

"The evening was absolutely delightful; Obadiah is a true gentleman, and his lips are as sweet as strawberry wine." Shadow looks at me inquisitively, surely doing her best to appreciate my enthusiasm. I continue to brush her mane with more vigor than usual. "The evening ended with a tender kiss on my cheek, just melting my heart." I run my hand across Shadow's face, stopping to kiss her on her nose, whispering, "Thank you so much for always being here."

There is a feel of bliss in the air. I fall back into a bed of hay, raising my legs high into the air. My chemise slips down around my thighs, exposing me to the fresh air. Wiggling my toes, my thoughts travel back in time to the moment of our excitement, realizing now that my love for Obadiah is genuine, sensing that his love for me is as genuine as mine is for him.

With all my daydreaming, time has slipped away. This is the day that I plan to finish my gown for the Christmas Ball. There are many more chores to complete before I am able pay attention to my own needs. I jump back onto my feet and hurry to finish my outside chores so that I might more quickly return to the house for breakfast.

∞

Entering the kitchen, I extend an invitation. "Mother, it is such a splendid day. Will you be joining me in the parlor later? I plan to put the finishing touches on my gown."

Mother is somewhat startled, as my entrance is a bit more audacious than usual. "Lucinda, I did not expect to see you up and about so early this morning." She continues to churn the cream. She asks, "Did you enjoy your day with Obadiah?"

It is difficult for me to tame the enthusiasm I am feeling. I respond, "It was absolutely wonderful!"

Mother looks up at me, smiling. "It would be a pleasure to watch as you finish your gown, but I have already committed my time to the Charitable Society this afternoon. We are gathering at Lois Chamberlain's house to knit socks for the State Lunatic Hospital." There is a moment of silence, followed by, "Maybe you might work to finish your gown this morning, and then join us. I am sure that Lucy will be there, and I thought maybe you could share the particulars of yesterday's exciting activities with all of us."

My thoughts immediately become absorbed with the intimate moments of last evening. Lost for words, I mumble, "It may not at all be of interest, it was just a barn raising." Mother surely detects my hesitancy. Returning to the original question, I respond, "Why, of course Mother, are you agreeable to finishing the chores here in the kitchen without my assistance?"

Mother responds, "Certainly. The cream is almost thickened and the cooking is done for the day. Your father has business in Auburn; I do not expect him home for dinner. As for us, Lois will surely have some baked goods and tea when we arrive."

∞

The gown is now complete enough for it to hang on the once-empty peg in my room. Approaching it, I recollect the morning I first dreamed of dancing with the faceless gentleman, in this most gracious gown. Now, it is more than obvious to me that the faceless gentleman is no other than my love, Obadiah. I remove the gown from the peg and find my way down the stairs to the parlor.

I lay the dress out on the floor, admiring the beautiful colors and patterns, saying to myself, "Just as I envisioned it." There is very little that needs to be completed; a few more stitches on the collar, and then the sewing on of the brass hooks. Taking a seat in my favorite chair by the front window, I pick up the dress and drape it over my legs. The work to complete it takes less than one half hour.

After sewing on the last brass hook, I cannot wait to try it on in its completed form. Standing, I lift the dress over my head, sliding it on over my chemise. After fastening the hooks, I take a twirl in it. The fit is perfect; I call out, "Mother, can you please come into the parlor? I have something to show you."

Mother is close by in the kitchen, and so appears immediately at the doorway of the parlor. "Lucinda, it is breathtaking. The floral pattern is lovely and I just adore the puffiness of the sleeves. You look like a princess; what a lovely gown."

I imagine myself dancing the minuet with Obadiah, moving gracefully about the room. Stopping, I express my thoughts to Mother. "The Christmas Ball is only four months away; it will be my dream come true evening."

∞

Mother and I decide to walk to the Chamberlains' house; the sky is clear and the temperature feels about seventy. Passing the Faulkner barn, thoughts of that horrid evening have become more distant than ever before. Instead, I am occupied by the promise of happiness that the summer has afforded me. As we pass the schoolhouse, Mr. Carter is on the granite step, calling out, "Good day to the Bixby ladies, and a beautiful day it is."

Mr. Carter is a very animated soul, with the patience of Job. I greet him by saying, "Good day, Mr. Carter! We are on our way to the Chamberlains' for an afternoon of knitting."

Mr. Carter responds, "Miss Bixby, would you be available to teach penmanship again next Wednesday, the 19th? The pupils are always asking for you."

"Most certainly. It is always such a pleasure."

When we reach the Chamberlains', we can hear the ladies in conversation though the open door and windows. Lucy appears at the front door, and with a surprised look, says, "Good day Mrs. Bixby; Lucinda, I did not know that you were coming." She enthusiastically comes toward me. She addresses Mother, "Mrs. Bixby, the ladies are in the parlor, and are expecting you. I would like to sit with Lucinda and hear all about yesterday's adventures."

Mother smiles at me, and then responds, "Thank you. Lucy, enjoy your visit."

Lucy takes my hand and leads me over to the stone wall to sit. Turning her head towards me she asks, "Was your day splendid? Did Obadiah finally kiss you?"

"Yes, Lucy, my day was certainly a splendid one. Obadiah arrived at my house earlier than expected, affording us much more time to be together." Doing my best not to leave out any of the important details, I share with Lucy as much of the day as I recollect. I go on, "When the men finished raising the main structure of the barn, it was time to dance."

Fervently, Lucy asks, "Did you dance with Obadiah?"

"Why, yes, I did. We began by performing the minuet, and then we danced together throughout the night. It was delightful."

Lucy is looking for more. "Did you travel home alone? The full moon was beautiful last night; did you stop along the way?"

I smile warmly toward Lucy, selecting my words carefully. "Yes, it was a beautiful night; and yes, we did stop for a moment along the way. We stopped alongside Singletary Lake; we simply embraced to keep warm, sharing with one another our innermost feelings."

Lucy, still appearing inquisitive, asks, "You have not answered me! Did he kiss you?"

"Yes, he did." I point to my cheek. "Right here on my cheek, just before we said our final goodnight."

It is obvious that Lucy expects more, but I do not feel it appropriate to share the details. I squeeze her hand gently, saying, "I just finished the gown I plan to wear to the Christmas Ball; would you like to come to my house to see it?"

Enthusiastically, Lucy accepts the invitation. "Yes, that is a splendid idea; the weather is perfect, and I had already planned to stop in to see Mary before the end of the day. I will visit her on my way back from your house."

We jump from the wall and brush ourselves off. I head directly into the parlor where the ladies are knitting. "Mother, Lucy and I are going to walk to our house; she would like to have a viewing of my new gown."

Mother responds positively, "Enjoy your walk; I will be along shortly."

Lucy and I have a skip in our step as we make our way down the road. As we approach the common, Ebenezer Goffe raises his hand, waving and shouting, "Good day, ladies! The perfect day for a walk."

"Good day, Mr. Goffe; it certainly is."

When we reach my house, Father is outside, unhitching Shadow from the buckboard. I am excited to see him. "Good day Father; how was your day?"

"It was very productive; I was able to finish the project I was working on in Auburn, allowing me to get back to some much needed work around here." Once Shadow is unhitched, he leads her back to the barn, asking, "Did you enjoy the barn raising yesterday?"

"Very much so; it was a marvelous day."

∞

The gown is lying across my favorite chair in the parlor. I promptly remove the dress that I am wearing, slipping the gown on over my head. I turn my back toward Lucy, asking, "Would you fasten me?"

Lucy begins to fasten each of the tiny brass hooks. "The pattern is wonderful." As she fastens the last hook, she remarks, "And the fit is perfect."

Lucy moves back a few steps, sitting in the chair where the dress was lying. I close my eyes and proceed to carry out the first few steps of the minuet. I finish with a curtsy, and then open my eyes to what looks to be a verily intrigued Lucy. Apparently unsure of what to say, she blurts out one word, "Magnificent." She stands to offer a few more words. "Your movement is exquisite and your gown is simply elegant."

Lucy takes her seat again, suggesting, "Sit with me for a moment. I have something to ask of you."

I take a seat next to her; she begins to speak softly and meaningfully, "You have changed tremendously during these summer months. Your demeanor has shifted from habitual

207

melancholy to extreme happiness." I am taken aback by
Lucy's observation; she continues, "Have you an idea as to the
cause? I might think it love, but Obadiah has yet to kiss you
intimately." She appears to become a mite uncomfortable.
"Or, maybe it is simply the freedom you feel when you dance."

I smile, and do my best to unravel the observations and
questions Lucy has posed. "You are very observant, and yes,
my demeanor has been mostly melancholic over the years since
we have met. This unfortunately was caused by a horrid event
that happened nearly ten years past, that has been impossible
for me to forget." I close my eyes for a moment, in full
expectation that I will relive that horrible evening in my mind,
causing my scar to become inflamed. Instead, I experience an
intense sensation of joy, and envision Obadiah's intriguing
smile, inviting me to dance.

"The events of this summer have led me to a new life, a life
bursting with happiness. It is not only dancing, and it is not
only love. It is dancing with the one I love." My eyes swell
with tears. "And this is truly what has helped me to bury that
horrid event of the past."

Lucy stands, taking my hands into hers. Lifting me from the
chair, she looks directly into my eyes. "I am so happy for
you."

TWENTY-FOUR

OBADIAH... *FRIDAY, AUGUST 14, 1840*

The afternoon sun shines through the shop window, flooding my workbench with light. The day has passed quickly, my attention consumed by the blissful events of yesterday. Lucinda is the perfect lady; my attraction to her grows stronger each day. Should I love again? Do I have a choice? Love does not show mercy; it is relentless. There is no choice.

Salome has asked that I look at her favorite cheese press to determine if it is feasible to repair it. The notches on the windlass have been chewed over the years, requiring that I reproduce it. Dennis was able to provide me with a suitable piece of three-inch round oak that required only a small amount of shaping on the lathe. The notches that engage with the pegs on the plunger are the most difficult to reproduce. Although the carving of the notches is tedious, it requires an element of mindfulness that engages me.

While working diligently on the final notch, I notice someone's feet approaching out of the corner of my eye. I recognize them as Salome's. They are always covered with dirt and soot, but enchanting nevertheless. She places her left hand on my shoulder, asking inquisitively, "Good day Obadiah; you have been out here since morning. What has you so occupied?"

"You had suggested to me that your favorite cheese press was in need of repair. I thought that it would be decent of me to attempt to repair it for you."

Surprised, she responds, "Dennis had looked at it, and thought it to be past its useful life."

Doing my best not to appear boastful, I suggest, "I would tend to agree with him, but you seemed to have a fondness for it that suggested to me that it was worth my while to spend an afternoon on it." I hold up the old windlass, explaining, "The press is in very good working order, it is just this piece, and the pegs on the plunger that are the problem." I point to the notches on the old windlass. "These have worn, causing them not to mesh properly with the pegs."

Salome nods her head, delighted that I would go to such a length to bring her happiness. She tenderly squeezes my shoulder, saying warmly, "I am going to miss you quite a lot when you move on." She captures me with her infectious smile. "It is past time for tea; Harriet is in the parlor and wishes for you to join her."

Appreciating Salome's kind notion, I assure her, "As soon as I am finished with this final notch, I will make my way in to share some time with Harriet. It is always such a pleasure."

Before taking her leave, Salome curiously inquires, "How did your evening go with Lucinda after we left? The minuet was even more delightful the second time. You make such an adorable couple."

"Our evening was wonderful; we danced till nearly midnight, followed by a blissful ride home in my carriage, guided by the light of the full Sturgeon Moon. I even had a chance to kiss her on the cheek, with great delight."

Salome contemplates my passion, suggesting, "It may just be that you do not move on quite as soon as you expected."

I ponder what she says, replying, "We will see."

∞

Returning to the tavern, I find Salome removing a delicious-looking apple tart from the Dutch oven that is warming over a heap of coals on the hearth of the fireplace. Moving it to a plate on the table, she warns me with a smile, "This is quite hot; you may want to give it a moment to cool before indulging." Salome hands me a cup of tea, reminding me, "Harriet is expecting you in the parlor."

The parlor is exceptionally bright this afternoon, the sun shining directly through the two windows on the west side of the building. Harriet is busy at work, knitting what appears to be a handsome-looking tippet. It is a light brown color, and has a thin, olive-colored border surrounding it. She looks up when she hears me, saying, "Good day, Mr. Griffiths. I am just finishing up on a tippet I am knitting to help warm my shoulders in the cold months ahead." She goes back to knitting, only to look up moments later, asking, "Are you going to take a seat with me?"

"Why, yes, I am. Let me put my cup of tea down and fetch myself a slice of apple tart. Would you like some?"

Harriet stops her knitting again to respond, "No thank you. I am most interested in finishing the last few rows of this tippet before retiring for the evening."

Returning to the parlor, Harriet remains intent on finishing her work, while I take a seat on the upholstered chair. The apple tart tastes as delicious as it looks. My cup of tea has cooled considerably, but remains warm enough to enjoy. Looking over toward Harriet, I ask, "Are you enjoying the summer days?"

Looking up at me, she continues to knit while answering, "It has been a most enjoyable summer, especially with my participation in the dance school." Her demeanor appears to change; she tilts her head. "But I am struggling with something that you may be able to help me with."

Harriet's innocence radiates through her inquisitive expression. With sincerity, I ask, "And what might that be?"

"I am struggling with the idea of eternity, and what it means to die."

It is obvious that Harriet has given considerable thought to the subject, otherwise she would not encroach on it. However, the subject of eternity is vast; it is quite a complex concept for the mind to comprehend. It is one of life's most thought-about conundrums, never understood with any certainty.

Knowing the strength of her young inquisitive mind, I pose the question, "Tell me: what are your thoughts on the subject?"

She stops her knitting, ponders the question, and attempts to answer me. "When I close my eyes at night to sleep, I too often find myself thinking of forever. I fear falling into an abyss that never ends. I try to think of Heaven, but it often does not help. During the day, when I am active, the concern is not as great."

Being sure to organize my words effectively, I respond, "Let me tell you a little secret; I too used to be quite frightened by the thought of death." Harriet places the tippet on her lap, paying all of her attention to my words. "It was love that changed me." She tilts her head, prompting for more. "Some three years ago, I found love in a young lady. Her name was Abigail. We shared every waking moment with one another; our joy for life was incredible, until she was suddenly killed in a freak accident."

Harriet places her hand over her mouth and spontaneously replies, "That's horrible."

"It was, until I realized how much I still loved her, and how much I felt her love still living in me. It is as if our souls were united as one, even though she was buried and I was alive."

212

Her head tilts to the other side. "Tell me more."

"Shortly after Abigail's death, I began to feel a desire to share the love we had for each other. Not the romantic love that we shared when she was alive, but a love more profound and lasting than that, a love that is a reflection of our true happiness together. I became more mindful of others; I began to experience the importance of helping others to find happiness, the same true happiness that Abigail and I shared."

Harriet has become enthralled by my story. I go on, "And so you see, I still do not know the truth about dying, but I no longer fear it, for I have been blessed with the wisdom to help others to find happiness. And with that, I have been showered with an untold amount of happiness of my own."

Looking at me with sincerity, she asks, "Mr. Griffiths, that is a wonderful story, but how does it alleviate your fear of death?"

Pondering, searching for the right words, I continue, "In the evening when I close my eyes for sleep, I know that the joy and happiness that Abigail had for the world remains alive in me. More importantly, it is alive in everyone that I encourage to find his or her own happiness. And so, when it becomes my time, I have a strong belief that the abounding happiness in my soul will live on in those that I have had the privilege of helping to experience a happier life. This brings me great comfort."

Harriet listens intently, appearing unsure of her next words. "Mr. Griffiths, I understand now, and you can be assured that the happiness you have brought me this summer will live on in my heart forever."

"Excellent, and you must promise me that you will share that happiness with everyone that you encounter in life."

"I promise."

213

TWENTY-FIVE

LUCINDA... *MONDAY, SEPTEMBER 21, 1840*

The air is surprisingly chilly this morning. The temperature must have dropped nearly twenty degrees overnight. There is a small fire ablaze in the fireplace of my room. Mother must have lit it earlier, although it has yet to make much difference. I reach for my knitted stockings, pulling them up past my knees. My feet are still quite frigid; I curl up under the quilt, massaging my toes with my warm hands. It helps. It is always difficult for me when summer fades and winter begins to enter the mind. However, the fall brings with it a joyous time of harvest, as well as the harvest dance.

On this day, the last day of summer, and the tenth week of dance school, I look forward to having the gents join us for an afternoon of dancing. This will be the first Monday that we will all come together at once, both ladies and gents, for an afternoon lesson. My thoughts turn to Obadiah and the many moments of happiness that we have shared throughout the summer. I am pleased that we will spend the last day of the summer dancing with one another, sharing our happiness together.

It is time now that I roll out of bed and begin the day. The sun has not yet risen, as it would have in July. The light of the fire is all that I need to make my way around the room. The water in the pitcher is too cold for a bath; I skip washing until later in the morning, when I am able to fill the pitcher with warm water from the cauldron. I slip on my petticoat and reach for my blue and green flannel dress that hangs on one of the pegs. I had removed it from my blanket chest last week, washing it in preparation for the colder days ahead. I did not expect to wear it so soon. I place my hair up into a bun and tie my cap on.

Ready for chores, I place two small logs on the fire to keep it going and hurry down the narrow staircase to the kitchen.

∞

"Good morning Mother; it was kind of you to set up a fire for me this morning. It is much chillier than I expected."

Mother is cutting the curd she has processed for making cheese. Watching her intently, the feel of the fire is wonderful on my back. It is hard to imagine that just yesterday the fire would have been uncomfortably warm. I ask if I might be of assistance. "Mother, is there something I can help you with before my chores begin?"

Mother smiles, assuring me, "Not now, my dear, but thank you. Once I have finished squeezing the curd dry and have it in the mold, you may help with the clean-up."

I respond kindly to Mother, "Yes, of course; it should take me no more than an hour in the barn."

∞

I step outside; the wind is blowing fiercely. I reach back into the house to remove a cape from the peg by the door and throw it over my shoulders. It feels as if winter has come, even though it is the last day of summer.

The barn shelters me from the wind; I am able to remove my cape to begin my chores while remaining comfortable. I place the milk pail under my cow's udder, positioning my stool such that it is easy to reach her teats. I begin to gently massage her udder to help let the milk down. When she is ready, I reach out and clamp the tops of two of her teats between my thumbs and first finger. Squeezing her teats with my other fingers, the milk begins to flow. My mind begins to wander, prompting me to recall the rare moments of intimacy shared with Obadiah over the summer. My love for Obadiah is profound; he is

215

constantly on my mind. Moving on to her other teats, I turn my attention to finishing my chores. Mother is expecting me to help her with the cleaning; I must hurry.

Shadow appears quite satisfied with the colder weather. When I am finished tending to her, I promise, "It is Monday, our day to pick up the ladies and go dancing. And of course, your day for a delicious treat." It has become a ritual for Charles to be present when we arrive at the tavern; he always has a treat for her.

∞

Back in the house, Mother has finished packing the curd into a mold and already has it on the press. While much of the cleaning is complete, she asks, "Lucinda, can you bring the whey out to the pigs and then wash out the pan for me? I will take care of the rest."

"Certainly. After that, I plan to finish knitting my armlets before leaving for dance."

∞

The sun is shining and the wind has diminished, making the walk out to the pig pen a tad more comfortable than earlier this morning. By the time I reach the pen, my arms are quite tired and the tips of my fingers feel frozen. The pigs both seem quite delighted with their morning treat. There is a pail of fresh water already drawn next to the well. I use it to wash out the pan and quickly make my way back to the house. The cold water on my already-raw hands remind me of the winter months that are ahead; I shiver with the thought of it.

∞

Placing the clean milk pan on the table, I move into the parlor. There are a few warm embers in the fireplace, remnants from this morning's fire. I wave my hands over the embers to warm them. The path of the sun is much lower now than it is during the peak of summer. It affords me some welcome warmth from the sunlight that seeps through the front window where I sit. Peering out of the window, I am captivated by the field of wild carrots that have all turned brown, watching their skeletons dancing carelessly in the breeze.

The armlets that I have been working on are nearly complete; I was hoping to finish them before the cold sets in. One is finished, and I am now knitting the final rows of the second one. Once the knitting is finished, I will sew them up, making them ready to protect my arms from the cold.

When it is time to leave for dance school, I poke my head out of the front door to check the temperature. While the mornings can certainly be quite frigid this time of year, the afternoons always tend to warm from the sun. Today is no exception; it feels to be at least sixty, nearly twenty degrees warmer than this morning. Nevertheless, I decide to keep my knitted stockings on and wear my flannel dress, in anticipation of a much colder ride home.

∞

Lucy and I have become quite close over the summer, contributing profoundly to my newfound happiness. Her friendship affords me the pleasure of knowing there is always someone to confide in, no matter how trivial the matter. She hops up on to the buckboard, sliding down the seat and up close to me. "Good day, Lucinda, you look to be dressed for winter." She smiles and squeezes my hand, asking, "Have you prepared yourself for a late night ride home with Obadiah?"

I turn to her, and softly reply, "If you remember, we are dancing with the gents this afternoon, leaving Obadiah free for the evening. One cannot be too prepared."

Shadow has become quite familiar with the route to the Lower Tavern; she takes us there with little encouragement from me. When we arrive, Charles is waiting with a pan of fresh oats and a bucket of water. Shadow and Charles have become quite good friends. "Good day, Charles; it has turned into a pleasant one, has it not?"

"Good day, Miss Bixby! It certainly has. Mr. Griffiths has asked that I help prepare his carriage for a journey later this afternoon. Will you be riding home with him?"

Getting down from the buckboard, I turn to Charles, suggesting warmly, "He has not invited me to do so as of yet, but your insight into the matter certainly suggests this as a possibility."

Visibly humored by my response, Charles proceeds to pay his attention to Shadow. I bid him farewell. "Have a blessed afternoon, and let us see at the end of the day who I ride home with, Shadow or Jasper."

∞

Lucy, Susan, Mary, Adelia, and I climb the stairs to the hall. Obadiah is at the doorway, as always, greeting each of his pupils as they arrive. The sight of him lifts my spirits to the sky. When we reach the doorway, he takes my hand as he did the first time we met, welcoming me with a kiss. Blushing, I return his kindness with a smile and a curtsy.

It is not long before everyone arrives and settles down in the chairs surrounding the hall. All appear quite well-behaved, a salute to Obadiah and his dedication to teaching fine manners to his pupils. Obadiah welcomes the class and begins the session. "Do not expect formal instruction today, but rather instead, a demonstration to me and your fellow pupils of the manners and skills you have developed over the past ten weeks of dance school." He appears quite excited to observe the fruits of his labor. "The first dance will be 'Constancy'—as you all know, one of my favorites. I want all of the gents to stand and politely invite one of the ladies to the dance floor. And, please do so with some restraint."

As soon as Obadiah speaks his last word, there is a burst of movement. It is obvious that most of the gents already have a lady of choice in mind. From the corner of my eye, I see Amasa Lathrop approaching me from across the room in a manner that is quite alarming. Almost out of breath, he anxiously inquires, "Miss Bixby, might I have the pleasure of this dance?"

Amasa is much taller than I am, and he displays an awkward demeanor. I stand and offer him my hand, responding, "The pleasure is mine." We walk together, taking our place at the head of the longways set.

Little Jim is ready to play; Obadiah makes his way directly toward us. I detect what appears to be a hint of jealousy. With a smirk, he addresses Amasa, "So I see that you have selected for yourself the most gracious of all the ladies." Amasa is noticeably uncomfortable. Obadiah clarifies, "To be taken only as a compliment."

Obadiah moves a few steps back and begins his instruction. "As always, we begin with our manners, followed by the first figure; with this dance, right hands 'round, and back again."

Little Jim begins to play; the entire longways set becomes animated. The pupils are in perfect step with the music; heads are bobbing up and down in unison. Obadiah is calling the figures with the pride of a successful teacher. It turns out that Amasa is a rather astute dancer. We remain partners for the first three dances.

The session passes quickly. Obadiah announces the last dance of the day; it is a cotillion titled "Marlbrouk." We practiced the same dance at the Chamberlains' at the beginning of the summer. Most of the folks have already selected a partner; Harriet is standing with Obadiah in what appears to be a deep conversation. I make my way over to them. "Harriet, would you be so kind as to be my partner for this last dance?"

Harriet appears elated with joy, "Miss Bixby, it is my pleasure to dance with you." Obadiah smiles warmly toward me.

Harriet and I take our place in one of the sets. I ask her, "Have you enjoyed the dance so far?"

Harriet looks to me, sincerely announcing, "With all of my heart and soul."

When the final dance is finished, Obadiah proudly announces to the pupils, "You have learned well, both the art of dance and the proper use of manners. We have only four classes remaining before the Harvest Dance on October 31. You surely will surpass my highest expectations by then."

Obadiah turns to Harriet. "And congratulations are in order for my youngest and most improved dancer. She has learned to dance without effort, displaying the perfect balance between freedom and poise."

Harriet blushes, and takes a well-deserved curtsy.

Obadiah approaches me, putting out his hand, asking, "Might you be interested in joining me in the parlor for a cup of tea? I would be delighted to carriage you home afterwards." Smiling, he adds, "I have already suggested the plan to Lucy, and she was quite agreeable to the idea." Charles was accurate in his observation earlier in the day.

With a feeling of delight, I quickly answer, "There is nothing more I would rather do than to spend the rest of the afternoon with such a delightful gentleman."

Lucy is watching from the doorway. I turn to her with a smile, nodding slightly, acknowledging that the plan is in effect.

∞

When the last pupil leaves, Obadiah and I go down the stairs to find Salome working busily in the kitchen. There is a delicious-looking cake, and a pot of freshly brewed tea on the table. The pot is rather odd. It features green glaze with a leaf pattern on the bottom; the top is molded to resemble a cauliflower and is glazed with a cream color. Salome observes my curiosity, adding, "Do you like it? Jonas informs me that it has been in his family for over fifty years. It is a wonderful piece."

I find Salome to be such a pleasant lady. I respond, "It is truly the most curious teapot I have ever seen."

Salome smiles; curiously, I ask, "And what kind of cake have you there?"

Salome is quick to reply, "It is a mountain cake, nothing more than a pound cake made with a variety of interesting spices."

She then points to a free-standing cheese press painted in blue. In a complimentary voice, she explains, "This is my favorite cheese press; Obadiah repaired the windlass on it last week and it is working as good as new."

Reminded of the small tabletop press that we use at home, I respond, "It is quite the elaborate machine; the color is most remarkable. Is it convenient to use?"

"It is, and since Obadiah has made the repairs, it works quite smoothly as well."

I slice off two rather large pieces of mountain cake and invite Obadiah to join me in the parlor, "Obadiah, might you pour us a cup of tea? I have enough cake for the both of us."

221

I look to Salome and ask, "Would you care to join us in conversation?"

"Thank you, Lucinda, but I have much work to finish up in the kitchen, and then I must return home to make preparations for my lady friends who are scheduled to arrive at six." She smiles, adding, "You and Obadiah enjoy some quiet time together. I will most assuredly see you again next Monday."

∞

The parlor at the tavern is a most accommodating room. Obadiah loves to stretch out on the upholstered chair; I find the sofa to be quite comfortable. The mountain cake is delicious and the tea is steeped perfectly.

Reflecting on all that has taken place since Independence Day, with much sincerity, I open the conversation by saying, "You must be quite pleased with everyone; they danced so well today. It amazes me how quickly the time passes. It feels like just yesterday when you first surprised me with a wet kiss to my hand. And, now, it is the last day of the most wonderful summer I have ever experienced."

Obadiah is noticeably moved by my sincerity. He takes a sip of his tea. Putting his cup down beside mine, he responds, "Lucinda, you have no idea the extent to which you have changed my entire outlook on life in these past ten weeks. I must also acknowledge, as we come to the end of my session in Millbury, I am somewhat at a loss to what might come next." His dark eyes have become fixated on mine. "Quite frankly, it is hard for me to imagine life without you."

It is difficult for me to hide the sensual desire that is boiling throughout my entire body. I want to embrace him in such a way that he will never let go. My eyes begin to swell with tears of happiness. "Nor I."

OBADIAH...   *WEDNESDAY, OCTOBER 14, 1840*

The sunlight peeks through the corner of the window, waking me from a sound sleep. Dennis and I had conversed in the parlor, sipping rum, until nearly three in the morning. The spirits have yet to dissipate, making my effort to sit up a bit more challenging than usual. I reach for the chamber pot and clumsily I attempt to relieve myself without puddling on the floor. The morning view from the edge of my bed is quite spectacular, this morning being no exception. The vivid colors of the trees announce the joyous completion of a blessed summer, and the beginning of a quiet time for renewal. I finish without incident, placing the pot back on the floor, slowly sliding it under the bed with my foot. Laying back down, I cannot help but to recollect the conversation from earlier this morning. It was a sincere effort on the part of Dennis and Salome to make me welcome here at the tavern for an extended visit. Surely in an attempt to provide me a permanent residence while courting Lucinda. Her presence in my life has changed my purpose for being; the invitation to remain in Millbury comes at the perfect time. It is settled; I must visit Lucinda this afternoon to share my intentions with her.

∞

I decide to finish a few things in the woodshop before joining Salome for breakfast. The walk down the path to the shop is rather chilly; my guess is that it is hardly forty degrees. The recent weather has been quite unpredictable. The first day of fall brought with it a hard frost, while last Tuesday, we woke up to a balmy morning that was undoubtedly in the mid-seventies. Even though this morning is on the chilly side, my intuition suggests that we are headed for a rather pleasant day; a perfect day for a carriage ride with Lucinda.

∞

The kitchen is abound with the smell of delicious food. Salome is at the table chopping an onion, preparing a batch of fried potatoes, no doubt. Fried potatoes have become one of my favorite foods. Salome prepares them by mashing up potatoes with plenty of butter, and then adding chopped onions with an interesting blend of herbs to the mix. She pan-fries them in lard; a delectable treat for sure. She also has eggs to fry and a good-sized portion of bacon to round out the meal. I am excited to share with her my decision. "Good morning, Salome. I want to thank you and Dennis for inviting me to stay on into the winter. I gratefully accept your invitation; I will be riding out to Lucinda's early this afternoon to share my intentions."

Salome appears rather delighted with my decision. "Good morning, Obadiah. I am sure that Lucinda will be quite pleased to hear." Turning to the salmon cabinet, Salome reaches into the drawer. "This letter came for you early this morning; the Postmaster dropped it by."

Salome hands me the letter; it is addressed from my father. A letter from my father is out of character; I open it with a heightened level of apprehension.

Dear Obadiah,

It is with sadness beyond my words that I write to you regarding the sudden illness that has consumed your mother in the recent days. The seriousness is concerning enough to beg your return as quickly as you are able. The doctor has gone to extreme lengths to relieve the hectic fever and coughing. Earlier this evening, after a two-day regimen of calomel and herbal treatments, he resorted to venesection. As a result, all optimism has vanished, leading me to beg for your immediate return.

From your father,
James Griffiths

My eyes swell with emotion; thoughts are racing unbridled in my mind. The grief radiates uncontrollably around me. Salome asks hesitantly, "What is it Obadiah? You look as if the letter carries extremely bad news."

I reply, "It does. My father has informed me that my mother is deathly ill; Father has summoned me to return to Providence as quickly as humanly possible." I begin to collect my thoughts. "Will you be so kind as to inform my students that I will be out of town for a period? I will make every effort to return for the Harvest Dance." Before giving Salome a chance to respond, I continue, "I must make the trip without my carriage to expedite my arrival. I will stop by Lucinda's house on my way to inform her of my situation."

Salome struggles for words. "Do what you need to do Obadiah. I will be sure to tie loose ends up for you here in your absence."

I quickly make my way up to my room to pack a few essentials into my satchel. The journey to Providence from Lucinda's should take me no more than five hours. That should have me in Providence by six if I do not meet unanticipated delays.

There is a slight knock on my door. I turn to find Harriet standing in the doorway. With the innocence of an angel, she attempts to comfort me, by saying, "Mr. Griffiths, I am so saddened to hear of your mother's sudden illness. Please, be on your way and allow me to tidy your room in preparation for your return." She is noticeably disturbed by the news, tentatively moving closer. She hugs me and her embrace is filled with compassion; my heart is warmed by her deep concern for me.

"Thank you, Harriet. Now promise me that you will practice your steps so that when I return for the Harvest Dance, you will make me proud."

"I promise, Mr. Griffiths."

∞

The ride to Lucinda's is quick; the temperature is kind, reaching into the mid-sixties, for sure. I tie Jasper to the post in the front of Lucinda's house and run to the front door. It is open, and so I knock rapidly, and then poke my head around the corner in hopes of seeing Lucinda sitting in her favorite chair; she is.

Lucinda appears quite startled by my unexpected visit. She places the trousers she is mending on the table. Standing, she reminds me, "Obadiah, I was not expecting you today."

"I apologize for the surprise, but I have some melancholic news to share with you."

Lucinda welcomes me with a warm kiss and says, "Tell me."

"My mother has suddenly become deathly ill; I must return to her side immediately. I expect to return to attend the Harvest Dance, if at all possible."

Lucinda squeezes my hands. "My dear Obadiah, this is terrible news. Please, my love will be with you on your journey, and my thoughts and prayers are with your mother." She embraces me warmly, whispering in my ear, "Be on your way, my love."

∞

The journey to Providence takes me down the road to Sutton and through Douglas. My thoughts are racing. I find comfort in the heartfelt send-off that I had received from both Harriet and Lucinda. Unfortunately, in my haste, I had forgotten to inform Lucinda of my decision to stay on in Millbury for the winter.

The time alone helps me greatly to collect my thoughts. I am convinced, more than ever, that meeting Lucinda was a sacred destiny; I want to spend the rest of my life with her. The remainder of my journey is both bitter and sweet, contemplating the loss of my mother in contrast with the bliss of knowing that my true love awaits.

TWENTY-SEVEN

LUCINDA... *SUNDAY, OCTOBER 25, 1840*

I gasp, trying to catch my breath. The room is dark; the nightmare was horrific. The quilt has fallen to the floor; I shiver from the cold. I reach for it, wrapping myself to fend off the bitterness. Closing my eyes, I curiously relive the obscureness of the dream. Obadiah is falling deep into a dark abyss; I reach pathetically with stretched arms to save him. The attempt is futile; he is gone.

It has been more than a week's time since Obadiah has left. My heart grows weary in anticipation of his return. I allow myself the pleasure to reminisce; the memories of the summer gradually become more vivid. My body begins to warm; a tingling sensation overwhelms me. The sincerity of his touch is divine, compelling me to convulse with pleasure.

The warmth is delightful, making it difficult for me to unravel from the comfort of the warmed quilt to face the cold air of the room. Being that it is Sunday, I have promised Mother that I would attend church with her. Just as I am preparing to get up, I see the glow of a candle making its way across the ceiling. I call out, "Mother, is that you?"

"Good morning, Lucinda, I thought I might start a fire for you to make it more comfortable to get dressed." Mother is standing at the top of the stairs now, her sweet face reflected in the candlelight. She adds, "I also brought you a pitcher of warm wash water."

The thought of remaining wrapped in my warm quilt for another fifteen minutes while waiting for the fire to take the chill out of the room pleases me. "Thank you, Mother, you are a blessing to me."

The dry kindling Mother uses to start the fire quickly ignites, encompassing the room with a warm glow. I delay until the fire begins to expire. Hesitantly, I unwrap myself, making my way to the fireplace to add more wood. My tender feet are quite sensitive to the chilly floor. I step closer to the fire, holding one foot over it at a time, allowing the flames to thaw my frozen toes. My stockings are hanging just close enough to the fire not to ignite. I gather them up, quickly moving to the blanket chest at the foot of the bed. The stockings remain quite warm; I pull them on, delighted by the added comfort they afford.

Washing with warm water in the cold air is quite the shocking experience. Nevertheless, the pleasure of cleanliness far outweighs the few moments of discomfort one must endure. Mother had warned me that the temperature has fallen to nearly thirty degrees. I will dress warmly for the ride to church. I slip on my heavy petticoat followed by my flannel dress. Staring at my reflection in the mirror, I am reminded of the pleasurable memories of the summer and the happiness they have instilled in my heart. No longer feeling vulnerable to the past, I happily pin my hair into a bun and tie my cap into place.

∞

Father has prepared the carriage for Mother and I. He has chosen not to join us for services, complaining that his lower back is in a great deal of pain. Massaging it, he says, "Sitting for two hours on a wooden bench would be torture." Handing me the reigns, he adds, "Enjoy the discourse; a visiting reverend is coming to speak about the immorality of dance—a subject you surely will be impartial to." Father smiles, knowing just how partial I am.

The journey to the church is rather chilly. Mother and I share a blanket to cover our legs; our capes are drawn tightly around our necks. Tentatively, Mother asks, "Are you at all concerned that you might be offended by what the reverend has to say?"

"Mother, I really have not given it much thought at all. To be sure, I am convinced that there is nothing immoral about the art of dancing." There is a long moment of silence before I ask, "Do you?"

Mother turns to me. "Let us hear what the good reverend has to say, before I answer that."

When we arrive, I guide Shadow to a hitching post and pull the reigns slightly. I whisper quietly, "Easy Shadow." I remove the blanket from our legs, folding it neatly. Stepping from the carriage, I bring the folded blanket with me, knowing the church will be just as chilly inside as it is outside. Mother ties Shadow to the post, and we walk toward the front of the church.

Reverend Holman is greeting everyone at the top of the stairs. The visiting reverend is nowhere in sight. Could it be that I do not have to endure the subject of the immorality of dancing? As we approach the reverend, he extends his hand to Mother, welcoming her. "Mrs. Bixby, it is a pleasure to see you." He then turns to me and says, "Miss Bixby, surely you will take interest in Reverend Parkman's discourse today. He has promised me that the content will be a compelling deterrent to the many youths who have flocked to the dancing school this summer."

A sudden chill overwhelms me. Looking directly into the reverend's eyes, I respond, "We will just have to see how compelling it is, won't we?" I quickly turn away, walking directly to our box, leaving Mother standing by the reverend. For the first time in months, the scar on my thigh begins to burn.

I sit, placing the blanket on my legs, anticipating the start of services. Feeling quite disturbed, I begin to chew on my fingers. Remembering the awful pain resulting from my last bout of finger chewing, I quickly place my hands on the bench and sit on them. The effort is very short lived; I begin chewing again. Mother takes her seat next to me, quietly asking, "Are you all right? Your response to the reverend was rather short."

"He has no right…" I stop and go back to chewing my fingers.

Mother respectfully reaches for my hand, gently pulling my fingers away from my mouth.

Reverend Holman takes his place at the pulpit. Raising his arms, he begins, "The Grace of our Lord, Jesus Christ, the Love of God, and the Communion of the Holy Spirit be with you all."

It is impossible for me to respond.

Everyone stands to sing the opening hymn; I remain silent.

When the hymn ends, we all sit. Reverend Holman introduces Reverend Parkman, who has been sitting behind the pulpit, out of my sight. "Let us all welcome Reverend Parkman, who is here to deliver his discourse titled 'The Immorality and Ruinous Tendency of Dancing School and Ball-Room.' "

Reverend Parkman approaches the pulpit; there is something horrifyingly familiar about this man. He begins by quoting Ezekiel: "*They shall teach my people the difference between the holy and profane, and cause them to discern between the unclean and the clean.*"

> The room darkens; a musty smell fills the air. His
> voice makes me tremble. I peer into his eyes; it
> all comes back. He pushes me to the ground,
> forcibly lifting my dress up around my neck. The
> stench of his breath is disgusting. I struggle to

push him off, but he holds me down. He aggressively claws at my breasts, trying his hardest to kiss my lips. I bite him hard on his upper lip, causing him to spit blood into my face. Continuing my struggle to get away, he slides his cold, miserable fingers deep into me, causing my entire groin to scream in pain. His eyes are dark and hollow, a pathway into his evil soul. He stands, and drops his trousers. I get up, quickly drawing my leg back, thrusting my foot directly into his groin. I fall back, piercing my leg on a pitchfork left carelessly on the floor. The last thing I remember is the excruciating burning pain between my thighs.

I relive the nightmare; for the first time, I remember everything. I can barely lift my head; I want to look once more to be sure. When I do, he is staring at me, speaking in an evil voice, *"That there is a hell, the pit of which is bottomless, and the flames of which are eternal."*

There is no doubt in my mind; this is the horrendous man responsible for my ten years of misery. All thoughts of happiness drain from my soul. My scar erupts in pain, the burning sensation proving more than I can handle. He continues to preach, *"Leaving, then, religion out of the question, I pronounce the exercises of the ball-room and the dancing school as too low and corrupting in their tendency, and as too directly immoral in their nature, to be countenanced for a moment by the respectable part of the community – a remark which will apply to this community."*

I turn toward Mother; she is intent on listening to this nonsense, spoken by the devil himself. I want to scream at her, telling her the truth of this beast. Instead, the chewing of my fingers becomes more intense. The resulting pain helps to relieve the overwhelming despair that is drowning me.

"Any individual, who laughs away the thoughts of death and eternity, who seeks the society of the gay and trifling, or the sensual and profane, for the express purpose of resisting the Holy Spirit, and overcoming his convictions of truth and of danger, may be, for aught he knows, making his damnation sure."

The overpowering cloud of shame that has plagued my life for ten years engulfs me. I murmur to myself, "I should have never flirted with that boy."

Mother turns to me. "Did you say something?"

"I am sorry; I was just thinking out loud."

His voice begins to tremble, *"But let me state still more definitely my objections to a dancing school. It is a school, in which the heart is rendered still more vain and unmindful of God, and indisposed to every thing serious. None but the vain will attend such a school."*

I am successful at ignoring his words for only a few moments, until his senseless babble begins to plague me again. *"I repeat – none but the vain will attend such a school. No one can go their time after time, and enjoy peace of conscience, whose moral feelings are not awfully blunted. Such a school tends to draw off the heart from God – to take the thoughts from eternal concerns – to give the mind a relish for carnal and sensual pleasures, and to create a love for a dissolute course of life. It is worse then, than simple lightness of mind – it is a course of conduct which has immortality stamped upon it, by the Bible, by public opinion, and by facts."*

The dark and musty memories of the past overwhelm my thoughts, reminding me of how this very man indulged his appetite and gratified his beastly passion on me. He speaks of damnation; he is damned.

"And will parents never open their eyes? Will you, can you, trust your children for instruction in the hands of those, whose hearts are so depraved, and whose minds are so entirely destitute of the fear of God?"

233

Mother remains fixated on the reverend's message. I fear his words have swayed her opinion. My thoughts immediately turn to Obadiah. He portrays himself as a man with a heart that appears to know only love. Have I somehow mistaken his beastly desires as love?

The words of the reverend empty my soul of all hope. *"But while on the subject of facts illustrative of the immortality of dancing schools, let me add – as you go thro' some of the streets in our larger cities, you will not unfrequently hear the fiddle, and the noise of dancing. And should you ask the citizens what it all means? They will tell you, that it means one of two things – the place is either a low grog shop, or it is the house of her, whose feet, says Solomon, go down to death, and whose steps take hold on hell."*

My willingness to do further battle with the eloquence of this man's interpretation of the Bible begins to weaken. I think of Obadiah again. Is it possible that I have been tricked by a wolf in sheep's clothing? I begin to have my doubts about the happiness that has lifted me from my despair. The cloud of shame becomes overwhelming; I was surely to blame for what happened to me.

Completely engulfed now by the dark abyss, I become entranced by his words. *"But, 2ndly, I am opposed to the dancing school, because of its interference with the work of the conversion of God. The company there to be met with, has got to be renounced, before the first step can be taken of the sinner's return and submission to God."*

The fear of God and the shame for my impurities consume my soul. How is it that I have allowed myself the pleasures of the sensual and profane? My stomach begins to churn with discomfort.

The words begin to clatter in my mind. *"No. It is to gratify a vain, sinful desire – to enjoy a lively and thoughtless season, to pass away the time without the usual cares and perplexities of the world – and to indulge in imaginations wild, corrupting and fatal in their tendency."*

Three of my fingers are bleeding due to the constant chewing. It is impossible for me to stop. I think of the overwhelming pain that resulted from my last infection; I welcome the pain as punishment that I certainly deserve.

Gradually, I become convinced that I have strayed from the righteous path; his words are making more and more sense. *"But I hope that you are all convinced, that the exercises of the dancing school, are a profitless waste of time. They lead to forgetfulness of God. They nourish sensual desires. They have often led to the seduction and ruin of the innocent. They are unfit for dying creatures."*

The fear of God and the fear of death rattle my soul. I must repent for my lost time in idleness and sensual pleasure. My stomach continues to churn with discomfort. I am compelled to extinguish the happiness of my summer from my soul.

"Once more, then, I would raise my warning voice, and urge you all to desist. For whether I have succeeded in fully illustrating it, or not; yet the difference between right and wrong, the 'holy and profane', or 'between the clean and unclean,' is as great, as broad, as distance between heaven and hell."

Mother turns to me, certainly recognizing the distress that has overcome me. Softly, she asks, "You appear unwell. Would you like to take your leave?"

My eyes swell with tears, my soul darkened by the memories of the past. I try to answer her; I am interrupted by the reverend's final words. *"Again I urge you to stop, lest in some sudden, awful moment, your way being dark, and your path slippery, your 'feet stumble upon the mountains' of everlasting ruin, of eternal night."*

At the conclusion, evil looks me directly in the eyes. I tremble with fear and vomit uncontrollably.

TWENTY-EIGHT

OBADIAH... *SATURDAY, OCTOBER 31, 1840*

Mother's face is still quite warm with fever. Last night was an improvement; the doctor was rather surprised by her slow but steady recovery. We had all thought the evening I arrived to be her last. I sponge the sweat from her forehead and face, doing my best to soothe her. "Mother, you continue to improve. Doctor is optimistic now that you will recover."

Her response is jumbled, but cohesive enough for me to understand. "Thank you for coming so promptly to my side. I promise you, I will get well." She smiles, and continues in a somewhat more demanding voice, "Is it not time for you to return to your Lucinda in Millbury? If I have my days correct, this is All-Hallows Eve, the night of your harvest dance. So go, and wish your dearest Lucinda my best."

It is hard to argue with Mother; I squeeze her hand with affection, promising my return. "You are most correct. I trust now that you will recover. I promise I will return to your side within the week to check on you. I will deliver Lucinda your warmest greetings."

∞

The journey back to Millbury is quite pleasant. The temperature is surely fifty; the sky is a clear blue with only a few scattered clouds. The trees are mostly void of their leaves, although the oaks appear to be holding on to theirs, as is quite usual for this time of year. I arrive in Douglas at nearly four; I should arrive at the tavern in plenty of time to prepare for the dance. I have not heard from Elias; it would be a pleasure to have him accompany Little Jim.

The pupils hardly need my instruction any longer, and so I anticipate the opportunity to dance with Lucinda. The thought of seeing her again causes a tingling sensation to run through my entire body. Jasper maintains a steady trot, assuring my arrival to the tavern before five. The closer I get to my destination, the more the excitement builds.

My journey to the tavern takes me past the Hutchinsons' house. The barn we raised in the summer is now complete. Stephen is sitting on the granite stone that serves as a step to the front door. I wave as I pass by, taking a right turn on to Millbury Street. Fond memories of Lucinda sitting by my side in the carriage on the night of the Sturgeon Moon begin to occupy my mind. I remember that most pleasurable night, and the love that has brought us so close together.

There is unfinished business. In my haste to return to my mother, I failed to inform Lucinda of my intentions to stay on in Millbury through the winter. I will share the surprise with her this evening, after the dance, when we have some time alone.

I slow Jasper to a walk as I pass Asa Waters's mansion; the Christmas Ball is now less than two months away. The thought of escorting Lucinda to such an elegant ball, in such a stunning home, excites me beyond words. The sights of Elm Street have become quite familiar due to the many trips I have taken to and from Lucinda's house in the past months. Turning onto Union Street, the journey to the Lower Tavern is nearly over. As I get closer, I see that Charles is sitting on the steps to the porch. Beside him, a pan of oats and a bucket of water. He sees me; standing tall, he begins to wave. Harriet is there as well, standing on the porch, waving enthusiastically. The warm welcome nearly moves me to tears. It is good to be back.

Jasper knows exactly where to go; Charles jumps from the steps, bringing the oats and the water with him. He is nearly out of breath. "Good day, Mr. Griffiths. Harriet and I have been awaiting your arrival. We both miss you so much."

I dismount from Jasper, untying my satchel from the saddle. "Good day to the both of you; I am very pleased to see you."

Harriet runs toward me, immediately asking, "Mr. Griffiths, how is your mother? Did she survive the week? I do hope so. She has been in my prayers every night."

"Yes Harriet, she is slowly recovering. Thank you for your concern." She appears quite excited to see me. I ask, "Are you ready for the dance tonight?"

"I am, Mr. Griffiths. Mother helped me to sew a new dress, just for the dance. It is beautiful; you will surely think so as well!"

∞

Charles and Harriet follow me up the stairs and into the tavern. There are a few patrons in the taproom; the parlor is empty. I turn left and down the hall toward the kitchen. The sight of Salome delights me. "Good day, Salome. It feels so good to be back."

She rushes over, warmly embracing me. Stepping back, she asks, "How is your mother?"

"The doctor expects that she will recover. I promised that I would return to her side by the end of next week. I presume it will be for only a short period; my plans are to return to Millbury before Thanksgiving."

Salome gently takes my hand, saying warmly, "That is such good news; your mother has been in our prayers."

Salome becomes a tad more animated. Letting go of my hand, she points to the table and excitedly announces, "Look at all of the baked goods we have prepared for the dance tonight. Harriet and I have been busy baking since yesterday."

The table is crowded with a variety of delicious-looking foods, with more in the bake oven. Smiling at Salome and Harriet, I say, "You have certainly out done yourselves!"

Salome surely recognizes just how ragged I look after my journey, suggesting, "You should take a pitcher of warm water up to your room to wash. There are clean cloths and soap by the basin."

Harriet adds, "I lit a fire in your room about an hour ago, to help ward off the chill."

"You are all so kind; it is a pleasure to be back. Thank you."

∞

When up in my room, I begin to remove the layers of clothing. I start with my boots and socks. This evening, I plan to wear my best trousers, vest, and topcoat. While it is true that I only have one such set, the thought of cleaning thoroughly and wearing them is appealing. I slip out of my trousers. Next, I remove my cravat and vest. Standing quite exposed, I sense that the air in the room has been warmed a bit by the fire, but remains quite chilly.

The mirror reveals a rather shabby-looking fellow. His hair is in a mess and his face is begging for a clean shave. The water in the pitcher remains steaming hot. I fill the basin with about an inch of water and soak one of the cloths. I lift the warm cloth to my face; the feeling is sensational. As it remains rather warm, I use it to scrub around my neck, followed by a washing of my hair. When finished, the cloth takes on a muddy look, as does the water in the basin. Agitating some soap in the water, I lather my face with the resulting froth as a preparation for shaving. Carefully, I run the straight edge across my face, leaving smooth and refreshed skin in its path.

The room has warmed considerably. I pour the dirty water from the basin into the chamber pot. I then refresh the basin with warm water from the pitcher. After rinsing out the cloth, I sit on the edge of the bed, washing my legs from my thighs down to my ankles. I scrub my feet, using the cloth to clean between my toes, rinsing it once more. I then use it to make one more pass over my legs and feet.

After refreshing the cloth with warm water, I pull my shirt up above my waist; I lay back on the bed. I place the cloth over my groin area, allowing the warm sensation to embrace me. Gently, I begin to wash. The pleasure of my own touch makes it challenging for me to rest, but time is racing, and the thought of seeing Lucinda is far more delightful than the activity at hand. I slide off the bed and remove my shirt. Using the clean cloth and the last of the warm water, I wash my upper torso, finishing with a thorough scrubbing of my hands.

∞

I arrive at the entrance to the hall just a few minutes before seven. I am pleased to see that Elias has been able to join us; he is conversing with Little Jim, Jonas, and Dennis. I take my place by the door to welcome the arriving guests. Adelia and her parents, Asa and Susan, are the first to arrive. I extend a warm welcome, "Good evening, Adelia; it is a pleasure to welcome you and your parents."

Adelia curtsies. "Good evening, Mr. Griffiths, it is a pleasure to see that you were able to make it back in time for the dance. How is your mother's health?"

"She is recovering; thank you for your concern."

Asa extends his right hand, placing it on my shoulder. Drawing me toward him, he whispers in my ear, "There was quite the controversial discourse at church on Sunday. A Reverend Parkman was doing his best to instill the fear of God and damnation into anyone attending dancing school. My understanding is that Lucinda was quite affected by it, bringing her to vomit by the end of the service." Squeezing my shoulder, he adds, "I sincerely hope that it does not have an ill effect on the attendance for tonight."

Surprised, and extremely concerned with the news of Lucinda, I thank Asa by saying, "I appreciate your telling me, let us hope that the effects are negligible."

Nearly a half hour goes by; a few of the more reliable pupils have yet to arrive. The most alarming absences are Lucinda and Lucy, who always arrive nearly on time. Elias and Little Jim look over to me, suggesting that it is about time to begin the music. Just as I begin to give up hope, Lucy and her mother appear from around the corner. Lucy appears to be somewhat out of breath and obviously distraught. "Mr. Griffiths, I am sorry for our tardiness. I have not heard from Lucinda since that horrible service on Sunday. I have tried numerous times to visit; Mrs. Bixby repeatedly announcing that Lucinda is not taking visitors."

Lucy, appearing to become further agitated, continues, "In a final attempt to speak with Lucinda, Mother and I made it a point to stop by her house this evening on our way to the dance, only to find her sitting in her parlor, apparently despondent from those evil words spoken by Reverend Parkman on Sunday." There is a slight pause. "It just makes no sense; Lucinda is quite an independent lady when it comes to such things."

My concern turns to alarm; should I stay, or make my way to Lucinda's side immediately? Quite unexpectedly, Lucy embraces me. Stepping back, she suggests, "Obadiah, your thoughts are quite obvious, it is surely best that you remain here at the dance with your pupils. You may want to visit Lucinda tomorrow in the late morning when she is alone. She most certainly will not be attending church services."

Lucy's attempt to remain rational is helpful. "I will stay, although not without serious despair."

Lucy takes my hand and gives it a gentle squeeze. She warmly assures me, "Everything will turn out splendidly; you just wait and see."

Letting my hand go, Lucy takes her leave.

Thinking quietly to myself, *This is not at all how I expected this evening to turn out.*

I am left standing alone by the door, my heart longing to be with Lucinda.

TWENTY-NINE

OBADIAH... *SUNDAY, NOVEMBER 1, 1840*

Dancing continued into the early hours of this morning,
Lucinda's absence was devastating. I lie in bed, patiently
waiting for time to pass by. I have realized little if any sleep,
tossing and turning, overwhelmed with thoughts of her. Elias
is sleeping soundly on the tick that Harriet placed by the foot
of my bed, his bouts of snoring increasing in frequency
throughout the night.

At the first notice of dawn, I rise to begin my day. The anxiety
of uncertainty has gotten the best of me. I try not to disturb
Elias in the process of dressing. Quietly, I close the door
behind me, heading directly to the kitchen. Salome is cracking
eggs into a bowl, preparing to make omelets no doubt. I greet
her.

"Good morning."

She jerks her head around. "Aha, you frightened me."
Surprise quickly turns to a welcoming smile, "Good morning.
Would you like me to pour you a cup of freshly-brewed
coffee?"

"That would be splendid; I predict it is going to be a long day."

Apprehensively, Salome inquires, "Lucinda's absence was quite
noticeable last night. Is she unwell?"

Doing my best to remain composed, I attempt to answer, "It is
rumored that there was a controversial discourse presented at
last Sunday's services regarding the immorality of dancing.
Lucinda was present; it presumably made her quite ill. I will be

calling on her this morning, with guarded optimism that she will receive me."

Salome appears quite saddened. "That is terrible; Lucinda was awaiting the Harvest Dance with much enthusiasm. I do hope she is well."

∞

I decide to take the carriage to Lucinda's, anticipating that we may want to converse without interruptions. I can do little in the way of preparation, since I do not want to presume the cause or severity of her apparent sadness. Familiar with the way, Jasper begins the journey; we head west on Union.

As we crest the hill onto the common, Simon and Hannah Bixby are approaching from the opposite direction. I gently pull back on the reigns, whispering, "Whoa, Jasper."

Simon brings Shadow to a halt, calling out to me, "Good day, Obadiah."

I reply, "Good day to the both of you."

In a rather concerned voice, Hannah warns me, "Lucinda is in a truly terrible way; the worse I have seen her in many years." Shaking her head in dismay, "She has been slipping deeper and deeper into a depression since last Sunday. I do pray that seeing you will bring her some relief. Thank you for making the effort."

I respond, "It is my pleasure. I was very troubled not to see her at the dance last night; I hardly slept at all, quite concerned with her well-being." Hannah nods her head, acknowledging my sincerity. Inquisitively, I ask, "Do you think that she will receive me?"

Simon quickly responds to my question, "If there is any one person that she will listen to, it would be you. My best wishes for your success."

Hannah nods in agreement, adding, "We will be away for at least two hours, longer if you wish."

"Thank you both. With luck, she will join me on a carriage ride."

Simon and Hannah offer me a departing wave as we continue our separate ways. Waving back, I become quite fearful that my hopes of talking with Lucinda might prove to be fruitless. We turn onto the common by Eliza Goffe's place, slowly proceeding to her house. When we reach it, Jasper walks over to the hitching post directly in front. I jump from the carriage and turn toward Jasper. Reaching out for the side of his face, I stroke him. "Wish me good luck with this."

∞

The front door is closed; there appears to be no movement in the house. I knock lightly on the door, trying not to startle her if she is in the parlor. After what feels to be an eternity, I try knocking again, this time a tad louder. After waiting another considerable amount of time, I decide to peep through the front window of the parlor. It is quiet; I do not detect even the slightest movement. I move to the other side of the house to peep into the front window of the kitchen. Nothing. My hopes to see her are diminishing.

Dejected, I turn to leave. I am stunned to see Lucinda embracing Jasper around his neck and whispering in to his ear. She appears ghostly; her hair is tangled and hanging on her shoulders. She is barely dressed, only wearing a chemise and knitted stockings. The cold does not appear to be affecting her, although the temperature has surely not risen to fifty.

I approach her; her attention remains with Jasper until I am only a few yards away. Lifting her head, she stares into my eyes. I am taken aback by the hollowness that I see in her stare; her soul has been gravely compromised by the sadness that has overtaken her. I slow my pace, doing my best to hold my composure; my heart and soul darken.

Gently, I reach out for her hand. She is startled out of her trance. Stepping back, she requests, "Please, do not touch me."

Startled, I stop, inquiring softly, "Lucinda, might we take a ride in the carriage? I promise that I will not touch you."

She slowly moves to the side of the carriage and climbs up on to the seat. I step up from the other side, being careful not to slide too close. The chill appears to be affecting her more now; she is shivering, crossing her arms and holding them close to her chest. Her head is drooped forward, her eyes fixated on her stocking feet.

I reach back to get the blanket from behind the seat. Unfolding it, I hold it up, asking her, "Would you mind if I wrap you?"

To my surprise, she answers with a slight twinkle in her eyes and a nod of approval. I am careful not to get too close; I manage to wrap the blanket around her shoulders and onto her lap. I take the reins into my hand and give them a slight shake. Jasper looks back at me with what appears to be an expression of hope, and then steps off.

We ride in silence for what feels to be hours, although surely no more than a half of one. Lucinda has not once lifted her head, nor moved even slightly from the position she started in. Wanting to break the deafening silence, I ask, "Lucinda, is there anything I might do to help ease your sadness?"

She turns her head slowly toward me, responding, "It was a mistake to believe that I could ever love. Earthly happiness is all vanity and vexatious to the spirit."

She turns her head back, all of this without emotion. Her response is disturbing; the Lucinda I fell in love with appears to have become possessed by the devil himself.

We have been riding in silence now for well over an hour, my hopes of conversation dwindling with each step that Jasper takes. Our journey has brought us back by way of Burbankville. When I reach Lovell's Hotel, I have Jasper turn to the right so as not to pass the church. With only a half mile left before reaching the common, I attempt to make further conversation, "Lucinda, I was in such a rush to be by my mother's side the last time we were together that I neglected to share with you that Dennis and Salome had invited me to stay on at the Inn through winter."

She again turns her head slowly toward me, staring into my eyes, silently demanding that I provide her the outcome of my decision. Cautiously, I continue, "I have accepted the invitation, so as to allow more time for us to be together."

Her reply is cold. "Obadiah, I am going to need time to think."

My heart is aching; my soul longing for the happiness once shared with this remarkable lady. I finally lose my composure; I reply briskly, "Think about what?"

Lucinda gently places her hand on the top of mine. "I am so sorry, but I do not deserve your love."

Her response takes me entirely by surprise. What could conceivably make her believe that she is not deserving of my love?

We continue our journey in silence, my mind dwelling on Lucinda's last few words. Her hand remains on mine, bringing me untold hope that our love is not lost.

∞

When we reach Lucinda's house, Jasper comes to a halt at the hitching post. Lucinda lifts her hand from mine and climbs down from the carriage. She removes the blanket from her shoulders, placing it neatly on the seat; she stops to stare into my eyes. "Obadiah, you must go on with your life. There would be no purpose in me destroying your good nature. I am convinced now: the darkness will never let me go. I'll always love you."

Lucinda slowly begins to make her way to the front door. I jump from the carriage; she stops and turns. "Please, give me time."

"Lucinda, every minute without you is a lifetime. Please, share your pain with me. Our love is surely strong enough to ease it."

"Obadiah, I need time."

THIRTY

LUCINDA...   *WEDNESDAY, NOVEMBER 4, 1840*

The screeching of the coyotes is more ominous than ever. I lay in the cold darkness of the morning, struggling to find even a dash of purpose for living. My fear of love has come back to strangle any hope of happiness. The pain of that horrible evening plagues me; my thigh is burning like wildfire. I play back the events of that night repeatedly, struggling to justify my innocence. Was it I that invited the beast to violate me? Was my flirting with young Amos the cause? Was it my fault? No one will ever believe in my innocence, especially Obadiah.

Rolling to my side, I curl up tightly into a fetal position. Two of my fingers are throbbing in pain from the constant chewing. The pain of my fingers and the burning of my thigh help to distract me from my fear and hopelessness. The morning dawns; it calls me to rise and begin my chores. If it was not for my love of Shadow, I may choose never to rise again.

Crawling out of bed and into the coldness of the day is a struggle for me. I have been wearing the same chemise and stockings for over a week; I have no ambition to change them. The mirror shares a reflection of despair; my hair is tangled and unkempt. I feel dirty.

∞

Passing through the kitchen on my way to the barn, Mother greets me, "Good morning, Lucinda. Are you feeling any better this day?"

Mother is obviously concerned with my appearance, although she does not bring attention to it. I condescendingly reply, "Good morning, Mother. Yes, I am doing my best to find cheer in the advent of a new day." She returns to her work, surely accepting that my disposition is unchanged.

I rush down the path to the barn. When I arrive, Shadow is munching on hay. She hears me; she looks into my eyes as if she knows. Her eyes invite me to find peace. I can see that she does not judge me; I can see that her love for me is unconditional. Why do I feel that people judge so harshly? It surely was not my fault.

Shaken by my state of confusion, I embrace Shadow around her neck. She is the only one that understands my plight. I whisper to her, "The perplexity of earthly life is far too difficult for me to navigate. My heart has become cold; my soul seeks the lasting peace of eternal life."

I step back; Shadow is staring at me in a peculiar way. It is as if she is trying to communicate with me, trying to find words to soothe me.

My journey back to the house from the barn is a tad brighter, Shadow having brought a glimpse of hope for my continued sanity. Although my thoughts remain tortuous, I feel the sudden urge to write, to seek sanity in a penned letter. My pace hastens, leading me straight to the parlor.

∞

Moving my favorite chair close to the table, I fill the inkwell and remove a large piece of paper from the drawer. Folding it in half, I begin to write:

Happiness

It is natural for all mankind to seek for happiness. They seek it in every direction, and in every circle in which they move. In every object they pursue their inquiry is, what happiness can I derive from it? One will seek for it amidst the gay, and thoughtless, because of the cheerful look, and merry laugh, which is generally found among the notaries of pleasure. Another will seek for it, in the rich and costly array of pride, and extravagance, thinking, it can be found, only in outward show. Another will seek for it in riches and laying up treasures for this world. While others are indulging their appetites and gratifying their worst passions, and seem to take pleasure in every sin. Others think the honour and applause of men, tends to promote happiness. Thus we see mankind dayly striving to obtain that object. They soon find that these sources fail them and they are left dissatisfied and unhappy. We find that there is no happiness, to be derived, from any of these sources, we are led to exclaim with the wise man, "all is vanity and vexation of spirit." Why are we so foolish, as to seek happiness in worldly pleasure? It tends to corrupt the mind, and destroy our health. Time is fast hastening us along, and we shall soon be separated from the things, and pleasures of this world; and if our enjoyments are numerous, and we are much attached to them; what can we have to support us in that trying hour when we must bid adieus to all these enjoyments? And if we are permited to arrive at old age, we cannot then enjoy the pleasures of youth, our powers and our faculties will decline, and the grave will be waiting to receive us. Or we are liable at any time to be laid upon a bed of death, and then if we have no other source of happiness, no treasure laid up in heaven, no friend, but earthly friends, we shall be led to sink down into despair. How much better for us, to stop our pursuit after the happiness of this world, and "lay up for ourselves treasures in heaven, where neither moth, nor rust doth corrupt nor thieves break through and steal."

Nov 4ᵗʰ 1840.   *Lucinda E. Bixby.*

Putting the pen down, I exhale with a sigh of relief. My thoughts are now concrete. One day, this letter will be of service to someone. Someone facing the same perilous struggle that I am now. I take it over to the chimney cabinet where Mother's small leather chest is. The chest is where she keeps her favorite letters and cherished personal belongings. I place it on the bottom for safekeeping.

THIRTY-ONE

OBADIAH... *SATURDAY, NOVEMBER 7, 1840*

Thoughts of summer consume my mind. My memory reveals nothing that would suggest that Lucinda is anything but worthy of my love. Certainly, controversy regarding the morality of dance would have little to do with that. Why, if that were the case, it would be me not deserving of her love. After all, I am the one who brought dance to Millbury, surely causing this distress. It all makes no sense.

I pull the blanket up around my neck; my bare feet become exposed to the chilly morning air. Quickly, I curl myself up, drawing my feet back under the cover. I pull the blanket up over my head. The warm air from my breath begins to bring me some comfort from the cold. After nearly ten minutes, I declare myself ready for the day. Reaching to the floor, I pick up my socks and struggle to put them on. I slip out of bed and hurry to pull on my trousers.

∞

The kitchen appears abandoned this morning. There is a pot of lukewarm coffee on the hearth sitting close to some dying embers. On the table, there is a plate with an omelet on it and some butter biscuits in a bowl. Salome is nowhere in sight. She has probably run off to complete more chores after preparing breakfast. It surely is difficult for her to maintain her house up the street, while at the same time operating the tavern. I take a large bite of omelet. It reconfirms; she certainly does a remarkable job of it.

Taking the final bite of a delicious biscuit, I wash it down with a mouthful of tepid coffee. Looking over at the wood box, I am reminded that there is at least a cord of wood outside that requires my immediate attention. Returning to my room, I tie on a cravat and slip on an older vest. I crack open the window to test the temperature; the sun is shining, but the air is a bit brisk. I throw on my barn jacket and begin my journey to the carpentry shop. The decision to wear a jacket was a good one, although most certainly after an hour of chopping wood the jacket will come off.

∞

I find the ax to be a tad dull; using the grinding wheel, I sharpen it to perfection. An ax cannot be too sharp. Chopping wood is one of those repetitive tasks, where your mood often dictates the overall worth of the experience. For me, a good mood most often leads to a time of spiritual reflection, a bad one leads to a time of agony sorting through complex thoughts that consume my mind. I am hardly an hour into it, and thoughts of how I might have upset Lucinda plague me. With each throw of the ax, the pain of losing her becomes more vexing.

After nearly eight hours, I am famished and dripping wet with perspiration. It must be after 3:00 and I have not eaten anything since breakfast. Although the air remains quite chilly, there is not a cloud in the sky, allowing the sun to shine brightly. Satisfied with the pile of wood chopped, I slip on my jacket and make my way back to the carpentry shop to hang the ax.

While following the path back to the tavern, I encounter a rather strange sight. A lone Eastern Blue-Tailed butterfly is perched on the branch of a young maple. Stopping to observe, I am intrigued by the gentleness of her motion. Her wings are a translucent blue, sparkling in the sun with each movement. The oddity of encountering such a sight this late in the season is perplexing. The recollection of Lucinda and the memorable encounter that we had with three such butterflies earlier in the

summer is simultaneously tender and heartbreaking.
Awestruck, I gently reach out toward her, prompting her to
move onto my out stretched finger. To my delight, she accepts
my invitation. Moments later, she flies away, fluttering toward
the heavens from whence she came.

∞

The kitchen remains quiet. There is new wood on the fire and
the cauldron of water is steaming. Harriet approaches from
the hallway by the parlor. "Good day, Mr. Griffiths. I have
drawn you a warm pitcher of water and placed it in your room,
along with two fresh washcloths. I observed how hard you
were working and thought you might appreciate the
opportunity to freshen up."

"Thank you, Harriet. That is very thoughtful of you."

"My pleasure, Mr. Griffiths. Would you like me to make some
tea? Mother has left us some gingerbread; I thought we might
sit in the parlor and engage in some conversation together."

Always appreciating Harriet's enthusiasm, I reply, "Of course,
it is always a pleasure. I will hurry to wash and change, and
meet you in the parlor in less than half an hour."

∞

The parlor is bright and warm; the setting sun is bathing the
room with positive energy. I take my seat in the upholstered
chair and stretch out my legs. Wearing clean clothes after a
thorough washing of the body is refreshing. Considering the
week's distressful events, I cherish the warmth of the sun and
the companionship that Harriet has afforded me.

Harriet enters the parlor. She is carrying a salver with a pot of
tea, two cups, and a good-sized portion of gingerbread on it.
Her smile is heart-lifting; she is the embodiment of humility
and kindness. She greets me. "Mr. Griffiths, you appear to be

very relaxed. This makes me quite happy inside." She continues her approach, placing the salver on the table next to me. "I warmed the gingerbread for us. I think it helps to soften the texture and certainly accentuates the taste of the ginger."

"Thank you, Harriet, your attention to detail never ceases to astound me. Please, have a seat and tell me what's on your mind today."

She pours us both a cup of tea and sits on the sofa next to me. Breaking off a piece of gingerbread, she reaches out and hands it to me. "Here, try it."

I take a bite, allowing the taste to settle in my mouth before swallowing it down. I confirm to Harriet, "The taste is delectable."

Harriet smiles; she asks inquisitively, "Mr. Griffiths, why has Miss Bixby disappeared from our lives? I miss her so."

I slowly take a sip of tea and place the cup back on the salver. The question is quite complex, the answer difficult to formulate. Harriet patiently awaits my reply. I do my best to simplify my response. "Miss Bixby will never disappear from us. Do you remember her exuberant love of life?"

Harriet tilts her head with curiosity. "I do; that is what I miss so much about her. Do you think that she will return?"

"Harriet, Miss Bixby has changed my life considerably, as she has yours. Our lives will always be heightened by the happiness she has brought us." Tears begin to form in Harriet's eyes, obviously yearning for more. "And yes, I do believe she will return to our lives. Once we work through whatever sadness plagues her."

"Mr. Griffiths, your perspective is always rooted in love, and the idea that love is a treasure that can never be taken from us." The tears begin to roll down her cheeks. "But I want so much to see Miss Bixby again."

"I understand Harriet, but worldly possessions are not permanent; all things on this earth will pass. As much as I believe that Miss Bixby will return to us, I accept that the love she has already instilled in our hearts will remain forever. And this brings me a much needed comfort."

"Mr. Griffiths, do you still love Miss Bixby as you did before?"

"Very much so."

Struggling with her words, Harriet asks, "Even though she has chosen to leave you?"

"Harriet, my love for Miss Bixby is unconditional. There is absolutely nothing that she could do to discourage my love for her."

Harriet, apparently confounded from my last remark, asks, "How can that be?"

"It is natural to feel displaced when someone you love changes direction in their life, no longer sharing in the same destiny. Nevertheless, that person is the same person that you had loved before. I believe that true love goes much deeper than the superficial. It is similar to the love that a parent has for their child."

Harriet appears to comprehend. "So you love Miss Bixby in the same way that I love both of my mothers, and my father."

"Yes I do Harriet; I also love her in a way that makes me want to hold her close to me. I promise, I will not give up my pursuit to reclaim her love. Miss Bixby will eventually regain her trust in me; love will prevail."

Harriet smiles. "I am sure it will."

THIRTY-TWO

LUCINDA... *MONDAY, NOVEMBER 9, 1840*

The overwhelming fear of the future has not subsided one small bit in the two weeks since my reencounter with evil. Each morning brings with it frightful expectations that my life will from now on remain void of happiness.

Having tossed and turned for the majority of the night, I am becoming more and more sleep-deprived. It is unclear as to what I detest the most: the encounter with that dreadful beast of a man, or the thought that I may have unknowingly enticed him. Either way, crawling from bed every morning has become a most ghastly task.

Dawn brings with it the dreary sound of pouring rain. The thought of struggling through another day frightens me, the rain accentuating that fear. I slip out of bed into the chilly air; my body so numb with fear that the cold is hardly noticeable. Moving toward the wall where my dress hangs, I cannot help but to stop for a moment and gaze at the telling reflection in the mirror. It terrifies me to lift my head, for fear of what I might encounter.

To my astonishment, I see innocence. Spellbound, I look deeply into the eyes of the beholder, beyond the superficial, deep into the soul that lies within her. Her soul dances; she is joyful to be alive. Her life is full of hopes and dreams; happiness abounds.

Shaking my head, the trance subsides. What remains is the reflection of a shattered woman. Becoming angry, I scream out, "I must NOT allow that beast to destroy my life!"

Surprised by my sudden boldness, there is a minute ray of hope that warms my soul.

My flannel dress is hanging on the peg adjacent to the beautiful gown I planned to wear to the Christmas Ball. I reach for the dress; pleasant memories of my summer with Obadiah creep into my mind. The happiness that those memories bring me begin to relieve ever so slightly the agony of the past two weeks. I resolve that Obadiah's intentions are pure. I ask myself, *Is it possible for him to love a broken soul?* Maybe it is.

The rain finally subsides; the sun peeks between the broken clouds. Taking a deep breath, I begin my way down the narrow stairs to the kitchen.

∞

Mother is busy preparing breakfast, singing cheerfully, "*Sweet, Oh, Sweet are the joys, Round Lil La's Cot Doth grow, the limpid stream like Lil La's voice, enchantingly does flow.*"

Mother's cheerful disposition is infectious, demonstrating to me further hope that there will be an eventual rise out of the bowels of this abyss. With an unexpected surge of enthusiasm, I greet Mother with a smile. "Good morning Mother; it is such a pleasure to begin the day with the sound of your beautiful voice!"

Mother stops, mid-phrase, to greet me, "Good morning, Lucinda. It is so wonderful to hear your happy voice. Did you sleep well?"

Doing my best to remain optimistic, I reply, "My evening was difficult, resulting in only an hour or so of sound sleep." Mother's cheerful face droops, displaying her obvious disappointment.

Trying hard not to disappoint her further, I smile. "But my morning has brought with it some unexpected happiness."

"This is wonderful news; you have been so melancholy the past two weeks. Would you care to share with me the cause?"

Being careful not to expose the deeper truth, I reply, "Well, of course, that horrid man has not the right to preach with such a deceitful tongue. The art of dance and good manners are not acts of evil." Taking a moment to breathe, I continue, "Why, he is the only evil that I encountered that day!"

"Lucinda, it was only his opinion. In speaking with Reverend Parkman after the service, he was quite concerned with your sudden illness. He appeared to be quite gentlemanly about it."

Unable to cope with any further discussion, I make my way to the back door shaking my head, "He is disgusting!" Trying again not to be a further disappointment to Mother, I assure her, "I must attend to my chores; it will be a delightful day."

∞

The clouds have returned, bringing with them the pouring rain. I dart down the dirt path toward the barn, nearly slipping on the mud that has puddled just outside the doorway. Although the temperature is rather pleasant for a November morning, the dampness of the rain causes me to shiver. I look around the barn in hopes of finding a blanket. Thankfully, I find one neatly folded on the carriage seat. I wrap it around my shoulders, waiting for the shivering to subside.

With the shorter days, the hens have nearly stopped laying eggs. I find two and place them into my basket. I place the stool and bucket in their proper place to begin milking the cow. Taking a seat on the stool, I begin to massage her udder. My mind relaxes; being here, in the barn with my animals, affords me a sense of happiness.

When I finish the milking, it is time for me to attend to Shadow. I embrace her neck, as I do every morning. Looking deep into her gigantic brown eyes, I encounter again that overwhelming sense of peace. "Shadow, you are such a wonderful friend." Letting go, I step back and reach out with my hands; I place them on her sweet face, whispering, "We are going to beat this."

The rain continues to pour down, making my walk back to the house rather treacherous.

Arriving back in the kitchen, I find that Mother has prepared a heaping plate of pancakes and a hot pot of fresh coffee. Drenched from the rain, I approach her. Unexpectedly, I embrace her, whispering in her ear, "I love you."

∞

The rain continues into the afternoon. The pile of clothes for mending has grown rather high; it is the perfect day to attend to it. Mother started a fire in the parlor earlier in the day, making the room quite comfortable. I move my favorite chair closer to the fire, placing the pile of clothes on the floor next to me. Sitting, I remove my wet stockings, allowing my feet to dry out and warm by the edge of the fire.

An unexpected knock at the door startles me. Putting down the dress I am mending, I venture to the foyer to see who it is. To my surprise, Lucy is standing on the granite step; she is soaking wet. I reach out for her hand. "Lucy, come in out of the rain."

As we walk toward the parlor, Lucy immediately begins to explain her surprise visit, "Lucinda, I have not seen you since that awful service, over two weeks ago. I have tried numerous times; I am worried sick about you. Are you well?"

Doing my best to alleviate her concern, I respond, "Yes, Lucy, I am quite well."

Placing a second chair close to the fire next to mine, I invite Lucy to sit. "You are drenched and shivering, please sit."

Before taking my seat, I encourage Lucy to remove some of her wet clothes. "Might I suggest that you remove your dress and stockings and hang them here by the fire? I will get you a blanket to cover up with."

Lucy reaches down and slips off her shoes and stockings. She hands the stockings to me and then stands to remove her wet dress. I exchange a warm blanket for it, hanging her dress next to the stockings. I take my seat by the fire, watching her wrap up with the blanket, trying to get a bit more comfortable. Curious as to why Lucy decided to walk in the pouring rain to visit me, I inquire, "Tell me, what prompted you to visit me on such a dreary day?"

"As I was saying, I have been worried sick about you. You are much too independent to be shaken by such nonsense. I was utterly shocked when you refused to attend the Harvest Dance. We worked so hard to prepare for it; Obadiah was so disappointed. Have you see him?"

"Yes, Lucy, I met with him a week ago on Sunday. We are just taking some time away from each other to sort things out."

"Sort things out? Sort what out?" Lucy is obviously unhappy with my answer.

It is becoming more and more difficult for me to mask the truth regarding my retreat from life. Lucy is quite exact in suggesting that I would not have reacted this way simply over the nonsense spoken by the reverend. I must find a way to rise above this darkness.

Lucy recomposes herself. "You have been so happy since you mysteriously lured Obadiah from me earlier in the summer." She smiles, surely referring to our first dance class. "And when you dance with him, it is obvious that your spirit is freed, allowing you to soar into the heavens." Becoming animated, she raises her arms, crying, "I have seen it, and there is absolutely no evil in it!"

I appreciate everything that Lucy is saying; our friendship is obviously stronger than I realized. I contemplate telling her the rest of the story, but refrain from doing so. I bend over slightly, reaching out for her hand, assuring her, "Lucy, you are a dear friend, and quite correct in your observation."

Thinking to myself that I must give her a better explanation, I manipulate the truth a tad. "Much of it is rooted in my anxiousness regarding the future of my relationship with Obadiah. Obadiah roams the countryside, staying for months in different locations. Why, for all I know, he has already left Millbury for someplace new."

Lucy seems quite surprised with my response, "Has he not told you? At the dance, Obadiah was quite vocal about the fact that he is going to be staying on at the Lower Tavern at least until spring."

Feeling very uncomfortable that I have misled Lucy, I do my best to respond with a reasonable bit of disbelief. "He did mention it, but I don't believe him."

Lucy adjusts herself in her chair, sitting up taller, wrapping the blanket tighter around her shoulders. With a voice of confidence, she becomes more resolute. "Lucinda, there is nothing grander than to be in love. I have been acquainted with you for years; we have become closer friends through the summer. You are in love with Obadiah, and he with you. As your dear friend, I am telling you to stop this foolishness. Please go and reconcile whatever differences you may have with him, and get on with it."

Lucy's passion for my well-being is moving, reminding me that happiness goes beyond one's self. Happiness touches the spirits of many. My reaction to that evil beast has been selfish,

both to myself and to those who care for me, especially
Obadiah. My eyes begin to swell with emotion; happiness lifts
my soul from the darkness. With enthusiasm, I confirm to
Lucy, "You are absolutely correct. There is no excuse for my
selfishness; it is time for me to move on!"

Lucy appears quite satisfied with my conviction; standing, she
points out that the rain has nearly ended. She informs me that
she has chores at home that are waiting for her. Removing the
blanket from her shoulders, she folds it and places it on the
table. She reaches for her stockings. Looking into my eyes,
she smiles. "They are dry, and warm." Sitting back down on
the chair, she pulls them on, quietly telling me, "The warmth
on my toes feels heavenly."

I hand Lucy her dress; she slips it on over her head. The tippet
I knitted for myself is draped over the back of my chair.
Reaching for it, I offer it to Lucy by asking, "Would you like to
wear this home? It will help ward off the chills of this dreary
day."

"Thank you, it most certainly will." Lucy wraps the tippet
around her shoulders, tying it closed.

Before leaving, Lucy embraces me, whispering in my ear, "You
are a strong lady; I truly admire you."

∞

The darkness of night arrives early; my spirit has remained high
since Lucy's surprise visit. Lighting a candle, I navigate the
narrow staircase up to my room. Placing the candle on the
blanket chest at the foot of my bed, I ready myself for sleep.
Removing all of my clothes, I stand stark naked in the dark
chilly room. At first, the reflection of the mirror is hardly
recognizable. Staring intently, the image of a princess forms.
Closing my eyes, I begin to twirl; my beautiful gown flows
graciously. When I finish my spin, I reach out elegantly to a

handsome gentleman with dark curly hair and beautiful dark eyes. His face is translucent and unrecognizable; his spirit is warm and full of life.

The brilliance of my vision subsides; I am left standing, stark naked in the middle of my room. I reach for my linen chemise and slip it on. Sitting on the blanket chest, I pull on my knitted stockings; I jump up into bed. Pulling the quilt up around my neck, I fold up into a fetal position; I wait for the heat of my breath to warm me.

Closing my eyes, I do my best to recollect the events of the day. Pleased with the progress I have made; I am encouraged in believing that the darkness will pass. Thinking quietly to myself, "I must see Obadiah; I must reveal the truth to him."

THIRTY-THREE

OBADIAH... *FRIDAY, NOVEMBER 13, 1840*

The afternoon turns out to be quite pleasant. The morning clouds have broken, allowing the sun to shine through brightly. Having spent most of the day chopping wood, I still have quite a bit of stacking to do before I am finished. Thoughts of Lucinda have rattled my mind ever since our last visit nearly two weeks ago. The last time we met, she had asked for time. My instinct is telling me that enough time has passed, and that a visit is in order. I sorely miss her.

Picking up the last two chunks of wood and placing them on the woodpile, I see Harriet running toward me from the house. She appears to be quite excited. Halfway down the path, she begins to shout, "Mr. Griffiths, Miss Bixby is here to see you! Come quick, come quick!"

When she reaches me, she is out of breath. She enthusiastically takes my hand and begins to pull, "Hurry, Mr. Griffiths; she is smiling and looking very pretty."

My response should be that of a mature gentleman, but to the contrary, I take Harriet's hand and we run together down the path toward the house. Harriet is panting, but manages to get a few more words out, "Mr. Griffiths, you were right, you were right, she did come back."

My mind is racing, prompting all sorts of thoughts. Is she here to reconcile? Maybe she wants to break it off for good, having had time to think through everything. It is silly for me to presuppose. I promise myself that I will not lose her. Harriet slows. "Lucinda is around the corner, on the porch with her brother Sumner and Salome. Should we not arrive composed?"

Harriet is right; we should take a moment before we arrive to gather our thoughts. We stop to take a few breaths. Continuing to hold each other by the hand, we walk slowly to the porch stairs together. I look up; Lucinda is looking down at me, smiling. My whole body warms with pleasure; her beauty is beyond the heavens.

Slowly, never taking my eyes off her, I make my way up the stairs to where she is standing, "Good day, Lucinda; you look lovely. It certainly is a surprise and a pleasure to see you." Turning to Sumner, I say, "Good day, Sumner; welcome to the Lower Tavern."

Lucinda responds tentatively, "Good day, Obadiah. My brother Sumner needed to pick up some supplies for my father here in town; he invited me along for the ride. I thought it time that we get together. If you would not mind giving me a ride home, we could talk then."

With little hesitation, I answer, "I would enjoy that."

Lucinda appears pleased with my answer.

I am surprised and cautiously optimistic; Lucinda's disposition seems warm and apprehensive at the same time. Salome is staring at me, smiling with that infectious smile. When she is sure that she has captured my attention, she winks, surely sending me her best wishes.

Sumner turns to me. "Obadiah, I must be on my way. I trust you will take excellent care of my sister?"

Responding to Sumner, I assure him, "Not to worry, I will be sure to return her home safe and sound."

∞

The final moments of the day's sunshine warm the parlor, making it the ideal place to continue our conversation. Salome has returned to the kitchen to prepare a pot of tea. Lucinda and Harriet each take a seat on the sofa. I am feeling rather shabby, so I say, "If you ladies do not mind, I would like to go up to my room to freshen up."

Lucinda seems comfortable with my request. "Take your time. Harriet and I will visit until you return."

I go by way of the kitchen to fetch a pitcher of warm water from the cauldron. Salome is removing a delicious-looking peach tart from the Dutch oven. She stops to wish me the best, "I am so pleased to see Lucinda casting a smile. My best wishes to the both of you. I know there is much for you to talk through, but it appears that she is going to give you a solid place to start."

Salome has been quite astute regarding the recent challenges that Lucinda and I have been facing. With much sincerity, I extend my appreciation, "Salome, you have been a true friend since our first meeting. Thank you for your support and your wisdom in helping me through these past few weeks."

The water in the cauldron is steaming; I draw a pitcher from it and head for my room. Salome reminds me with a smile, "The tea will be ready within fifteen minutes; let us not keep your lady friend waiting."

My room is quite chilly, despite the pleasant weather we are having. Quickly, I remove all my clothes, beginning the arduous task of washing my naked body in a cold room. The warm washcloth feels wonderful, but air-drying in a chilly room, not so much. It does not take me long to finish, knowing that Lucinda is in the parlor waiting for me. Once dressed, I take a quick look in the mirror. I could use a shave, but decide that getting back to Lucinda is more important.

∞

Upon my return to the parlor, the three ladies are conversing amongst themselves. Salome pours me a cup of tea. "Obadiah, would you like a taste of peach tart with your tea?"

Apprehensively, Lucinda suggests, "Obadiah, we have much to discuss, and the sun has already settled. Perhaps we should be on our way shortly."

Not knowing whom to answer first, I quickly respond to Salome, "Thank you, but maybe just tea."

Turning my attention back to Lucinda, I respond, "I agree, we should soon be on our way."

Salome accommodates the request by saying, "Harriet, it is time for us to clean up and prepare ourselves for bake day tomorrow."

Harriet appears a tad disappointed with having to break up the conversation, but responds cheerfully, "Yes Mother, right away." Turning toward Lucinda, Harriet offers warmly, "It was so good to see you; I am so happy for the both of you."

Lucinda stands and reaches out for Harriet's hand. Giving it a squeeze, she reminds Harriet, "You are a blessed child. It is my pleasure to have you as a dear friend."

∞

Taking our leave from the tavern, Dennis greets us as we approach the carriage. "Salome informed me that you would need the carriage this evening. Charles and I have prepared it for you. Jasper is well fed and has had plenty of water. I put an extra blanket on the seat to help you to ward off the chilliness."

Turning his attention to Lucinda, Dennis adds, "Lucinda, it is such a delight to see you again. I do hope we see more of you in the coming months."

Lucinda appears warmed by the invitation. "We will see."

Lucinda places her hand on Charles's shoulder. "How is my favorite young man? Shadow most certainly misses you."

Charles perks up. "I am doing quite well; please say hello to Shadow for me. I look forward to seeing her again soon."

∞

We begin our journey by taking Union all the way down to Main Street. We then head north on Main toward Worcester. The sky is clear; thousands of sparkling stars are twinkling throughout. Unfolding the blanket from the seat, I place it over Lucinda's legs. While thrilled with her sudden willingness to talk, I prepare myself to convince her of my love.

As if she has a lens into my soul, Lucinda begins to speak: "I am sure you are questioning my change of heart in the matter of the tragic discourse presented some weeks ago."

The tone of her voice concerns me. I respond with confidence, "That you have made the effort to be with me is encouraging. My love for you has grown stronger in your absence."

She slides closer to me, placing her hand on mine. "This has been a very trying time for me. My love for you is beyond words, beyond this world. My fear is that I am not worthy of your love."

My heart stops; my response is stern. "How is it possible that you feel unworthy of my love? You are the perfect lady for me; we are perfect together."

She slides closer, squeezing my hand. "Ten years ago, I was flirting with a boy at a church function. The Reverend Parkman was leading us in prayer. He stopped abruptly, scolding me unmercifully. His eyes penetrated mine, putting the fear of God into me."

"Lucinda, you were only flirting. That is certainly not a sin."

"Obadiah, it gets much worse. That beast secretly followed me down the road. Sneaking up on me, he grabbed me and dragged me into the Faulkners' barn near my house. I struggled with him, but his strength overwhelmed me; he tossed me to the ground and pulled my dress up around my neck, exposing me. He jumped on me and told me that if I wanted to flirt, I should flirt with someone who can satisfy my desires. He grabbed for my breasts, and then tried to kiss me. I bit his upper lip hard, making it bleed. He spit his disgusting blood on my face."

Lucinda is crying; it appears that she is finished. I do my best to calm her by saying, "Lucinda, it is over now."

"It is not over! He jammed his fingers deep inside of me, the pain was unbearable, I screamed. Then he stood up and dropped his trousers, exposing his disgusting self. I struggled to my feet and kicked him as hard as I could. That is when I fell back, gouging my leg on a pitchfork carelessly left on the floor. The last thing I remember is the excruciating pain between my thighs."

Lucinda is shaking uncontrollably now. Stopping the carriage, I turn to her and embrace her tightly. "Have you ever told anyone about this?"

She responds, "It was my fault. I should have never been flirting. No one would have believed in my innocence."

Doing my best to comfort her further, I say, "Lucinda, this was never your fault. I cannot imagine how you have lived with this secret for so many years."

"Obadiah, there is something else. Reverend Parkman is the horrible beast that delivered the discourse at the church three weeks ago. He has come back!" She pauses a few moments. "You see, I am not worthy of your love; it was my fault. I surely enticed him."

Embracing her tighter, I do my best to reassure her, "Lucinda, this was not your fault. You did nothing wrong; you are most worthy of my love. I assure you, the Reverend Parkman will bring you no more harm. I'll make certain of that."

Lucinda begins to calm; her arms find their way around my waist, warmly returning my embrace. Tears leak from her swollen eyes; her innocence glimmers in the light of the partial moon. We gaze deeply into one another's eyes. She appears frightened. We continue to gaze. Slowly, by the grace of God, her quivering lips transform into a sweet smile. I lean down to kiss her; the taste of her lips is sweeter than the nectar of gods.

∞

Pulling the reins slightly, I prompt Jasper to continue the journey. There is a welcomed sense of tranquility that surrounds us. Lucinda softly breaks the silence. In her sweet voice, she says, "Obadiah, I missed you so."

Her words are comforting to my soul. I respond, "My dearest Lucinda, you have been in my thoughts every minute of every day."

As we approach the turn up by Dr. Jewett's place, I pull back slightly on the reins, bringing Jasper to a stop. Turning toward Lucinda, I whisper, "I am honored that you have trusted me with your secret. It will remain safe with me, forever."

Her response is warm and articulate. "The burden of it has weighed heavily on my soul for many years. This most recent encounter released a fury of emotions, nearly enough to end my life. Your acceptance of me for who I am warms my soul, and that gives me tremendous hope for our future."

I sense a longing for further dialogue. I continue, "Life is precious, but it is never without suffering. It is finding the strength to eradicate the suffering that brings us to happiness."

Continuing the conversation, I share with Lucinda, "Earlier this summer, I met a most gracious lady; her name was Jerusha. When she was your age, the love of her life vanished without trace. When I met her, she was a frail forty-three years of age. She spoke openly of her suffering, but was never able to eradicate it. We talked late into the evening. Although she found some peace in the memories of her love, she was regretful of wasting her life away in a melancholy state. Rather than embracing the happiness that she had shared with her fiancé, allowing it to help define her life, she instead held onto the suffering of her loss."

Lucinda appears entranced by my story. I continue, "In the ten years since that horrifying first encounter, you have suffered enormous pain. Pain that has dampened your spirit, crippling your capacity to love freely. Maybe this recent encounter was a blessing in disguise, encouraging you to share your pain with me, eradicating the suffering once and for all."

Lucinda embraces me affectionately, whispering, "I love you."

Looking deep into her eyes, she allows me a glimpse into the depths of her soul. "Lucinda, my love for you is unconditional; it will always be. You must promise me that no matter what happens in the future, the happiness that we share will always have a place in your soul. That it will always be there to help define you. That it will give you the wisdom to eradicate suffering and allow you to live your entire life full of happiness."

We kiss warmly; she replies, "I promise."

THIRTY-FOUR

LUCINDA... *THURSDAY, NOVEMBER 19, 1840*

The fire in the parlor has burned down to embers; I add three pieces of wood, blowing gently on it with the bellows. The flames jump from the dying embers, as if woken from the dead. Mother has gotten far behind in her shoe work. I promised I would help her while I wait for Obadiah. He is going to Providence to see his mother; he plans to stop by on his way there. She is doing much better, his promise to return to her delayed, due to his concern for me. My bouts of sadness have subsided decisively in the past week, having had the pleasure to visit with Obadiah three times since last Friday.

Mother has placed all the shoe work that needs attending to on the table. Sitting in my favorite chair, I peer out of the front window. The field leading to the pond has transformed once again, covered delicately by a glistening blanket of fresh snow. While not enough to delay Obadiah's journey, the high wind and chilly temperatures will surely make the trip an unpleasant challenge.

The instructions that Mother left for me are quite clear: close ten pair of thicker shoes, stamp out eighteen pair, and prepare twelve threads for tomorrow. I am expecting Obadiah to arrive within the next hour; I begin sewing, in hopes of getting a good start on the work before he arrives.

Looking out the window, I watch as the wind blows quite furiously, causing the snow to form random clouds against the background of a blue sky. The cold air is finding its way through the cracks around the door and windows, leaving in its path trails of fresh snow on the floor and the sills. I place three more pieces of wood on the fire in the parlor and I check on the kitchen fire to be sure it has enough wood. Putting three more pieces on it as well, I decide to prepare a pot of tea for when Obadiah finally arrives.

Sitting back down on the chair, I gaze again out of the front window. It is rather ironic that the snow can appear so inviting from the inside of a warm room, knowing how cold and dangerous it can be while in its midst. As I begin sewing my third shoe, I see Obadiah coming down the road from the direction of the common. Jasper is pacing himself, prancing delicately in the nearly six inches of new snow that has fallen since last evening.

Obadiah opens the front door, entering into the foyer. He heads directly over to the kitchen fireplace to stand on the hearth, close to the fire, allowing the snow to melt from his boots. He warms his hands by the fire, then removes his boots, leaving them on the hearth. Removing his hat and cape, he places them on the kitchen table. Looking over at me with a warming smile, he suggests, "Good day, Lucinda; the perfect weather for a ride through the woods."

I approach him. "Let me warm your sweet soul with a kiss."

Each time that we kiss, it is more exciting than the last. Embracing him tightly, I invite him to sit with me in the parlor. "Would you be so kind as to move a couple of chairs close to the fire while I finish the preparation of the tea?"

"It would be my pleasure; hurry along, I must be on my way soon enough to have plenty of time to avoid the dark."

When I arrive back in the parlor, Obadiah has removed his topcoat and vest. Sitting by the fire with his feet propped up on a piece of wood sitting precariously close to the flame, he appears quite relaxed.

Placing the pot of tea on the table, I ask, "Would you like some gingerbread to go along with your tea?"

He replies, "No, thank you. I had quite a hearty dinner just before taking my leave from the tavern. But a hot cup of tea sounds delightful."

After pouring a cup of tea for the both of us, I take a seat next to Obadiah by the fire. I take the liberty of placing my feet next to Obadiah's on the same piece of wood. Rubbing the sole of his foot with my toes, I ask, "When do your plans have you returning to Millbury? You had mentioned a few weeks; have you decided on a particular day?"

"Why, yes, I believe I will be traveling back on the afternoon of December eighteenth; it is a Friday. That affords me plenty of time with my mother; hopefully it gets me back before any extreme weather sets in."

I remind Obadiah, "The Christmas Ball at Mr. and Mrs. Waters' house is taking place on the following Thursday evening. I am so excited."

Looking at me with excitement, he replies, "I have played it over and over in my head a thousand times: Lucinda and Obadiah, gracefully dancing the opening minuet with one another, as if Heaven exists right here on Earth."

I close my eyes, sharing with Obadiah the pleasure of our love.

We sit by the fire; just being in one another's presence is a blessed event. Again, I begin to massage the bottom of his foot with my toes; I try desperately to get a rise out of him. He turns his head toward me; he stares directly into my eyes, hinting quietly, "My dear, are you trying to start trouble?"

I forewarn him, "My mother is just moments from returning, so you must be quick."

I slide from my chair, quickly moving to my knees. I snuggle up close to him. His lips are delicious. My hand enjoyably finds his pleasure point; I work to bring him to that state of bliss. His gasp of joy confirms my success.

He immediately responds by moving his hand up and under my dress. While my desire is burning with vigor, it is certain that my mother will arrive home in just moments. I move my hand around his neck. Pulling him close, I whisper, "There will be plenty of time for that when you return from Providence."

Seemingly satisfied with my answer, he sits back in his chair appearing quite relaxed. I stand, making some hasty adjustments to my dress.

The front door swings open; Mother announces her arrival, saying, "Good day, everyone, quite a breezy day we are having." Stomping her feet on the hearth in the kitchen to remove the snow, she shouts out, "Obadiah, it is getting quite late in the day. Are you still planning to travel to Providence?"

"Yes, Mrs. Bixby, we were just finishing up with our visit. It is certainly a pleasure to see you again."

Mother has become quite fond of Obadiah, surely hoping that one day he might become my husband. Whenever she brings up the subject, I do my best to shrug it off. Although, frankly, the time is approaching when my hopes to become Mrs. Griffiths will be satisfied.

Obadiah stands as Mother enters the parlor. "Please, take my seat by the fire to warm yourself. I must be on my way to Providence; riding in the dark is much too challenging, especially in the snow."

Mother appears pleased with the invitation, promptly sitting and pulling the chair closer yet to the fire.

∞

Obadiah and I take hands and walk over to the kitchen. I reluctantly help him with his vest and topcoat, wishing he did not have to leave for such a long time. Sitting, he reaches for his boots that have been warming on the hearth. After slipping them on, he stands and holds his arms open. He smiles at me with that enchanting smile, luring me directly toward his warm body. His embrace is heavenly; my heart throbs with desire.

Just as I am about to release him, a sudden fear overcomes me. My hold on him tightens. "Please be careful; I cannot imagine my life without you."

It feels as if an eternity passes, Obadiah surely searching for the proper words before responding, "My return is certain, my love for you eternal. I will forever be with you—that is my promise."

THIRTY-FIVE

OBADIAH... *WEDNESDAY, DECEMBER 16, 1840*

My longing to return to Lucinda has become intolerable, resulting in my heartfelt desire to proceed with my travels back to Millbury sooner than planned. Moving over to the window that faces into the street, I am intrigued by how busy everyone appears so early in the morning. Travelers are carefully navigating horses and carriages about the hectic street. People are darting in and out of storefronts, cheerfully engaged in conversation.

A gray hue paints the sky; the stillness of the air is a strong indicator of an impending storm. I must do my best to begin my journey no later than one. Having left the bulk of my personal things in Millbury, I only have a few articles of clothing to pack.

∞

As expected, the packing of my satchel goes quickly; I hurriedly work to tidy up the room. Although the short stay with my parents has been wonderful, my heart yearns to be with Lucinda.

My mother has recovered completely from her bout with consumption; it is a pleasure to see her attending to her chores with a sprightly bounce in her step. She has prepared a delicious-looking mince pie; it is one of my favorites. I share my appreciation with her. "Mother, the mince pie smells delightful, as always. Will Father be joining us?"

With a sigh, she informs me, "Father was summoned to the docks this morning to assist in the unloading of a cargo ship that arrived late yesterday afternoon. He extends his regrets for not being present to wish you a safe journey and assured me that he would be here in spirit."

The sincerity in my mother's eyes remind me of the struggles my father has had holding down a job. I respond kindly, "I understand; Father must work when work is available."

The mince pie is more delicious than it appears. Mother has been preparing mince pies for me since before I can remember. Typically a Christmas treat, Mother decided to surprise me by baking one early this year, so that we are able to share in the tradition. When I was young, I always enjoyed watching her prepare the Christmas pie. First, she minces the meat and vegetables into a fine paste, and then she folds in fried apples. She finishes by mixing in a generous sprinkle of sifted sage. I compliment her on the delectable taste. "You have outdone yourself with this pie; the sweet savor of it will most indubitably stay with me throughout my afternoon's journey."

Mother, who has finished with her dinner, is peering out of the front window. She warns me, "There is a flurry of snow in the air; you should consider beginning your journey soon."

The thought of riding for five hours in a snowstorm does not appeal to me. I ask, "Does it seem as if it will turn into a severe storm?"

Mother responds, "It is difficult to tell; but you are very welcome to stay here for another night if you wish."

I look out the window to observe for myself. "It appears only to be a flurry; I will leave immediately and return if it becomes severe."

∞

Jasper is ready for the journey; he has had plenty to eat and drink throughout the morning. I throw the saddle over his

281

back and fasten it; I tie my satchel to the saddle. Mounting him, we make our way out of the barn. Mother is on the porch; I wave and shout out, "I love you, and give my best to Father."

There has been little accumulation of snow thus far, only a scattered flurry from time to time. The roads from Providence remain busy with activity. When we venture out on to the main road to Douglas, the scene becomes rather serene, albeit ghostly. I reveal to Jasper my hopes for the future. "There is no doubt that Lucinda would be a wonderful wife." His ears perk up a tad. "I have decided that I will ask for her hand in marriage at the Christmas Ball."

After an hour passes, the snow becomes heavier. Being a rather warm snow, it clings to the evergreen trees, prompting their branches to sag under the load. Less than three inches of new snow have fallen. That, on top of the few inches remaining from Sunday's storm, makes the going slow, but certainly not treacherous.

I am nearly three hours into the journey; the wind has picked up and the temperature seems to be dropping significantly. I pull the rein slightly. "Whoa, Jasper." I dismount, landing in snow that has piled up at least another four inches. I fumble with the buttons of my trousers, eventually undoing a few, allowing me just enough access to piss. The stream forms a hole in the snow, steam hovers over it; the feeling is delightful. With only two more hours left to travel, I remain quite optimistic that I will arrive safely at the Lower Tavern in time for a late supper.

Four hours have passed; the storm has become relentless. The wind is blowing fiercely; the snow is blinding. I am surely getting close to Douglas where I will find a bed for the night. Jasper has slowed his pace dramatically; he is doing his utmost not to succumb to the rising snow.

A sudden crack fills the air. Before I am able to react, a falling branch sweeps me to the ground; I land hard on my right side. Fortunately, the snow softens the landing; nevertheless, an excruciating pain radiates from my right thigh. I lay for a moment, trying not to panic. Attempting to unfold my right leg from under my left, the pain shoots up from the injury, radiating throughout my entire body. I do my best to posture myself in such a manner that would allow me to better see where the pain is coming from. I roll to the left in an attempt to sit up. In doing so, I notice that the snow has turned blood-red under my right leg; there is a protuberance of some sort under my trousers. I reach down to pull them up. The pain is excruciating; there is a tree branch protruding from a large laceration on my inner thigh. I black out.

When I come to, over an inch of fresh snow has fallen on me. Jasper remains by my side, uncertain as to what to do. The pain in my leg has subsided somewhat, but I find it impossible to muster the strength to move. The blood continues to leak from my wound, although it has slowed, surely due to the cold. Coming to the unfortunate conclusion that I am unable to move on my own, I whisper to Jasper, "Go; find your way to safety at Lucinda's."

Jasper, obviously unsure of his next move, lowers his head down next to my left arm. He offers a slight nudge. I respond, "Please, Jasper, you must find your way to safety. Go now." Reluctantly, Jasper begins to walk away. He looks back several times, surely hoping that I will call for his return.

The fear of dying consumes me. The pain has diminished; my body is warming. The uncontrollable shaking is intense. I drift in and out of consciousness. The fear that I am about to drift away without seeing my lovely Lucinda again is more painful than the gaping hole in my thigh.

The feeling of warmth gradually turns to a raging heat; my body is burning up. I attempt to remove my cape; I begin to burrow myself into the snow. Slowly, the pain along with the fear begins to subside. There is a sense of stillness encouraging me to surrender.

I drift quietly into a state of bliss; the light is warm and inviting. My thoughts become clear; flashes of light present vivid images of my happiest of times. The distinct savor of the mince pie lingers in my mind. Thoughts become lucid; I envision myself dancing with Lucinda. I promise her that my love will remain forever. As the vison becomes clearer, I can see that we are at the Christmas Ball. We are dancing in the midst of a thousand blue butterflies. She twirls; I reach out my hand. She looks me directly in the eyes, promising, "You will remain in my heart forever. I love you."

THIRTY-SIX

LUCINDA... *THURSDAY, DECEMBER 17, 1840*

The howling of the wind startles me out of a deep sleep. The lower sash of my window is rattling in the frame, inviting tiny squalls of snow to leak through the cracks and blow freely around the room. The embers glowing in the fireplace are begging for fuel to keep them alive. The wind that penetrates the many openings to the inside blows frigidly across my face. Coming to grips with the inevitable, I roll out of bed to add some pieces of wood to the fire. Getting down on my hands and knees, I give them a good blow from the depths of my lungs; the fire comes alive, throwing off a burst of warmth.

The refection in the mirror tells all: it portrays a smile that reaches from ear to ear, revealing the sentiments of the happiest lady alive. The Christmas Ball is only one week away, the return of my Obadiah from Providence only two days. I never imagined the happiness that one summer could bring to a lost girl, fearful of love.

I slip on a petticoat and my flannel dress; I brush the snarls from my hair. The stockings I am wearing are a heavy knit. They cover my legs nearly four inches above my knees, affording me some added warmth on this chilly morning.

∞

Looking forward to starting the day, I prance down the narrow staircase to the kitchen where I find Mother beginning preparations for breakfast. "Good morning, Mother; it appears that we have had quite a fierce storm last night."

Cracking eggs into a large bowl, Mother acknowledges, "Good morning, Lucinda. Yes, what started as a mild storm turned violent quite quickly. The cold and wind has prevailed into this morning. Certainly not an evening to be out in the elements, that's for sure."

The comfort of the kitchen fire is making it difficult for me to commence my short journey down the path to the barn. Nevertheless, I throw my cape on over my shoulders and open the back door. The wind blows a squall of drifting snow into the kitchen but the blazing fire melts it before it can settle. With a concerned voice, Mother warns, "Walk carefully and please do not dally out there."

∞

The snow has conveniently drifted from the path for most of its length. Unfortunately, there are nearly two feet that have drifted up against the side door of the barn. The snow is light and so I am able to push it aside with my hands quite easily. Shifting enough to allow me to open the door, I step in. Wearing my mittens over my armlets provides me enough protection from the cold snow to keep my hands and arms warm. Fetching eggs is an easy chore, for there are none. After milking the cow, I tend to Shadow, who appears quite comfortable in the wake of the storm. The water in her bucket is covered by an inch of ice; I chip at it with an ice pick, removing the pieces one at a time. With the ice removed, I place it within her reach. Our morning embrace is tighter and longer than usual; the softness of her mane is particularly inviting today. Stepping back, I share my feelings with her. "Good morning, Shadow. You are staring into the eyes of the happiest lady in the land."

∞

Jaunting back to the house, I pay little attention to the wind and blowing snow. Mother has prepared a large plate of fried eggs with chunks of bacon and bits of onion, making them that much more appetizing. Serving myself a rather large portion, I take a seat at the table with Mother. The frost that has accumulated on the front window obscures the view. Squinting to get a better look, I am surprised to see a horse standing by the hitching post near the road. Rushing over to the window to get a more thorough look, I call out to Mother, "There is a horse out there; it appears to be Jasper."

Quickly, I throw on my cape and hurry to the front door. The snow has drifted nearly a foot against it; I push it hard to clear the way. Running down the front path, I yell out, "Jasper, what are you doing here?" In a state of confusion, I look hither and thither for Obadiah, to no avail. Turning back to Jasper, I say, "You look frozen." Leading him by the rein, we head toward the barn.

Thankfully, Shadow and Jasper are not strangers. Charles had a habit of putting them together at the tavern during my many visits as a way for them to "get acquainted." Shadow remains quite settled as I position Jasper next to her in the stall. Untying the satchel from the saddle, I hang it on a peg with the sleigh bells. I then remove the saddle and hang it as well. Moving the bucket of water over, Jasper immediately begins to drink. Turning to Shadow, I make a request: "Jasper needs a friend right now, please watch over him. I must go and find Obadiah."

My mind is whirling with confusion; where is he? Rather than taking the path directly to the back door, I take the path to the road in hopes of finding him. Where do I look? The road is covered with snow; I look as far as I can in both directions. I do not see anything that looks out of place. Fear begins to plague me and I murmur aloud, "Where could he be? He was not supposed to leave Providence until tomorrow." Lowering my head with worry, I rush back to the front door.

Upon entering, I call out, "Mother, it was Jasper for sure. He was saddled and Obadiah's satchel was still attached." I take a few breaths. "I am truly worried. We must prepare the sleigh and make the journey to the Lower Tavern. I am sure we will find him safe there."

∞

We have not used the sleigh yet this year. Father is out of town for a few days and so I have to prepare it for travel by myself. The barn is not large enough for us to store everything that we have properly and it takes me nearly an hour to rearrange things so that I have clear access to it. The anxiety is killing me. Pulling it slowly toward the large door in the front of the barn, I appreciate that it is light enough for me to handle on my own. Once in position, I bridle Shadow and lead her to the front of the sleigh. I harness her to it and then tie Jasper to the back. Taking the satchel from the peg, I place it under the seat in the sleigh. The sound of sleigh bells may help relieve the anxiety so I decide to attach them to the harness. When finished, I assure both horses, "Be patient, I will run to get Mother."

∞

Mother and I return to the barn within fifteen minutes. Sliding the door open, I tell her, "Be sure to bring enough blankets to stay warm." I lead Shadow out of the barn far enough to allow Jasper to clear the door. Mother carries two heavy woolen blankets and jumps up onto the seat. I slide the barn door closed and jump up next to her. I give the reins a shake, shouting out, "Let's go."

With sleigh bells ringing, we head down the road toward the common. With the newly fallen snow, I estimate that between six and eight inches have accumulated. We take our left at Eliza Goffe's place; there are large branches that have broken from trees lying in the road. The fear that Obadiah was caught in the fury of the storm resurfaces, causing me to blurt out, "Mother, I truly hope that he is safe."

We pass over the Gowan Bridge; Adelia's beautiful mansion comes into sight on the right side of the sleigh. The view is magnificent, the freshly fallen snow sparkling in the sunlight. The Christmas Ball is only a week away; what if he is lost forever? I turn to Mother once more, looking for assurance. "Surely he is safe."

Mother takes my hand in hers and gives it a gentle squeeze. "Let us get to the tavern before we make any further judgements."

∞

When we arrive, both Harriet and Charles burst out of the door and onto the porch. Harriet yells out, "Miss Bixby, what are you doing here? It is such a delight to see you!"

Charles comes running down the steps, raising his hand to the side of Shadow's face, touching her gently. "Good day, girl."

When he recognizes that Jasper is tied to the rear of the sled, he adds with excitement, "That is Jasper; where is Obadiah?"

My heart sinks with Charles confirming that he is not here at the tavern. I respond to both Harriet and Charles, doing my best to remain optimistic. "Good day to you both. We found Jasper at our house this morning. We had hoped that we might find Obadiah here at the tavern with you."

Harriet answers from the porch, "He is not here, but please, you and your mother must come in to warm yourselves."

I pick up Obadiah's satchel and jump down from the sleigh; Mother follows. Harriet and Charles show us the way to the parlor. Harriet yells down the hallway to the kitchen, "Mother, Miss Bixby and her mother are here for a surprise visit. Come quickly."

Taking a seat in Obadiah's favorite upholstered chair, I invite Mother to take a seat near me on the sofa. Salome enters the parlor. In a surprised voice, she inquires, "What brings you out on such a chilly day? We do not expect Obadiah until Saturday. Not at all to suggest that we are not pleased to see you."

As reality begins to set in, I do my best to stay composed. I begin to speak, my eyes swelling with tears. "Good day, Salome. Please, take a seat." Salome sits on the sofa between Harriet and Mother. I continue, "Earlier today, I found Jasper standing in the road by my hitching post. He was saddled and Obadiah's satchel was still attached." I lift up the satchel to show her. I go on, "I looked everywhere for any sign of him, but to no avail. Not knowing what to do next, I thought that he may have come here." Tears are dripping from my eyes as I finish my thought. "But obviously, I was wrong."

It is apparent that Salome is doing her best to comprehend all that I have just said. However, to my surprise, Harriet responds first, "Miss Bixby, this is terrible news. But Mr. Griffiths would not want us to cry; he would want us to be strong and to hold onto hope."

Salome contributes, "Yes, there is always the possibility that he was knocked from Jasper and has found his way to safety."

From the upholstered chair, I have a clear view of the open door that leads to the taproom. Dennis is standing in the doorway, in conversation with one of the gents that is seated at a table. The room is dark and smoke-filled; I can barely make out that there are two additional men at the table. They are all smoking and drinking mugs of ale. Dennis looks over at me; he immediately suspends his conversation and makes his way toward the parlor.

As he approaches the door, he tentatively raises his hand to greet us. "It is the Bixby ladies. Welcome."

He passes through the doorway, seeming somewhat absorbed. I ask, "Dennis, is there something troubling you?"

"Yes, it has to do with the conversation I was just having with those three gents at the table. They rode up from Providence this morning on their way to Worcester. About three miles south of Douglas, they came upon an unfortunate situation. It appears that a fallen branch had swept a man from his horse in the storm. They found him frozen to death on the side of the road, a branch protruding through a nasty laceration in his thigh. Poor man; such an unfortunate fate."

The room begins to spin; the world around me becomes nauseating. I scream out, "Tell me, tell me it is not true!"

THIRTY-SEVEN

LUCINDA... *THURSDAY, DECEMBER 24, 1840*

The flow of tears has been continuous since last Thursday. I thank God for the many people that have helped to comfort me through these very trying days. The loss of Obadiah has brought me to the brink of lunacy. This, the long-awaited day of the Christmas Ball, shall end in misery, like every other day since his passing.

Lying in bed, I am numb from head to toe. Rays of sunshine come and go; the sash rattles, suggesting another squally day. The wind is blowing around the frigid air, chilling me to the bones. Rolling over under the quilt, I face away from the sun; I stare at my beautiful gown. All of those dreams of happiness stolen from me, never to be returned. I have made the decision not to leave my bed until this dreadful day is finally over. Mother has kept the fire going, checking in on me from time to time.

The door to my room opens; I hear quiet footsteps coming up the stairs. Mother sees that I am awake. "Lucinda, I brought you some chowder. You must eat to keep your health." She puts it down on the side table. Bending over, she embraces me, kissing me on the cheek. In a soft voice, she says, "You may not understand now, but attending the ball would be a great step toward healing. You must trust me."

Understanding her love for me, I respond, "Mother, how can that be? I so loved Obadiah; how could attending a dance without him be healing?"

Her eyes tearing up, she responds, "It most certainly would be. You must trust me."

"Mother, I love you, but I cannot."

Obviously disappointed, she takes her leave from my room. I contemplate her request.

∞

More than an hour passes. The chowder was delicious; I have not eaten anything substantial for nearly a week. The thought of going to the privy outside is met with much disapproval on my part. I decide that the chamber pot is a much superior alternative. I slip out of bed into the chilly air. Squatting, I hold the pot in place and begin my business.

I hear the door open and the distinct pitter-patter of feet coming up the stairs. Happening much too quickly for me to react, I choose to stay squatting.

Somewhat embarrassed, I look up to see Harriet standing by my bed. Bewildered by the sight, she inquires, "Miss Bixby, why are you using the chamber pot in the middle of the day?"

Not really knowing how to respond, I finish, I stand, and I smile. "Miss Bixby is a bit confused since the loss of Mr. Griffiths." Being surprised to see Harriet in my room, I inquire, "And so, to what do I owe this visit?"

Harriet appears to accept my explanation without further questioning, responding, "Adelia Waters dropped by our house yesterday to share with us her concern that you may not attend the Christmas Ball tonight. She was gracious enough to invite my mother, father, and me, in the hope that we might convince you to come. She knows how close we are to you."

It is quite touching to experience the outpouring of love that so many of my friends and family have shown me. Tears cause my eyes to swell again; I do my best to explain. "Going to the ball would incite so many memories of Obadiah; it would bring me to my knees in sorrow."

293

Tears from Harriet's eyes roll down her cheeks, "Miss Bixby, Mr. Griffiths made me promise that I would share all of the happiness that he brought me throughout the summer with everyone I encounter. There is no other person in the world that I want to share his happiness with more than you."

We are both weeping now, but the weeping has transformed from cries of desperation to cries of joy. Harriet has reminded me of the promise I also made that the happiness Obadiah and I shared would always hold a special place in my soul, that I would forever keep him alive in my heart and that our happiness together would always help to define who I am.

Reaching my arms out, I call to Harriet, "Come, give me a hug." Harriet, looking a tad surprised, moves toward me. Once we are embracing, I whisper softly in her ear, "It would be my honor to accompany you to the Christmas Ball tonight. Moreover, thank you for reminding me that the treasures of happiness are never destroyed. They will always be with us here on Earth and in the heavens above."

Harriet appears quite satisfied; she is quick to remind me, "You must hurry; we do not want the ball to commence without us. Mother and Father are in the parlor with your mother and father; Jasper is hitched to the sleigh, waiting for us. We have little time to waste."

I quickly move to the front of the mirror to determine what I must do to fix my hair. It is a snarled mess. Turning to Harriet, I ask, "Would you run to the kitchen and fetch me a pitcher of warm water from the cauldron? That would be so helpful to me."

Harriet, excited to help, takes the pitcher from the stand and trots quickly down the stairs. I can hear her yell into the parlor, "Miss Bixby is going to the ball, yes she is!"

I take my beautiful gown from the hook that it has been hanging on since summer. Just the feeling of it excites me. Laying it on the bed, I take a seat on the blanket chest. I remove the stockings that I have been wearing for the past week. Harriet arrives with the pitcher of warm water, pouring a good amount into the basin. She then soaks a clean washcloth and brings it over to me. I immediately begin to wash my legs, quickly moving down to my feet. Once satisfied, I remove a clean pair of stockings from the blanket chest and pull them on.

Continuing to wash, I change into a clean lower-cut chemise. I slip on my fancy petticoat. I ask Harriet to rinse out the washcloth while I again look into the mirror to determine the best approach to fixing my hair. Using the rinsed cloth, I scrub my hair as hard as I can bear. Using a comb, I straighten it out. When finished, I shake my head, encouraging my natural curls to return.

Harriet is watching with amazement as I transform myself. A headband of dried flowers is hanging on a small nail just above the fireplace. Taking it down, I lay it on the blanket chest next to where Harriet is sitting. She carefully picks it up. Looking at it with a blessed smile, she turns to me, sharing, "Miss Bixby, this is beautiful."

"Thank you, Harriet. I made it when Obadiah and I were first invited to the ball."

It is time to put on the gown. Moving toward the bed, Harriet watches me as I hold it up, admiring its beauty. Slipping it over my head, it falls perfectly on my shoulders; it drops to the exact right length. Harriet helps me to fasten the hooks up the back. When finished, I twirl, admiring the beauty of the dress as it floats elegantly through the air. Placing the headband of flowers on my head, I return to the mirror for a look.

Quite excited, Harriet gasps, "You look like a princess!"

We hurry together down the stairway and into the parlor. Mother and Father are visiting with the Fishers, awaiting our arrival. Excitedly, Mother stands and shares with me, "You look so beautiful."

For the first time in my life, I notice that Father's eyes are swelling with tears. He adds shyly, "Enjoy your evening, Lucinda; you look gorgeous."

Thanking them both for their heartfelt compliments, we take our leave.

∞

The Fishers' sleigh has two seats. Salome and Dennis sit in the front, and Harriet jumps into the back, waiting for me to join her. First, I must give my Jasper a hug. "I love you so."

Jumping into the seat next to Harriet, I pull a blanket up around us and reach my arm around her shoulder. With sleigh bells ringing, we begin our journey to the Christmas Ball. The temperature promises to fall into the single digits tonight; we have plenty of warm blankets and are wrapped tightly in our woolen capes.

Sleighs and carriages line the street in front of Adelia's beautiful house and there is a path of lanterns leading from the street to the front door; it is magical. The four of us begin to walk together up the path. A wave of sadness overwhelms me, wanting so much to have Obadiah by my side. Closing my eyes for just a moment, the promise I made Obadiah helps me to recover some happiness. When we reach the front door, Adelia opens it. She welcomes the Fishers and gives Harriet a warm hug. I overhear her whisper, "You did it, you got Miss Bixby to come! God bless you."

When I enter the foyer, Mr. Waters is there to greet me, "Lucinda, may I take your cape?"

I respond to him politely, "Yes, you may, thank you."

∞

When he returns, he takes me gently by the hand and leads me onto the dance floor. To my utter surprise, all of the guests are standing in a large circle, all holding candles in Obadiah's honor. Mr. Waters turns to me. "We know that Obadiah would have wanted to dance the first minuet with you. In his name, we would be honored if you would help by bringing his blessed spirit upon us this Christmas Eve."

Standing in awe, the music to our favorite minuet begins; I close my eyes and begin to dance. At first, it is quite awkward. Opening my eyes, for just a moment, I see the hope that so many hold for me; I embrace the love that fills the room. Closing my eyes, I allow the music to absorb me. I move with all the elegance of a princess.

As I come to the end of the dance, I open my eyes. Lifting my head, the loveliest of paintings, depicting a beautiful field of green grass against the perfect blue-sky backdrop, captivates my attention. A thousand blue butterflies flutter in the sky; happiness moves me to tears of loss and joy.

Closing my eyes, I take my last twirl. I reach out my hand; his dark eyes stare directly into mine. I promise him, "You will remain in my heart forever. I love you."

THIRTY-EIGHT

LUCINDA... *FRIDAY, JULY 23, 1909*

Looking back now at the *Summer of 1840,* I am able to recollect the happiest of times. From that memorable moment on the Fourth of July, when I first laid eyes on Obadiah, until I bid him farewell that cold day in December, Obadiah swept into my life; he healed my broken past. I think sometimes that he was an angel sent to me from Heaven. His manners were divine; his presence was always a blessing. He brought with him a spirit of love; a love that continues to dance in my heart to this very day. I vividly remember that anyone who had the blessing to know Obadiah became a more loving soul. Remember little Harriet? She grew up to become the most vibrant soul I have ever come to know.

To be frank, it took me quite some time to accept the death of Obadiah. While my dance in his honor at the Christmas Ball was an important first step, I slipped in and out of sadness for many months that followed. Eventually, the spirit of Obadiah's happiness became a power that animated my soul, just as he promised.

I will never forget the sparkle in Asa Waters' eyes when he first laid eyes on me the night of the ball. He was so excited to share the joy of Christmas with me. Asa Waters became ill the following year; he passed peacefully at his beautiful home on Christmas Eve of 1841.

I met and married a wonderful gentleman in the summer of

1844. He had lost his wife Emerline to pleurisy fever in February of that year, only ten days after the birth of his second daughter, Frances. The gentleman's name was Andrew. Shortly after Emerline passed, he changed his daughter's name to Emerline. He also had a daughter Caroline, who was two at the time I met him. It turns out that I was unable to bear children; his children were a blessing to me. Unfortunately, young Emerline contracted bilious dysentery when she was five years of age. She died in September of 1849. My sweet Caroline still comes to visit me here in Worcester from time to time.

Andrew and I lived a happy life together. Taken from me in 1884, at the age of seventy, he left with me nearly forty years of happiness.

Yes, there was suffering along the way, as there always is.

However, as Obadiah taught me, happiness always prevails, if you allow it.

AUTHOR'S NOTES

Summer of 1840 is a work of fiction. However, many of the novel's main characters are based on real people. As recorded in the Vital Records of Millbury, MA, Lucinda Elmina was born to Simon and Hannah Bixby on July 23, 1815. In a letter written to Lucinda by her mother Hannah Bixby on July 10, 1843, Hannah suggests to Lucinda that a Lathrop Bugbee stopped by and offered up that he knows a "gent" that wants a wife. The letter goes on to describe the gent as "*hansom and industrous.*" With this, we can be quite sure that Lucinda was twenty-five years of age and unmarried when she sat down on November 4, 1840 to pen the letter entitled "*Happiness.*"

While Obadiah Griffiths is a fictional character, his Uncle John was known as an itinerant dance master who traveled through New England in the late 18th century. Many of the dances referred to in the novel are taken from the works of John Griffiths. References to manners are taken from his pamphlet entitled, "*Instances of Ill Manners, to be carefully avoided by Youth of both sexes.*"

In Chapter 1 of the book, I introduce Mr. Benjamin Franklin Hallett. Mr. Hallett was an actual person who delivered his oration to the people of Millbury one year earlier, on July 4, 1839. I took the liberty to reference the primary source of his oration at the celebration on July 4, 1840 at the Congregational Church. In Chapter 3 of the book, I introduce Reverend Motte who delivers a sermon at the Congregational Church in Millbury entitled, *The Christian Patriot.* The primary source has Reverend Motte delivering the sermon at the South Congregational Church in Boston on that same day. In both cases, I used direct quotes from the primary sources to better authenticate the sentiment of the times.

In Chapter 27, I introduce another fictional character by the name of Reverend Parkman. Reverend Parkman delivers a sermon written by Reverend Dana Goodsell entitled, *"The Immorality and Ruinous Tendency of the Dancing School and Ball-Room."* The primary source has Reverend Goodsell delivering the sermon in Plainfield, MA on February 10, 1839. There is absolutely no connection between Reverend Goodsell and the fictional character, Reverend Parkman, except the delivery of the sermon. Reverend Parkman, and the story behind his character, are fictional.

In the writing of the book, I referred to an original map of Millbury, MA dated 1851. Although the map is dated eleven years later, I felt that historically, the use of an original map brought a stronger realism to the story. Wherever possible, I used other sources to authenticate the actual people and places that would have existed in 1840. One of those primary sources was a survey map of Millbury dated 1830.

During the initial research for the book, I spent hours at the America Antiquarian Society scrolling through two of the more popular newspapers of the time. The Massachusetts Spy was an excellent source for advertisements and news of the times. The National Egis was my source for the daily weather. It was recorded at the State Lunatic Hospital in Worcester.

Finally, the map of Massachusetts that was printed in 1836 was an excellent map to guide Obadiah in his travels from Providence, RI and throughout Massachusetts.

ACKNOWLEDGEMENTS

WITH THANKS

To my wife, Vicki, for keeping it real, as she always does;

To my daughter, Kelly, the first reader of the manuscript. She struggled through the first draft, one chapter after another, as I wrote them, encouraging me to continue;

To my first editor, Samantha Friedlander, who worked on the book during her final semester in high school. She edited, researched, and suggested the moment of reflection used in the last chapter of the book;

To Ryan Beckman, who interprets life in the 1830's at Old Sturbridge Village in Sturbridge, MA. Our many fireside chats at the Bixby House helped to bring life to the cooking scenes in the book;

To Tom Kelleher, historian and curator at Old Sturbridge Village, who has been invaluable as a mentor and teacher of Early American History throughout the many years I have had the pleasure to know him;

To the many folks at the American Antiquarian Society, who helped me to navigate the vast collection of primary sources in their collection, many that were used to bring life to the characters and scenes in the book;

To the members of the Millbury and Sutton Historical Societies, who helped me to pull together a reasonably accurate account of the two towns as they would have been in 1840;

To Rebecca Beall, Curator of Collections at Old Sturbridge Village, for taking the time to show me the beautiful gown that Lucinda wore to the Christmas Ball;

To Roberta DeCenzo, Historic Records Consultant at the Wayside Inn in Sudbury, formerly known as the Red Horse Tavern, who sat with me for a good part of a day in the archive room as I collected historical facts regarding Jerusha Howe;

To Barb Finer and Pat Ram, for reading and commenting on early versions of the manuscript;

To Mary Chabot, for her help in copy editing the fourth draft and suggesting that she would "recommend" the book to others;

To Elise Martorano, for her enthusiasm and for her extremely helpful copy editing and editorial comments;

To George Fogg, who taught me everything I know about English Country Dancing;

To all the rest of you, too numerous to mention, who encouraged me along the way.

BIBLIOGRAPHY

Primary Sources

Hallett, Benjamin Franklin *Oration before the Democratic Citizens of Worcester County, Massachusetts, at Millbury, July 4, 1839* E.W. Bartlett Worcester 1839 Harvard College Library

Motte, M. I. *The Christian Patriot – A Sermon Delivered at the South Congregational Church, Boston, July 5th, 1840* Folsom, Wells, and Thurston Boston 1840

Goodsell, Dana *The Immorality and Ruinous Tendency of the Dancing School and Ball-Room A Discourse Delivered in the First Congregational Church in Plainfield, Massachusetts, February 10, 1839* David Kimball Concord, NH 1839 American Antiquarian Society, Worcester, MA

The Ball-Room Instructer; Containing A Complete Description of Cotillons and other Popular Dances. With Illustrations. Written and Arranged for Amateurs in Dancing Huestis & Craft New York 1841 American Antiquarian Society, Worcester, MA

The Slaves Cry Volume 1 New London, CT 1844

> On Tuesday, July 14, 1840, Mrs. Chamberlain quotes from the document at a dance gathering in her home.

Map of the Town of Millbury in Worcester County H.F. Walling, Engineer, O. Harkness, Assistant 1851

Survey Map of Millbury, MA 1830

Map of Massachusetts, Connecticut and Rhode Island Constructed from the Latest Authorities Packard & Brown Hartford 1836

> This map was helpful in defining routes traveled by Obadiah throughout the book. It is very detailed.

The Massachusetts Spy, Newspaper Published Weekly in Worcester 7/1/1840 thru 12/30/1840

> I used various articles and advertisements to bring more authenticity to the book. In particular, there are descriptive articles about the July 4th celebration in surrounding towns.

The National Egis, Worcester Newspaper Published Weekly in Worcester 7/1/1840 thru 12/30/1840

> This newspaper published the weekly weather from the State Lunatic Hospital in Worcester. In writing the book, I used the records, where available, to recreate the actual weather of the day.

Howe, Jerusha

> Thanks to Rebecca at the Wayside Inn in Sudbury, MA for sharing original letters written by and to Jerusha Howe. Having spent many of evenings at the Wayside Inn, and sharing in the many stories describing "The Ghost of Room 9", the few chapters that took place at the Red Horse Tavern were quite personal to me.

Bixby, Hannah July 10, 1843

> There were many original letters to and from members of the Bixby family that helped me to better understand the relationships of the time. In particular, a letter from Hannah to Lucinda, describing Hannah's preparation for the 4th of July celebration, helped to bring to life the first chapter of the book. It was also interesting to read that Hannah was trying to find Lucinda a husband in 1843.

Bixby, Lucinda November 4, 1840

> The original letter entitled "Happiness" is reproduced in full in Chapter 30. It was my intrigue over this letter that prompted me to begin writing the "Summer of 1840."

Secondary Sources

Centennial History of the Town of Millbury Massachusetts Davis Press Worcester 1905

History of Sutton Massachusetts 1704-1876; Including Grafton until 1735; Millbury until 1813; and Parts of Northbridge, Upton and Auburn Compiled by Rev. William A. Benedict, A.M. and Rev. Hiram A. Tracy Sanford & Company Worcester 1878

Vital Records of Millbury, Massachusetts to the End of the Year 1849 Franklin P. Rice, Worcester 1903

Vital Records of Sutton, Massachusetts to the End of the Year 1849 Franklin P. Rice, Worcester 1907

Ancestry and Life of Josiah Sibley Compiled by Robert Pendleton Sibley, John Adams Sibley, James Longstreet Sibley Library of Congress 1908

Genealogy of the Descendants of Joseph Bixby 1621-1701 of Ipswich and Boxford, Massachusetts Willard G. Bixby, New York 1914

A Collection of the Newest Cotillions, and Country Dances; principally composed by John Griffiths, Dancing Master, to which is added, Instances of Ill Manners, to be carefully avoided by Youth of both sexes Printed and Sold at Northampton, Massachusetts. (Price Nine Pence) [1794]. *American Antiquarian Society.*

The Reshaping of Everyday Life 1790 – 1840 Jack Larson, Harper & Row, New York, 1988

ABOUT THE AUTHOR

Arthur Martin holds a M.Ed. in Religious Studies and interprets the history of Early American Dance at Old Sturbridge Village in Sturbridge, Massachusetts. "Summer of 1840" is his first novel. He lives in Sutton, MA with his wife Vicki and their Chihuahua named Jerusha.

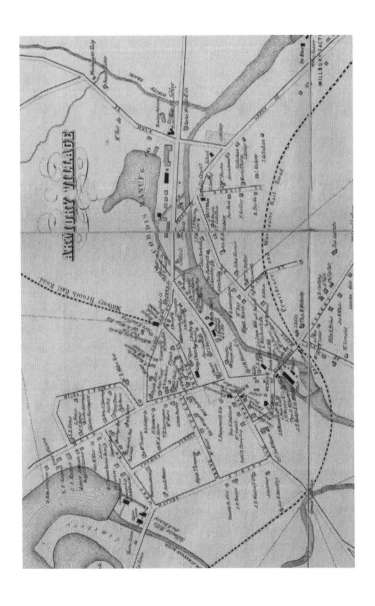

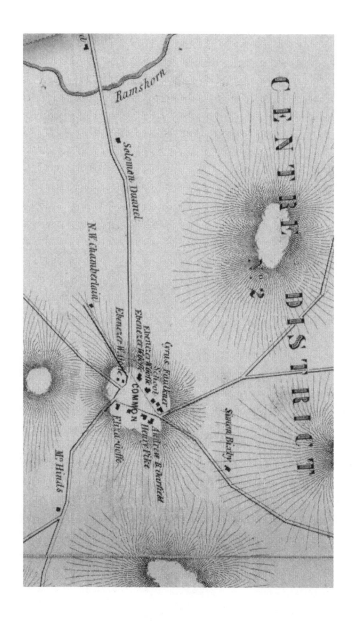

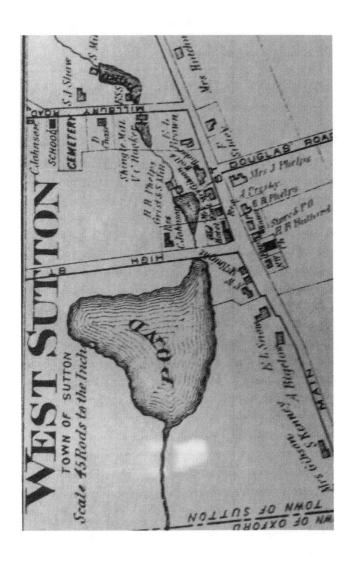